SHADOW HUNTERS

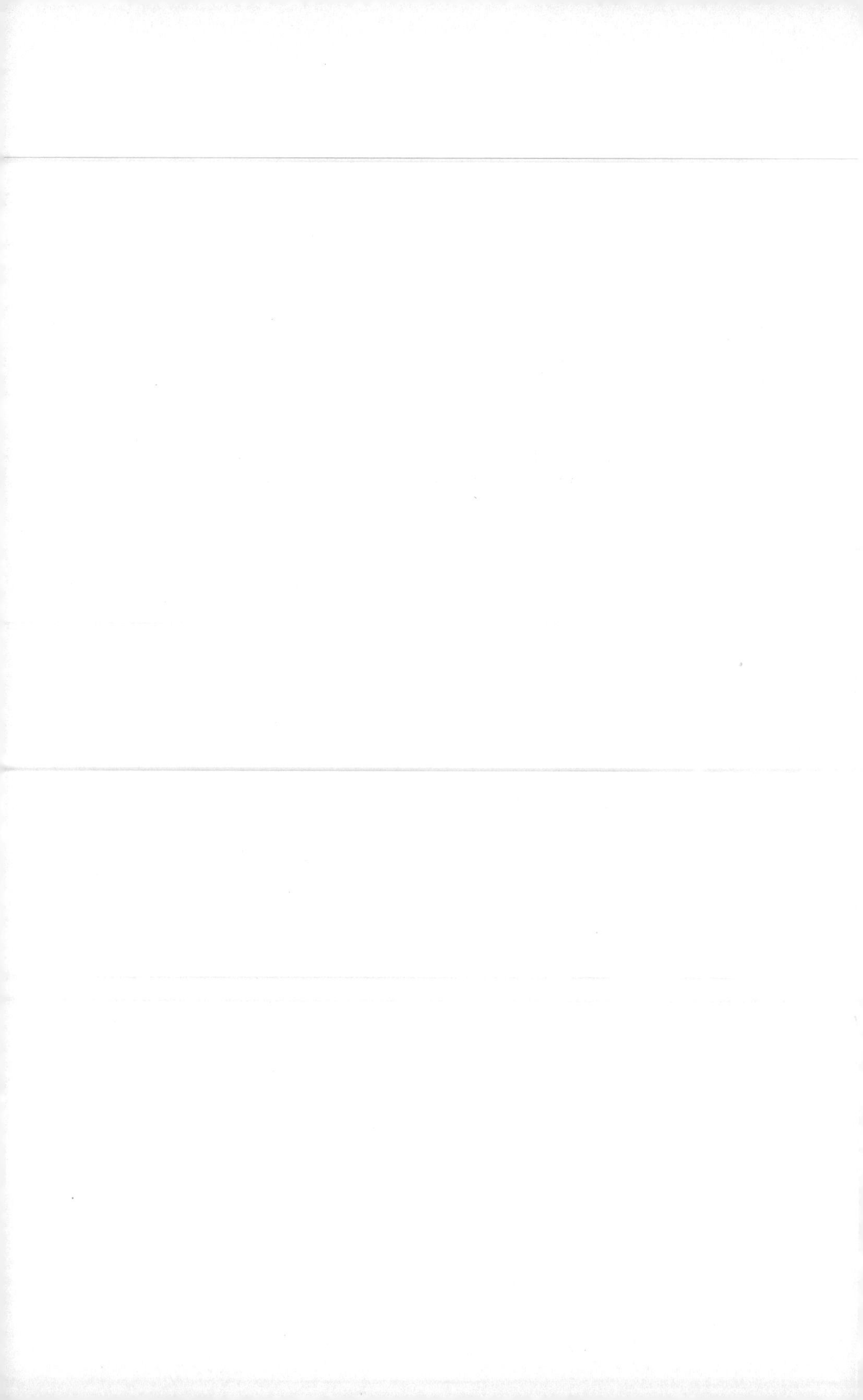

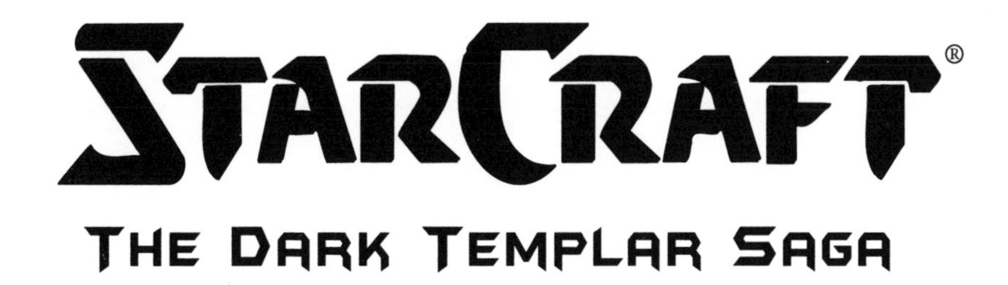

THE DARK TEMPLAR SAGA

BOOK TWO OF THREE

SHADOW HUNTERS

CHRISTIE GOLDEN

This book is a work of fiction. Names, characters, places, and incidents are products of the author's imagination or are used fictitiously. Any resemblance to actual events or locales or persons living or dead is entirely coincidental.

ISBN: 978-1-9456831-1-4

First Pocket Books printing November 2007
First Blizzard Entertainment printing March 2018

10 9 8 7 6 5 4 3 2 1

Cover art by Glenn Rane

Printed in China

This book is dedicated to Chris Metzen, Evelyn Frederickson, and Andy Chambers, with deep appreciation for their support, enthusiasm for my work, and their abiding passion for the game of StarCraft.

PROLOGUE

IN THE DARKNESS, THERE WAS TERROR.

The news had come three days ago from Artanis, the youthful new leader. The unthinkable was happening. Their world was about to be destroyed. Aiur, beautiful, beloved Aiur, which had seen and survived so much, would soon become unrecognizable.

Come to the warp gate, they had been told.

Hurry.

At first, everyone had tried to gather too much, of course. Evacuation is never a leisurely business and there was much to choose from: beautiful homes filled with beautiful things. Cherished family heirlooms? Precious khaydarin crystals? Clothing for the journey? All this and more eventually was discarded as of no value at all as the true urgency of the situation became starkly clear. Heavily armored shuttles and small atmospheric vessels were crammed with too many people, or departed without enough, all heading for the single functional warp gate left on the entire planet. Scouts flew escort when they could, firing at the waves of maddened, disoriented zerg that covered the once-lush earth like a sickening living carpet. Reavers trundled into the worst of it, the automatons saving lives while dragoons and zealots slaughtered zerg by the hundreds. The best they could hope for was to clear enough space so that the shuttles could disgorge their precious living cargo within reach of the gate.

The gate was large and wide, but not sufficiently large or wide to accommodate the terrified crowds that surged toward it. A long line of stalwart high templar stood, the last bastion of defense between the fleeing crowds and the monsters who had nothing but the urge to kill driving them.

Ladranix stood among their number. His once-gleaming gold armor was covered with ichor, melted in spots where acid had splashed on it. Beside him stood Fenix, an old friend from many battles, and the terran Jim Raynor, a new friend who had proved himself but recently. It was all happening so quickly—the courageous death of the noble Executor Tassadar, the revelation of the existence of the dark templar and word of reunion with their once-shunned brethren, the descent of the zerg.

Now they were fleeing to Shakuras, those who could make it. Those who had transportation, who could still walk or run or crawl through the portal. Smoke filled the air, and the sounds of battle, and the horrific chittering of the zerg as they came in wave after wave to slay and be slain, by the protoss or their own kind, it mattered not to them.

But the protoss themselves uttered no sound. Briefly, Ladranix permitted himself to wonder what the terran thought of it all. If only he could "hear" in his mind what Ladranix heard—the fear, the resolve, the rage; Raynor would not think the protoss a silent race as he likely did now.

And then the gate flickered. The emotions that were already buffeting Ladranix like something physical increased, and even he, mentally disciplined as he was, staggered briefly under the telepathic bombardment.

"What the hell's happening?" Raynor shouted, habit, even though the terran knew that all he needed to do was think the words and they would be heard.

The response came back at once, from whom Ladranix was not certain. His focus was on rending to pulp the four zerglings who were scrabbling and tearing at him. *We are disabling the gate. We must. Several zerg have already gotten through. We cannot risk more. Shakuras must survive. Our people must survive. I only hope we are not too late.*

Aiur has fallen.

A psychic wail went up and Ladranix actually stumbled for a dangerous moment. Horror. Anguish. Loss—aching, wrenching loss. What would they do? How could they go on? Alone, alone, so alone . . .

There was nothing to be done but fight. *Flee!* Ladranix sent with all the energy that was in him. The shocked protoss recovered, and scattered every which way.

Grimly, Ladranix and the others kept killing, hoping to buy the few seconds or moments that would mean life to others. He knew their own lives were already lost.

CHAPTER ONE

IN THE DARKNESS, THERE WAS ORDER.

Her haven was inviolable. She was queen of all she surveyed, and her vision was vast.

What those who served her unquestioningly knew, was her knowledge. What they saw, was her sight. What they felt, were her feelings. Unity, complete and utter, shivering along her nerves, racing in her blood. A unity that began with the lowest and most base of her creations and ended with her.

"All roads lead to Rome" was a saying she remembered from when she was weak and fragile, her mighty spirit encased in human flesh, when her heart could be softened by such things as loyalty, devotion, friendship, or love. It meant that all paths led to the center, to the most important thing in the world.

She, Kerrigan, the Queen of Blades, was the most important thing in the world of every zerg who flew, crept, slithered, or ran. Each breath, each thought, each movement of the zerg, from the doglike beasts to the mighty overlords, lived but by her whim. Lived to service her whim.

All roads led to Rome.

All roads led to her.

She shifted in the damp, dark place, flexing wings that were sharp and bony and devoid of membrane as she might have rolled her neck to ease tension when she was a human woman. The walls pulsated, oozing a thick, viscous substance, and she was as aware of that as she was of the larvae hatching in the pods, as she was of an overlord on a distant planet assimilating a new strain into the whole. As she was of her own discontent.

Kerrigan rose and paced. She was beginning to grow impatient. Before her arrival as their queen, she knew, the zerg had had a mission. To grow, to absorb, to become perfect, as their creators had wanted them to be. Their creators, whom they had turned on without so much as a breath of conscience. Sarah Kerrigan understood the idea of "conscience." There had been moments, even in this glorious new incarnation, where she had had twinges of it. She did not see such a thing as a weakness, but as an advantage. If one thought like one's enemies, one could defeat them.

The zerg were still on that mission under her guidance. But she had brought something new into the mix: the pleasure of revenge and victory. And for too long now, she had been forced to rest and recover, lick wounds, and fall back on the original mission.

Certainly, she had not been idle over the last four years. She had rested here on Char, had found new worlds for her zerg to explore and exploit. The zerg had thrived under her leadership, had grown and advanced and improved.

But she hungered. And that hunger was not sated by moving from planet to planet and simply re-creating and improving zerg genetics. She hungered for action, for revenge, for pitting her mind—keen even as a human's, awesome in its ability now—against her adversaries.

Arcturus Mengsk, self-styled "emperor" of the Terran Dominion. She'd enjoyed playing with him before and would again. It was why she had let him survive their last encounter, why she'd even tossed him a few crumbs, just to ensure he'd make it.

Prelate Zeratul, the dark templar protoss. Clever, that one. Admirable. And dangerous.

Jim Raynor.

Unease fluttered inside her, quickly quelled. Once, before her transformation, she had cared for the easygoing marshal. Perhaps she had even loved him. She would never know now. It was enough that thoughts of him were still able to unsettle her. He, too, was dangerous, although in quite another way than Zeratul. He was dangerous for his ability to make her . . . regret.

Four years of waiting, gathering strength, resting. She had been sick of slaughter, but no more. Now that she—

Kerrigan blinked. Her mind, processing at light speed, sensed something and latched onto it. A psionic disturbance, far, far distant. Of great magnitude—it would have to be for her to have picked up on it from so far away. But then again, she herself had been able to telepathically contact Mengsk and Raynor when she was undergoing her transformation—touch their minds and cry out for aid. Aid which had not come in time, and for that, she was grateful, of course. But what was this, that sent ripples out as if from a stone tossed into a lake?

It was fading now. It was definitely human. And yet there was something else to it, a sort of . . . flavor, for lack of a better word. Something . . . *protoss* about it.

Kerrigan's mind was always on a thousand things at once. She could see through any zerg's eyes, dip into any zerg's mind as she chose. But now she pulled back from all the ceaseless streaming of information and focused her attention on this.

Human . . . and protoss. Mentally working together. Kerrigan knew that Zeratul, the late unlamented Tassadar, and Raynor had shared thoughts. But they'd created nothing like what she now sensed. Kerrigan hadn't even realized such a thing was possible. Human and protoss brains were so different. Even a psionic would have difficulty working with a protoss.

Unless . . .

Her fingers came up to touch her face, trailing along the spines that lay like Medusa locks on her head. She had been remade. Part human, part zerg.

Maybe Mengsk had done the same thing with a human and a protoss. She wouldn't put it past him. She would put very little indeed past him. She herself might even have been the one to give him the idea.

She'd been what was known as a ghost herself, once. A terran psychic, trained to assassinate, with technology that enabled her to become as invisible as the ghost for which she was named. She knew that people who trained in this program were made of stern stuff; the people who put them through the training, heartless.

Ripples in a pond.

She needed to go to the source.

What had gone wrong?

Valerian Mengsk couldn't believe what he was seeing. His ships were just . . . sitting there in space while the vessel with Jacob Ramsey and Rosemary Dahl aboard made a successful jump. They were gone. He'd had them, but now they were gone.

"Raise Stewart!" he snapped. His assistant, Charles Whittier, jumped at his employer's words.

"I've been trying to," Whittier stammered, his voice pitched even higher than usual in his agitation. "They're not responding. I can't raise anyone at the compound either."

"Did Dahl's ship manage to emit some kind of electromagnetic pulse?" It was a possibility, but not a likely one; all of Valerian's ships were well protected against such things happening.

"Possible, I suppose," Whittier said doubtfully. "Still trying to raise—"

Eight screens came to life at once, with nearly a dozen people talking simultaneously. "Talk to Ethan," Valerian ordered, leaning down to mute all the other channels. "Find out how it is that he managed to let them slip through his fingers. I'll talk to Santiago."

Santiago did not look like he wanted to talk. Valerian would go so far as to say the man looked positively rattled, but the admiral managed to compose himself.

"Sir," Santiago said, "there was . . . I'm not sure how to explain it—some kind of psi attack. Ramsey rendered us all completely unable to move until he jumped."

Valerian frowned, his gray eyes taking in images of the others on the vessel. They all looked shaken in one way or another, but—was that young woman over there *smiling*?

"Let me speak with Agent Starke," Valerian said. If somehow Jacob Ramsey and the protoss inside his head had indeed been able to send such an attack against his best and brightest, Devon Starke would know the most about it.

Agent Devon Starke was a ghost, one who had come perilously close to becoming a literal one a little more than a year ago. That was when Arcturus Mengsk had decided that the ghost program needed a serious overhaul.

"They are useful tools," Mengsk had said to his son. "But they are double-edged ones." He'd frowned into his port. Valerian knew he was thinking about Sarah Kerrigan. Mengsk had helped Kerrigan escape the ghost program, and for that he'd won passionate loyalty from the woman. Valerian had seen holos of her; she'd been beautiful and intense. But then when Kerrigan had outlived her usefulness, started to voice questions, Mengsk had abandoned her to the zerg. He thought they'd kill her for him, but they had another idea. They'd taken this woman and turned her into their queen. Thus it was that Mengsk had unwittingly created the being who was now probably his greatest enemy.

Valerian was determined to learn from his father, both the good lessons and the painful ones. A ghost who was loyal to you was a good thing; letting one out of your control was not.

So when Mengsk decided that he would terminate—in a controlled environment this time—fully half the current ghosts in his government, Valerian had spoken. He'd asked to have one.

Mengsk eyed him. "Squeamish, son?"

"Of course not," Valerian said. "But I'd like one to help me with my research. Mind reading is a useful thing indeed."

Arcturus grinned. "Very well. Your birthday's coming up, isn't it? I'll let you have your pick of the litter. I'll send their files over to you tomorrow."

The following afternoon, Valerian was perusing a data chip containing the files of two hundred and eighty-two ghosts, two hundred and eighty-one of which would be dead within thirty-six hours. Valerian shook his head at the waste. While he understood that his father was dedicating all his resources to rebuilding his empire, it seemed a poor decision to Valerian to simply terminate the ghosts. But it was not his place to challenge or even seriously question his father on such decisions.

Not yet anyway.

One file in particular stood out. Not because of the man's history or his physical appearance—neither was remarkable—but because of an almost offhand notation about Starke's area of specialization. "#25876 seems to excel in remote viewing and psychometry. This predilection is counterbalanced by a proportionate weakness in telepathic manipulation and a less efficient method of termination of assignments."

Translation—#25876, known now by his birth name of Devon Starke, didn't much care to plant mental orders for suicide or murder, and didn't like to kill with his own hands. Devon Starke could do these things, certainly, which was why he had not been terminated before now. Mengsk wanted tools he could use immediately. Later, when the empire was firmly established, there would be a place for those who could, say, tell who had held what wineglass and where their families might be hidden away.

But that was later, and at this moment Mengsk wanted to keep the best assassins and at the same time send them a very firm message about what would happen to them once they were no longer useful to him.

Valerian knew well what had happened the last time Mengsk had a ghost who was "problematic." Mengsk did not want that to happen again.

So for his twenty-first birthday, the day he had come of age, his father had given him another human being as a gift. #25876 had been freed from the cell where he had been awaiting death. The neural inhibitor that had been deeply embedded into his brain as a youth was removed, and Starke was permitted to remember his identity and history. He was also permitted to know why he'd been spared, and who had chosen him.

He therefore was utterly loyal to Valerian Mengsk.

Starke's face appeared on the screen. Devon Starke was, like Jacob Ramsey, someone you wouldn't give more than a passing glance. Slight, shorter than average, with thinning brown hair and an unremarkable face, the only memorable thing about Devon was his voice. It was a deep, musical baritone, the sort of voice that immediately caught and held one's attention. And because being memorable was not exactly what being a ghost was all about, Devon Starke had gotten used to seldom speaking.

"Sir," Devon said, "there was indeed a psychic contact from Professor Ramsey. But I wouldn't call it an attack. A delaying tactic, maybe, to allow them time to escape." A pause. "Perhaps we should continue this conversation in private? I can step into my quarters and have you patched through."

"Good idea," said Valerian.

At that moment, Charles Whittier turned and looked at him, visibly upset. "Sir—I think you should hear this. Someone named Samuels; he says it's urgent."

Valerian sighed. "One moment, Devon." He punched a button and turned to the screen Charles had indicated.

Samuels, dressed in medical scrubs and looking a bit panicked, was gesticulating. The sound came on in mid-sentence. "—critical condition. They're operating on him now but—"

"Hold on a moment, Samuels. This is Mr. V," Valerian said, using the false name he had adopted when working with most underlings. Very few knew his true identity as the Heir Apparent to the Terran Dominion. "Calm yourself and speak clearly. What's going on?"

Samuels took a deep breath and ran his hands through his hair in what was obviously a nervous gesture. Valerian observed that Samuels' hands were bloody and that the man's fair hair was now clotted with the substance.

"It's Mr. Stewart, sir. He was injured when Ramsey and Dahl escaped. He's in critical condition. They're working on him now."

"Tell me what happened with Dahl and Ramsey."

"Sir, I'm just a paramedic, I don't know much about what went on, only that we have wounded."

"Please, then, find someone who does know, and have him or her contact me at once." Valerian nodded to Charles, who continued speaking with the flustered paramedic. Briefly, he permitted himself to wonder why someone who was trained in handling life-and-death situations was so upset by what had happened.

He switched back to Starke, who was alone in his quarters. "Do we have privacy?"

Devon grinned. "Yes, sir." Devon had, of course, read the minds of the rest of the crew to make certain that their line was not being tapped. Having a ghost was so terribly convenient.

"Continue." Valerian placed his hands on the table and leaned down closer to the screen.

"Sir . . . as I said, it was psychic, but it wasn't an attack. There was nothing hostile or harmful about it. Somehow, Ramsey managed to link our minds. Not just mine to his . . . all of our minds. Everyone in this immediate area. And not just thoughts, but . . . feelings, sensations. I—"

For the first time since Valerian had known the man, Starke seemed at a complete and utter loss for words. Valerian could easily believe it, if this was indeed what had happened. This was protoss psi-power, not human. Only a tiny fraction of humanity had any psychic ability at all, and only a small percentage of those could do what the ghosts could do. And from all accounts, even the most gifted, most finely trained human telepaths were pitiful compared to an ordinary, run-of-the-mill protoss.

He hungered to hear more, but he could tell that Starke was in no real position to tell him. Pushing aside his impatience and burning curiosity, Valerian said, "I'm recalling your vessel and two of the others, Devon. We'll discuss this more when you've had a chance to gather your thoughts."

Starke gave him a grateful expression and nodded. His image blinked out, replaced by that of the vessel floating serenely in space.

Valerian tapped his chin thoughtfully. Now he understood better why the paramedic he'd spoken with seemed so shaken and distracted. If Devon had the right of it—and knowing his ghost, Valerian was certain he had—then the man had just undergone what was possibly the most profound experience of his life.

Not for the first time, Valerian wished he had the freedom to have been present when these miraculous things were happening, rather than hearing about them secondhand. To have been with Jake Ramsey when he finally entered the temple. To have felt this strange psychic contact that Devon was certain wasn't an attack. He sighed. *Noblesse oblige,* he thought ruefully.

"Sir, I have a Stephen O'Toole who says he's now in charge," Whittier said. At Valerian's nod, Whittier put the man through.

Valerian listened while O'Toole related what had happened. Rosemary Dahl had managed to take Ethan Stewart hostage, using her former lover to get to the hangar in Stewart's compound. Once inside the hangar, fighting had broken out. Apparently someone named Phillip Randall, Ethan's top assassin, had been killed—the witness said by the professor. Ethan himself had gotten a round of slugs in the chest from Rosemary. Fortunately a team had been on hand with sufficient time to get Stewart into surgery, although the prognosis was not good.

Valerian shook his head as he listened, half in despair, half in grudging admiration. Jacob Ramsey and Rosemary Dahl were proving to be more than worthy opponents. The problem was, he'd never wanted them to be opponents at all. None of this was supposed to happen. Rosemary, Jake, and Valerian should have been together in his study, sipping fine liquor and discussing the magnificent archeological breakthroughs Jacob had made. And perhaps that would yet happen.

It was a pity about Ethan. Valerian had poured a great deal of money into financing Ethan Stewart. If he died, it would be quite the loss.

"Thank you for the update, Mr. O'Toole. Please keep Charles apprised of Mr. Stewart's condition. I've recalled three of my vessels but am leaving the others there for the time being. I will be in contact."

It had been touch-and-go for a long while. Ten more minutes and it would have been too late. As it was, Ethan Stewart was a mess. Whoever shot him had done so at close range, but had been a bit impatient, which had meant he hadn't stopped to make sure he'd finished the job. Paramedics had snipped off just enough bloodstained clothing to get an IV in one arm and lay bare the bloody chest, impaled with several spikes. The chief surgeon, Janice Howard, had deftly removed the spikes, and they lay in a glittering crimson pile on a table near the bed on which Ethan rested. One had gotten too close—she'd had to suture up a slice to his heart. But Ethan was incredibly fit and apparently as strong-willed in an unconscious state as he was while waking, and against all odds, they'd saved him.

She was closing up the chest cavity, daring to think the worst was over, when suddenly a harsh, wailing sound cut through the air and the room's lighting changed from antiseptic white to blood red. Howard swore. "Hit the override!"

For a second, her assistants just stared at her. She knew what the sound meant, and so did they, but Janice Howard had taken an oath, and even if the base was under attack she wasn't going to stop in the middle of a life-and-death operation.

"Hit the damn override!" she yelled, and this time the assistant obeyed. The sound of the Klaxons dimmed and the light returned to normal. Howard gritted her teeth, calmed herself, and returned to the delicate job at hand. She was almost done. A few moments later, she'd finished stitching up her employer like a cloth mannequin and let out a long sigh.

"Someone find out what's going on," she said. Samuels nodded and began trying to raise someone from security. She wasn't overly worried for her personal safety or that of her team; the compound was complex and well guarded and the medical wing was located deep inside. Of more concern to her were the casualties elsewhere on the base. They'd already weathered one attack today; she wondered how many people they'd have to stitch up when it was all over.

She stepped back, peeling off her bloody gloves and disposing of them while her assistants cut away the rest of Ethan Stewart's bloodstained clothing.

"Can't raise anyone," Samuels said. "Everything's down."

"Keep trying," Howard ordered, fighting back a little flutter of panic.

"Huh . . . this is weird," Sean Kirby said. Howard turned to look at him and her eyes fell to Ethan's left wrist.

The clothing on the right arm had been cut away so they could insert the IV, but they'd ignored his left arm until now. The wrist was encircled by a small bracelet which had been taped to his skin. No, not a bracelet, a collection of wires and hardware—

"Shit," moaned Howard, darting forward, blood still on her upper arms. She grabbed at Ethan's hair, knowing now that it wasn't hair at all, hoping she wouldn't find what she knew she would, and tugged off the hairpiece.

A delicate netting of fine, luminous wires was wrapped around Ethan's bald pate, held in place by small pieces of tape.

Damn it! There'd been no time to check for such things, he'd been within minutes of death when they'd found him and the surgery had begun almost immediately. It'd taken six hours. How long had he been wearing this thing before then? What kind of damage had it done? Why was he wearing it anyway, Ethan was no telepath—

Gunfire rattled in the corridor. All heads turned toward the doorway. All heads but Janice Howard's.

"We're medical staff; they won't kill us, whoever they are," said Howard, hoping to calm them. Howard did not look at the doorway, instead bending over Ethan and starting to remove the tape that fastened the softly glowing wires to his cleanly shaven scalp. She didn't know much about these things. Every instinct told her to just rip it off, but she feared that might damage him further.

More gunfire, and screams. Horrible, shrill, agonized screams. And a strange, chittering sound, a sort of clacking.

"What the . . . ," whispered Samuels, his eyes wide.

Howard thought she knew what it was. She was pretty sure everyone else in the room had guessed as well. But there was nothing to be done, except their jobs. There were no weapons in an operating room;

no one had ever expected they would need them. And if the sound came from the source Howard thought it did, it was unlikely that any weapon any of the doctors and assistants could wield would do anything but make them die slower. They had a patient. He came first. With hands that did not shake, she continued to unfasten the tape.

The screaming stopped. The silence that followed was worse. Howard removed the last piece of tape and gently disengaged the psi-screen.

A bubbling, liquid sound came from the door and a harsh, acrid odor assaulted her nostrils. Coughing violently and holding the psi-screen net in her hands, Howard turned. The door was melting into a steaming puddle, the acid that had dissolved it now starting to eat through the floor. Framed in the hole that was now the doorway to the operating room were creatures straight out of nightmares.

Zerg.

Her team stood frozen in place. The zerg, strangely enough, also did not advance. There were three of them that she could see, standing almost motionless. Two of them were smallish; she'd heard the term "doglike" used in training to describe zerglings, but now that she beheld them, they were nothing so pleasant. They waited, incisors clicking, red human blood shiny on their carapaces. Above them, its sinuous neck undulating slightly, towered something that looked like a deranged cross between a cobra and an insect. Scythelike arms, glinting in the antiseptic light of the operating room, waited, presumably for the order to slice off heads.

The zerglings drooled, fidgeting a little, moving slightly into the room so as not to be standing in the puddle of acid. The medical team backed up as if the creatures were indeed dogs, sheepdogs from old Earth, herding them into the corner. They went, terrified into obedience, confused that the creatures they were told would rip them to pieces on sight were not doing so. Thinking that maybe they might be deemed unimportant, and live to talk about the encounter over a beer somewhere someday.

Howard hoped that too. But she knew in her gut she was wrong.

The zergling in the lead was staring at her intently, and Howard knew without knowing how she knew that someone other than the creature was looking through its eyes. Those black eyes, flat and emotionless, went from her face to her hands to the prone form of Ethan Stewart on the bed.

The cobralike thing—hydralisk, that was the name; somehow it was important to Howard to use the proper term for things, even now when the properly named hydralisk was about to kill her and the thought made hysteria bubble up inside her—reared back and spat something on Ethan. It was a strange gooey substance, and as she watched, it spread, rapidly encasing him in some kind of webbing or cocoon.

Attacking her patient.

"No!" Howard cried, the paralysis broken. A saver

of lives to the last, she sprang forward. The zergling whirled on her, chittering with excitement, happy to be freed from its command to sit, to stay; by God it really was like a dog, wasn't it—

She heard the screams around her as she hit the ground, and after that, heard nothing more.

CHAPTER TWO

IN THE DARKNESS, THERE WAS PAIN.

Jake Ramsey swam unwillingly back to consciousness and the dull throbbing ache that had awakened him. Eyes still closed, he lifted a hand to his forehead and probed gingerly at the crusted blood that covered a good-sized lump, then hissed as the pain went from dull and throbbing to knife-sharp.

"You hit your head when we jumped," came a cool female voice.

For a long, confusing moment, Jake didn't remem-ber any of it. Then it all came tumbling down on him.

He was on a stolen ship, fleeing from Valerian Mengsk, son of the emperor. Valerian wanted him . . . wanted him because . . .

Because you have the memories of a protoss preserver in your mind, came Zamara's cool voice inside his head.

Oh yeah, thanks for reminding me, Jake thought sarcastically.

He sat up slowly. His head spun and he made no further movement for a few minutes, fighting back nausea. It was all coming back to him now. The offer that Valerian had made, hiring a "crackpot" archeologist like Jake to explore a dark temple of unknown alien origin. Full funding, full support, state-of-the-art equipment—it had seemed too good to be true. And of course, like most things that seem too good to be true, it had been. There'd been this one little catch.

Jake had been ordered to get inside the "temple," as Valerian was fond of calling the construct. Jake had done so, deciphering the riddle that had blocked entrance to the innermost chamber of a labyrinthine creation. And inside that chamber . . . inside, Zamara had been waiting. Waiting for someone to figure out the secret, waiting for someone to whom she could deliver the precious burden of an entire race's memories.

He'd almost gone mad. She'd had to rewire his brain. It had been too much for him to handle, an onslaught of memories of a time known now as the Aeon of Strife, when the protoss had been violent and ruthless and seemingly lived to slaughter one another. Even now, those first few flashes of memories, exploding into his brain without context or explanation, made him break out into a cold sweat.

It was necessary. And you are . . . undamaged.

Tell that to the lump on my head, he thought back.

Suddenly Jake had gone from an expendable crackpot to someone—hell, call it for what it was, some "thing"—of great value to Valerian and the Dominion. Rosemary "R. M." Dahl, the woman who had supposedly been appointed to keep him safe, had turned on him and his entire team. The marines who had delivered the archeologists to the planet with friendly well wishes and affable smiles now came back for them, but this time the team were prisoners, not guests. It had been the coldest of comforts when, unexpectedly, the marines had included Rosemary and her team as their prisoners as well.

It was Rosemary who had spoken to him a minute ago, Rosemary who was piloting this stolen vessel. Jake got to his feet, gripping onto the back of a chair for support. His head hurt like mad, but he tried to ignore it, and he turned to face the woman who had once been betrayer and was now comrade.

She had been strapped into her seat when they made the jump, and so, unlike Jake, had escaped injury. Strapped in and lost in a place of complete and total union with every mind in the vicinity. Jake had instigated the melding, shocking and upsetting the protoss inside him. As part of this process of integrating the memories she carried into his brain, Zamara had guided him to and through one of the most pivotal moments in protoss history—the creation and discovery, for it was both, of something called the Khala. It was a union not just of the minds but of the hearts and emotions of the protoss. Within this space, they did not simply understand one another, they almost became one another. It had been profound and beautiful, and it was only Jake's desperate need to save himself, Zamara, and Rosemary that had enabled him to pull out of the link and hit the button that would allow them to elude their pursuers by leaping blindly around the sector.

Jake, however, had *not* been safely strapped in, and he winced as he looked at the blood on the panel where he'd banged his head.

Rosemary's blue eyes flitted over to him, then down to the panel. "Panel's fine," she said. Doubtless it was meant as a reassurance. Even if it wasn't, he decided he'd take it that way.

"Well, that's good."

Rosemary grimaced. "It's about the only thing that is. That was a very rough entry. We're going to have to land somewhere and repair shortly—where, I have no idea, as I don't even know exactly where we are yet. I woke up to life support on the fritz and got that taken care of. Navigation's iffy and one of the engines has been damaged."

She looked up at him. "You don't look so good either. Go . . . do something about that."

"Your concern is appreciated," he said.

"Medkit's in the back, on the top shelf in the locker," Rosemary called. Jake made his way to the back of the vessel, opened the locker, and found the kit. He poured some sanitizing cleanser onto a pad and, peering into the small and barely adequate mirror fastened to the locker door, dabbed at his face. A nanosecond later he fought the urge to leap to the ceiling and scream—the cleanser stung like hell. The cut was, of course, not nearly as bad as the mask of blood on his face indicated. Head wounds bled a lot. The lump was still tender but it, too, was not too bad. Gritting his teeth against the pain, he swabbed at the cut, soiling pad after pad.

"How long have I been out?" he called up to Rosemary.

"Not that long. Maybe five, ten minutes."

That was good. Minor concussion then, nothing too severe.

How are you doing in there, Zamara?

He caught a brush of amusement, but Zamara seemed a bit distracted. *Well enough, Jacob. Thank you for inquiring.*

Everything okay?

I am simply considering what to do next.

"So Jake," Rosemary continued as he fished around for a bandage. "That . . . experience . . . before we jumped—what the hell did Zamara do to all of us? I've done a lot of drugs in my day and that was, by far, the strangest and best trip I've ever been on."

There was a time when both Jake and Zamara would have bridled at the thought of something as profound and sacred as union within the Khala being compared to a drug trip. But now that both of their minds had blended, even briefly, with Rosemary's, now that both had had a hint of what it had been like to *be* her, the condemnation was cursory and half-hearted. R. M. was using terms she knew to try to describe something far beyond what any human had ever experienced. No disrespect was intended.

"I've told you about the Khala, the Path of Ascension," he said. He found a bottle of plastiscab and gingerly applied a layer over the cut. It warmed up almost immediately, and he winced a little. He disliked the stuff, but it worked. The layer of plastic that would form in a few seconds would protect the cut quite efficiently, although sometimes removal of the plastic bandage led to reopening the wound; someone hadn't thought things through very well. He replaced the bottle and put the kit back on the shelf. Making his way to the cockpit, he continued. "It's how the protoss were able to come together again and rebuild their society after the Aeon of Strife."

R. M. had found a tool kit and was now lying underneath the console, unscrewing a panel. A cluster of wires dropped down a few centimeters, and there was a soft glow of chips in their tangled center. Briefly, Jake had a flash of another memory Zamara had shared with him—that of a strange chamber created by beings known as the xel'naga, the benefactors and teachers of the protoss. Jake had relived the memories of a protoss named Temlaa. Temlaa had beheld the bizarre and terrifying sight of writhing cables emerging from walls to fasten onto his friend Savassan. Though the outcome had been wholly positive, it had deeply disturbed Temlaa and, through that long-ago protoss, Jacob Jefferson Ramsey in the here and now.

His head suddenly hurt again.

"Yeah," Rosemary said. "Go on."

"Well . . . it didn't look like we were going to be able to escape Valerian and Ethan's ships."

"No kidding," R. M. snorted. "Five Wraiths and a Valkyrie from Val plus whatever Ethan wanted to throw at us."

Rosemary's voice was completely calm as she mentioned Ethan Stewart's name. It was as if he were a stranger to her, and after Ethan had betrayed R. M. so badly, Jake supposed she thought of him that way. Nevertheless, even if someone had betrayed him—as indeed, the woman lying in front of him busily rerouting wiring had—he couldn't have done what Rosemary had—fired a rifle at point-blank range into the chest of a former lover. Ethan had dropped like a stone, blood blossoming like a crimson flower across his white shirt.

Jake looked away. He was grateful for Rosemary's coldheartedness in a way. It'd saved his life and Zamara's more than once.

I told you we would need her, Zamara reminded him.

Yes. You did.

"So?" Rosemary prompted, her eyes on her work.

Jake continued. "Well . . . I knew what had happened to the protoss when they first were exposed to the Khala. And I thought, what if I shared that feeling with everyone in the surrounding area?"

Rosemary fixed him with intense blue eyes. As always, Jake felt something flutter inside him at that gaze. "You linked everyone in the Khala, Jake?" Anger and a hint of fear flitted across her face. He didn't have to read her thoughts to know what she was thinking—was she going to have her brain rewired, as his had been?

"No, no," he said. "That's not possible. We're not protoss, for one thing. Our brains can't handle something like that directly. And even the protoss needed to touch the khaydarin crystals to experience it, at least at first. Not sure about it now; Zamara hasn't taken me that far yet. What I did was share the memory of how it felt, and for a brief moment I opened your minds to each other. You all—we all—did the rest."

She regarded him for a few seconds, then shook her dark head. "Wow" was all she said, but it was heartfelt.

"Yeah," Jake replied, his monosyllabic comment equally sincere. He wondered, as he had right before they had made the jump, if something more lasting than his immediate escape would come of that instant when, for the first time, nearly a thousand humans had had the briefest, palest hint of what it was like to have minds and hearts joined as one.

He hoped so.

Rosemary swore. "I thought as much. Rot in hell, Ethan."

"What's wrong?" Jake asked worriedly.

"He's got a tracking device integrated into the navigation system. He—"

—sticks it in there, a tiny little thing, easy to miss if you didn't know what you were looking for and if you didn't know the bastard's little trick of—

"Hey!" Rosemary's voice cracked like a whip, and the anger that rolled off her was a one-two punch. Jake blinked. She was out from under the console and jabbing a finger in his face so fast he'd barely seen her move. "Get the *hell* out of my head! Don't you dare do that again without asking me. Do you understand?"

She was angry out of all proportion to what she was thinking, but Jake knew that wasn't the point. She had very recently been through a profound experience that she was still trying to integrate. And besides, although he was getting used to the idea of his thoughts being known by another as they popped into his mind, Jake well remembered the outrage he himself had felt when it started to happen.

The color was high in her cheeks, and her blue eyes sparkled. Jake winced. "Sorry," he said. "I just was anxious to know what had happened and I didn't even think about it. It won't happen again."

That is not a safe promise to make, Jacob, came Zamara's warning voice. *There may be a time when we need to violate it.*

She's proven herself amply, in my opinion. You're so used to doing this casually, as part of who you are. For humans, it's much more an invasion of privacy.

Rosemary does have difficulty trusting others, Zamara agreed.

That's the understatement of the year.

Rosemary searched his gaze and then nodded. She took a deep breath, composed herself, and returned to her task. "This is an old trick of Ethan's. He integrates the tracking device completely into the navigation system, so that every adjustment and every coordinate goes right back to the source. You don't just know where this ship is, you know where it's been. It's also impossible to remove."

Jake blanched, and he felt Zamara's concern as well. "What does that mean?"

"It means we need to get an entirely new nav system."

He stared at her. "How are we going to do that? We're on the run in case you haven't noticed."

"I have a good idea where we can start looking safely. But first, I want to have a look at the damage. I'll suit up and check it out. You and Zamara . . . don't touch anything."

She scooted out from under the console and got lithely to her feet. Purposefully, she strode toward the locker and began to suit up for a space walk.

She is deliberately withholding information. She will not tell us where she intends to go.

Let her cool off, Jake replied to Zamara. *She's mad, and I don't blame her a bit. That was a stupid thing to do. I guess that bump on the head rattled me more than I thought.*

If an alien consciousness inside one's mind could sigh, Zamara did. *When this is all taken care of and the vessel is repaired, our destination must be Aiur.*

Jake thought about the homeworld of the protoss. Lush, verdant, tropical. Rich with vegetation and animal life, dotted with heart-stoppingly gorgeous relics of the xel'naga in their strange, twining, mysterious beauty. He smiled softly.

Rosemary, now encased in a suit that would enable her to move around in the cold darkness of space, threw him a glance and scowled a little. "See that light?" She pointed to the console. He looked where she indicated and saw a small button, currently dark. He nodded. "Once I get outside and the doors seal shut again, it's going to turn green. It'll stay green the whole time I'm out there. If it turns red and an alarm starts sounding, I'm in trouble. At that point I will give you permission to read my mind so that you can get me safely back inside. Got that?"

"Yes," he said. He understood what she was saying. She was putting her life in his hands.

"Okay then." She moved to the back of the cabin and touched a button. A door irised open and she stepped through without a backward glance. A few seconds later, the button came to life, glowing green just as R. M. had said. He sighed. His head was still hurting.

We will head for the underground chambers that Temlaa and Savassan discovered. There is great technology there. It will help me to complete my mission and keep my people safe.

Jake asked excitedly, "The chambers? That underground city?" Zamara had given him only the briefest tantalizing glimpse of the vastness that comprised the hidden city of the xel'naga. Most of Temlaa's memories concerned a few very specific places, one of which was a chamber in which the desiccated protoss bodies had been stored. He wanted to close his eyes and relive that memory, now that Zamara had informed him that was their destination, but he had a duty. Rosemary had entrusted him with her safety.

I will watch over her. You may revisit the chambers if you wish.

Jake nodded, trusting Zamara, and closed his eyes.

There was the memory, first Temlaa's, then Zamara's, and now his: as pure and perfect as if it were actually unfolding before him rather than being recollected.

In the center, hovering and slowly moving up and down as it had no doubt done for millennia, was the largest, most perfect crystal Jake had ever seen. It pulsated as it moved languidly, and Jake realized that this was the source of the heartbeat sound he and Savassan had been hearing for some time now. For a long moment he forgot his fear and simply gazed raptly at the object, seduced by its radiant beauty and perfection of form.

In all the memories I hold, Zamara said, *all the things I have beheld and touched and known—there is nothing like this crystal, Jacob. Nothing.*

He sensed her awe and shared it. He thought he caught a fleeting tinge of hope so intense that he might even have called it "desperate." Jake began to query Zamara, but at that moment the door irised opened and Hurricane Rosemary stormed in. He blinked, suddenly realizing that about twenty minutes had passed without his even being aware of it.

"This is why you never jump without proper preparation," she said as she removed her helmet. "We'd have had to replace quite a bit even without Ethan's little tracking device."

"All right," Jake said. "If we have to, we have to. But we need to do it quickly. I've been talking with Zamara, and she thinks we need to get to Aiur."

Shedding the rest of her suit and hanging it back up in the locker, Rosemary turned to him. "Aiur? Why?"

"Remember those caverns beneath the surface I told you about?"

"Yeah . . . some kind of underground city." Rosemary's anger was now directed at the damage the ship had taken rather than at Jake. She actually looked interested in his comments. "We're going to get to see that place then?"

"Looks like. Zamara thinks there's some technology there that can help her. Help us."

Rosemary was regarding him thoughtfully. "You know, Professor, if there actually is ancient, advanced technology sitting quietly forgotten beneath the surface of Aiur . . . that really *could* help us."

"Rosemary—"

"Jake, listen. We're being hunted by the son of the *emperor,* for God's sake. We had to fight our way to get where we are right this minute and we'll have to keep fighting unless we do something about that. Look—I've cast my lot in with you. We've got to trust each other. I'm not going to rat you out, but this is a big net that's been cast for us. We might be able to make a trade with Valerian: our lives for whatever technology we can give him."

Out of the question.

I'm not telling her that, Zamara. She makes a good point.

This is my people's heritage we are discussing, Jacob. Our legacy. Protoss knowledge belongs to the protoss, not a terran emperor who will exploit it and use it for harm.

You killed a lot of terrans for protoss knowledge. And now Rosemary and I are on the line for it too. If this gets Rosemary and me out of danger, I'm all for it.

There was silence from the alien inside his head, and Jake realized that Rosemary was looking at him expectantly.

"Well?"

"Uh—well, Zamara's not too keen on the idea," Jake said truthfully. "But we can talk about it when we get there."

R. M. nodded. "We're not going to get there at all unless we haul ass and effect repairs pronto." She moved past him and slid into the seat. He took the chair beside her, although he knew nothing about the dozens of lights, buttons, and switches in front of him.

"Now let me see . . . Good! I was right in my hunch about where we are. So that means that . . . "

She punched a few more buttons and a star chart came up. Rosemary nodded, pleased. "Excellent." She laid in a course.

"So where are we going?"

She gave him a grin. "Back in time, Jake. Back in time."

CHAPTER THREE

IN THE DARKNESS, THERE WAS HARMONY.

Unified, single-minded of purpose, seven beings were one. Each contributed to the whole, was present and yet subsumed, the magnificent, powerful, deadly *one* greater than the individuals who comprised it.

It . . . *he* . . . moved languidly now, but could move almost at the speed of thought when roused to action. Radiant at his center, his glow was shadow.

He stirred as the ripples of something brushed his mind. Something familiar. Something he wanted destroyed. Something that threatened him and his task.

Preserver, a part of him named the loathed quarry.

How can this be? A preserver, in such a place? wondered another part.

And there is something else. It is not pure protoss mental energy. It has been tainted—or augmented. It is difficult to know which.

How and why, tainted or pure, it does not matter. It must be found and stopped. Like all preservers. Other parts, once individuals, now fractions of the whole, murmured their discontent.

Preservers were a dire threat, perhaps the only true one this being, naming itself in his multiple consciousness Ulrezaj after the most powerful individual that comprised him, had ever discovered. Preservers knew too much. And so Ulrezaj had been attentive to any signs of them, tracking them down one by one and snuffing out their fragile little lives until soon there would be none left. There were only a handful as it were, and they had never been many. It was a foolish way to carry information, inside a mortal shell that was so easily crushed.

The seven-who-were-one turned their formidable mental powers toward this strange sensation, this ripple in a dark, still pond.

Ulrezaj would find the renegade preserver. He would find it, he would destroy it, and the threat the protoss posed would be no more.

And then Ulrezaj would continue in his glorious work.

Valerian wielded his sword like all the demons of hell were attacking him.

Parry, stroke, whirl, slice, impale—the imaginary foes attacking him from all sides at once fell before him. He leaped up as a nonexistent sword sliced at his knees, lunged forward, turned, and blocked a fictitious attack. Tucking his sword, he ducked, rolled forward, and came up fighting. Sweat plastered his fair hair to his forehead, dappled his upper lip, slicked his chest. His heart thundered in his ears and despite all his training his breath was coming in little gasps. He had never practiced with such focused intensity before in his life, and he craved the peace he knew would come after such exertion.

He finished the routine, twirled the sword expertly over his head, sheathed it, and bowed. Valerian never forgot to bow, no matter what. To bow was to remember one's opponent. And Valerian always, always remembered who he was fighting.

There came a tentative knock on the door. "Come in, Charles," Valerian called, pouring himself a glass of water and drinking thirstily.

While Whittier always looked as if something was wrong, this time the distress on his face was more pronounced than usual. "Sir," Whittier said, "it's His Excellency. He wishes to speak with you at once."

Valerian's stomach tensed, but years of practice at hiding his emotions enabled him to respond calmly. "Thank you, Charles. Tell him I will be there in a moment."

Whittier gulped. "Sir, he's pretty impatient."

Valerian turned cool gray eyes upon his assistant. "I will be there in a moment, Charles," he repeated in a soft voice.

"Of course, sir." Whittier closed the door.

Valerian wiped his face with a cloth, composing himself. After the debacle at Stewart's compound, he'd known he'd be hearing from his father soon.

Off the beaten track the planet might have been, but word of zerg in terran space would have gotten to Arcturus at light speed. He finished his glass of water, changed his shirt, and went into Whittier's office.

Whittier jumped at the sound of the opening door. Valerian sighed. Whittier was an extremely capable assistant and Valerian relied upon him a great deal, but the man had the constitution of a rabbit.

"Thank you, Charles, put him through," Valerian said. He returned to his training room and went to the small vidsys that was set up in a curtained-off area. Steeling himself for the confrontation—for he knew such the conversation would be—he touched a button.

The visage of Arcturus Mengsk appeared. Mengsk was a big man, and managed to convey that even on a small screen. His hair was thick, if more salt than pepper these days, as was his mustache. Piercing gray eyes met those of his son.

"Four years with no sign of the zerg, and then all of a sudden they show up on a remote planet which happens to be where you've set up a former black marketer. I didn't get where I am today by believing in coincidence. Anything you care to tell me?"

Valerian smiled. "And good afternoon to you too, Father."

Arcturus waved a hand. "Rule number one for running an empire, son: when the zerg are a topic of conversation, the niceties go out the airlock."

"I'll remember that. The situation is under control, Father."

"Define 'under control,' and tell me why the zerg are there in the first place."

Valerian debated. He could remain silent, or lie, or tell the truth. It was too late to sweep everything completely under the rug. But the most important thing to Valerian was that Mengsk not know about Jake's . . . unique situation. Valerian still held out hope that he and Jake could sit down as fellow lovers of archeology and discuss the wonders he had discovered. If Mengsk learned about it, Jake would be snatched from Valerian's hands and his mind poked, prodded, scanned, and eventually rendered inert. What Arcturus wanted was an edge, some new technology, some new and better way to smear his enemies into paste. He cared nothing for the glories of a vanished civilization or unequaled cultural insights.

Quickly, Valerian tried to think what Arcturus would know already, and would likely know shortly. The emperor would know that three of Valerian's ships had been there, and from their logs probably that three more had been recalled. Depending on the condition in which the zerg had left the hangar, he could possibly know that a ship had been stolen and others had been sent after it. Jacob Ramsey's name might be in some log somewhere, but Valerian knew Ethan would not have left any traceable information about the archeologist or his discovery. Ethan would have kept that sort of thing carefully locked up in his head. Which, sadly, had likely been ripped from his shoulders or dissolved in acid. No one had been left alive, either in the compound or in the ships in orbit above the planet.

"I spoke with my contact there before the zerg descended," Valerian said, choosing his words carefully. "One of their ships was hijacked several hours before the zerg attacked. It could be that this was part of a personal grudge against Stewart. My sources indicate that the pilot was formerly romantically involved with him. Perhaps she led the zerg to him for some reason."

Mengsk made an annoyed sound. "The zerg aren't a wandering pack of wild dogs that just happen to catch your scent. They're directed within an inch of their disgusting little lives."

Valerian shrugged. "If they were directed, then they left immediately. They must have gotten what they came for."

That much at least was true. He had feared, when word came of the attack, that somehow Kerrigan had gotten wind of what had happened with Jake and had sent her zerg to claim him. How, he had no idea. They had come, descended, wreaked the havoc that was synonymous with their name, and departed.

A thought occurred to him, one that bothered and pleased him in equal parts. Still seemingly casual, he said, "Stewart was indeed a former black marketer. I used him for my own ends, but it's possible he was a double agent of sorts. I don't suppose he was working for you in any sort of capacity?"

Mengsk's jaw tightened almost imperceptibly. Few who didn't know him as well as Valerian did would have noticed.

"It's possible. I don't know every single person in my employ." Arcturus chuckled. "You have a mere handful, my boy. But don't worry, I'll soon give you more—maybe more than you can handle."

Valerian smiled. He wasn't certain he had guessed correctly, but it was, as Mengsk had just said, a possibility.

"I look forward to the challenge, Father. If he was not working for you, then perhaps for an enemy? I'm sure you have more than a handful of those."

Now Mengsk did frown. "Also entirely possible. Humans have been in league with Kerrigan before now." His gray eyes looked pensive. It was with difficulty that Valerian smothered a smile.

Maybe Ethan had indeed been playing both sides. It didn't matter now. What mattered was that even in death, Ethan was serving Valerian well. He had distracted Arcturus from the real target, which was the escaping vessel.

"I assume your people are there?" he asked his father.

"Of course."

"I will set mine to locating the hijacked ship then."

"If you feel it necessary," Mengsk said. "If anything else turns up, you are to notify me immediately. Anything that's of sufficient interest to warrant a zerg incursion into my space, I want to know about."

Valerian nodded. "Likewise. Stewart was my man. At least"—he smiled in what he hoped was a sufficiently self-deprecating manner—"I thought he was."

Mengsk chuckled, then his face was replaced by the official insignia.

Valerian was both pleased and uncomfortable with how the exchange had gone. He did not like misdirecting his father, but he knew—he *knew*—that Ramsey would be destroyed if Mengsk had him. He hoped that soon he would have Ramsey safely in his hands and this would no longer be an issue.

"Sir?"

Valerian realized he'd been staring at the now-dark screen for some moments. He turned at the sound of Devon Starke's melodious voice.

"Devon," Valerian said warmly, indicating a chair. "It seems I pulled you out just in time."

Starke nodded his thanks and took a chair. He smiled slightly.

"Not for the first time, sir. But yes, our recall was quite welcomed once we heard what had happened with the zerg."

Valerian didn't ask if Starke thought the zerg had come for Ramsey. That was his father's problem, not his. He needed to find Jake and Rosemary before Mengsk did.

He posed this problem to Starke. "They can be tracked, sir. All of Stewart's vessels have tracking devices hardwired into their navigation systems.

I have the sequence we need to look for." The ghost tapped his temple.

Valerian smiled. "Excellent. Now. Tell me about this psychic . . . I'm not sure what to call it."

Emotions flitted across Starke's thin face. "I've never experienced anything like this, sir. I know what you told me—that Ramsey had been attacked by a protoss and that knowledge had been rather forcefully placed into his brain. But I shouldn't have been able to sense that. Not at the distance I was from his vessel. It was . . . a sense of unity. Of dissolving barriers between people."

"Linking minds?"

Starke considered. "That, yes, but that was almost secondary. I can link my thoughts to yours. I can read your thoughts. Theoretically, linking to a third is not such a leap. We can't do it, not yet, although I've no doubt your father and others are hard at work on that."

Valerian smiled dryly. "No doubt at all."

"This was much more than that. Sir, I fear you'll think I'm waxing overly poetic if I say it felt less like linking minds and more like . . . linking *souls.*"

Starke spoke in a soft tone, his musical voice giving the words an extra resonance. The hairs rose on Valerian's arms.

"No, Devon. I don't think that's overly poetic at all. But please continue—this is fascinating."

Starke nodded. "I knew the thoughts and the feelings of everyone in all six of our vessels and everyone in the compound. I . . . It's as if I *was* everyone. All of them, all at the same time."

"All? Including Rosemary and Jake?"

Devon made an annoyed face. "Yes. But I fear I was unable to concentrate on Ramsey as hard as I should have. I was taken by surprise and rather overwhelmed by the entire thing. I can only imagine what it must have been like for nontelepaths to experience this. Sir, I felt their fears and their hopes, knew their worries and secrets. I almost became them."

Here he hesitated. Then he added, "And . . . they became me."

Valerian raised a blond eyebrow. "So. Ramsey now knows that I have a ghost on his trail."

"If he didn't suspect it already, then yes, sir, I expect that he does. Our only consolation is that Ramsey isn't as comfortable holding this information as he might be. I can't tell you for certain what I remember, and I've been undergoing training for such things since childhood."

Valerian nodded slowly, thoughtfully. "And you think this was done as a delaying tactic? This . . . psiburst?"

Starke hesitated. "Yes. But more than that. It was . . . I'm sorry, sir, but it was beautiful. Profoundly moving. If we could all stay in that space, really stay in it—there'd be no need for empires."

Although it would be understandable and even expected for Starke to mutter against Mengsk, considering how close he had come to dying because of an order from Valerian's father, the ghost had never voiced such sentiments. He knew that his employer was struggling with the same issues that beset all children of great parents—how to step out of their shadow without knifing them in the back. He knew Valerian's interests lay outside of conquest and more in cultural development. So Valerian was surprised to hear even this slight rebuke coming from Devon's lips.

"Nor should it be used as a tool for such," Valerian said mildly. Color blossomed in Starke's cheeks, but he remained silent.

Valerian realized he'd been right not to tell his father about Jake. What Jake had accomplished had provided perhaps the most powerful mental and emotional experience humanity had ever known. And Arcturus Mengsk, so single-minded in his purpose as to be almost pure in it, would view this ability as a weapon. He would obtain peace with it, yes, but only under his terms.

"When you have time, I want you to write down everything you remember," Valerian told Starke. "But first—we must find Jake and Rosemary."

CHAPTER FOUR

ROSEMARY'S SHORT-NAILED FINGERS FLEW OVER the console, setting in the coordinates immediately after they materialized in normal space. She leaned back, stretching, and finally it seemed as if she had relented enough to tell Jake and Zamara where they were headed.

"We need to replace the navigation system as well as some other parts that were damaged in the jump. That's not as difficult as it might sound, because system runners are great little vessels. They're not pretty, but boy are they functional, and they built thousands and thousands of them. They ended up being a sort of blueprint for most of the systems in place in any size ship today. So they don't require special equipment—you can swap things in and out pretty easily and pretty quickly. They're designed to keep going no matter how badly you have to patch them up. That's why they're so beloved by black marketeers."

"You sound like you've done this a lot," Jake said.

"I have," Rosemary answered. "Hell, Jake, I've done pretty much anything that's dangerous, illegal, or fun."

She offered a grin to Jake, still stretching in a fashion that brought a bit of color to his face. The grin was playful and uncomplicated, and he'd seen so precious little of either from her that he almost forgot to smile back. He realized that now that her anger at him had passed, she was starting to enjoy this. She was, as she had just said, in her element.

You were right to bring her along with us, Jake said. *I have no idea how to even pilot a ship, let alone repair one or navigate. And as for—*

His mind's eye filled with the image of Rosemary blowing the face off a former colleague who'd turned traitor. Of her whirling precisely and calculatedly shooting someone who'd spat at Jake. And then he thought of what he'd done—or, rather, what Zamara had done, using his body—to one Phillip Randall, prized assassin of Ethan Stewart.

You could have learned how to fight and kill on your own. We did not need her for that.

I don't want to learn to be like her in that way, Zamara. Or like you—not about that. I don't want that at all. The very thought seemed to make his headache return.

There are many things you do not want to do, Jacob Jefferson Ramsey, and yet you must do them.

There was a hint of sorrow emanating from Zamara, even while making this firm statement. Jake knew that the protoss disliked using him so, though there was never any question that she would. This was a new development in their relationship; it had certainly not been present at the outset. She had been grimly determined to see her mission through, and her lack of concern about him had been as impersonal as it was implacable. That had changed over the last several days, as she had given him more and more information, more memories.

Will there be more? Memories, like what you did with Temlaa and Savassan?

Yes. There is much more that you still need to know. More that you must understand before I can give you the final piece. I would not burden you with such if it were not absolutely necessary.

That's the least of my concerns about the situation. Now that I understand what to expect, I . . . am enjoying learning about your people. As an archeologist I find it fascinating.

"Well, it's a good thing you're along for the ride then," Jake said lightly to Rosemary. The entire mental exchange with Zamara had taken just a couple of seconds. "So, are you going to tell where you're taking us? You said something about going back in time?"

"Like I said, I had to cobble things together. I know all the spots to get spares. This one happens to have some historical significance about it. Ever heard of a little thing called the Battle of Brontes?"

"It sounds familiar."

She gaped at him. "Familiar? Where were you when all this stuff went down?"

"On a little planet called Pegasus, happily forgotten by the rest of the sector. We heard about the bigger events, sure, but I never followed the battles. Just the big things. Like the zerg and the protoss and the wiping out of entire colonies."

She shook her head. "Wow. Huh. I never thought of myself as being particularly up on current events, but I suppose you have to be, if you want to know which side your bread's buttered on. Anyway, there was a Confederacy general named Edmund Duke. There was a pretty major skirmish here against some of the Sons of Korhal. After a space battle, salvagers, scavengers, and thieves usually move in to take whatever is left . . . but our buddy Val's dad is rebuilding an empire and he needs all the ship parts he can lay his hands on. This place has become a salvage yard for the Dominion, and we will need to be careful getting in, and getting out. We're just about in viewing range." She hit a couple of buttons. "Ah, there we go."

Rosemary had brought them to a graveyard. Jake thought that it had indeed been a significant battle, to leave this much wreckage. He wondered if any effort had been made to find the bodies, or if they were out there along with pieces of ships, spinning slowly in starlit darkness, nothing more than space junk now. Some of the vessels appeared largely intact, others were obviously unspaceworthy pieces of debris.

"Okay, so far so good," said Rosemary, breaking his train of thought. "No sign of a welcoming party coming to intercept us. Chances are we haven't been noticed yet. We go in dark and drift in . . . just another piece of the junk." She touched a few controls and the power went down with a soft sigh. Jake and Rosemary were enveloped in dim starlight as the controls went dark. "Slow and unnoticed," Rosemary said. "More people than us know about this place. There's usually a lot of unsavory types here even with the Dominion's presence—smugglers and pirates and so on. There'll likely be a couple of Wraiths beating a patrol around the place, but we've got a system runner, so we should be able to outrun them if we're spotted."

Jake felt a twinge of amusement at the thought of Rosemary's referring to anyone else as "unsavory types." That sensation was shortly replaced by unease as they moved toward the dead ships. His headache increased as they passed several tense moments while the ship drifted closer and closer to the debris field. Finally, they were in among the pieces of wreckage. Giant parts of ships loomed past and Rosemary slowly brought minimal power online and used the runner's thrusters to avoid hitting any of the other vessels.

"No company yet—good. Let me risk some quick scans to see if we can find what we need." Jake was glad Rosemary seemed to know what she was doing. She was calling up information, her blue eyes scanning it quickly, and finally she nodded. "A compatible nav system right there, as well as some drive and life support components we need. May need work, but probably nothing I can't handle. Looks like we finally caught a break. Let me remove this one and then I'll go get the other."

Slowly, carefully, R. M. maneuvered the system runner until it was only about ten meters from the vessel in question. Rising, Rosemary located a tool kit, dropped down to the metal floor, and slid under the console. Jake watched in silent admiration as she unfastened the plating, reached into a jumble of wires and glowing chips, and inside of fifteen minutes removed a fairly large navigation unit. As they lifted the frame holding the nav system out, she pointed with a scowl to a glowing green circular component in the heart of the frame.

"There's our culprit."

"Are you going to destroy it?"

She shook her head. Her silky black hair flowed with the movement. As was always the case, Jake wished he could touch it without getting punched.

"We have a better use for it. All right, time to go get its replacement. Same deal as the last spacewalk, Professor. I go out, you watch the little light."

"Will do."

They carried the nav unit into the docking chamber, and she went into the back room and suited up. The door closed and a few moments later the light illuminated green. Jake waited until he saw her floating past, the tether secure on her body, nav unit in tow, directing herself purposefully to the Wraith they had pulled alongside of, and then got himself a coffee. It was much, much better than what passed for the beverage on the marine vessel the *Gray Tiger.* He supposed he shouldn't be surprised. This was a black marketer's vessel, after all. While he was up, he opened the medkit and found something for his headache.

The thought of the *Gray Tiger* made him think of his friends who had died aboard that ship. He wondered if he would ever remember them without this rush of commingled guilt and pain.

Eventually you will be able to. Once you fully understand what it was for which they died.

Don't suppose you're going to tell me this century?

Zamara chuckled at his turn of phrase. *There are things you must know first, as I have told you repeatedly.*

Be happy to learn them, so long as you watch out for Rosemary.

Of course.

Jake took another sip of the coffee, looked at the green light, smiled to himself, and closed his eyes.

Jake stood with the rest of the templar as their fallen brother, their leader, their friend, made his final voyage. Jake was not a young protoss, and this was not the first friend to whom he had bade farewell. But it never got easier.

Zoranis had been popular with his people. Thousands had turned out for this solemn ceremony, lining the Road of Remembrance for almost its entire length. The Road of Remembrance led from the provincial capital of Antioch, wound for several kilometers west, and ended at the ruins of an ancient xel'naga temple. Broken steps led up to a flat surface with a pool that collected rainwater. Here, the honored dead were ritually bathed, dressed for burial, left for a day's cycle under the watchful care of loved ones so that the sun, moon, and stars would shine upon them, and then laid into the earth for their final rest.

While the ritual itself was ancient, performed by each tribe even back during the Aeon of Strife, the Road had come into existence only after the protoss had embraced the Khala. The Road of Remembrance was a physical symbol of the Path of Ascension. As all protoss were joined in the Khala, so now all veterans and protoss of note, no matter their caste, were given the honor of traveling the Road of Remembrance. Jake had seen artisans, scientists, templar, and members of the Conclave alike being borne on a floating dais, a stasis field surrounding their bodies with a halo.

This was the first time he had walked beside the body of a high templar, though, and he hoped it would be the last.

Zoranis had fallen in honorable combat. He was not one to sit back and let others take all the risks while he made all the decisions. His choice had cost him his life, but had won the battle—as had his decision to have his second-in-command fight beside him.

The young protoss Adun was already becoming something of a legend. He had fought at Zoranis's side for over eighty years now. Few had seen a more graceful warrior in physical combat or a more intelligent strategist. Some petty folk had implied that Adun was the real driving force behind most of Zoranis's decisions over the last fifty years. Jake actually hoped so. Because if it was true, then Zoranis's good leadership would not have died with him.

He walked solemnly, his heavy, formal robes brushing the earth. On either side of the white-paved road were lines of mourners. They were hunched over, shaking, their skin mot-tling in the unmistakable sign of grief. Zoranis was not only well liked, but well loved.

In the Khala, there was nothing but heart, and hearts were full today. Jake let the respect, admiration, and sorrow wash in and around and through him, adding his own genuine grief to the mix.

Beside him walked Adun. Young, vibrant, intense, and strong, he was everything the templar were supposed to be. As an active warrior—Jake was too old to participate in combat, though he had excellent tactical knowledge—Adun wore his armor, and it gleamed golden as the sun that glinted off it. A half a head taller and a bit larger than any of the other templar, he was a commanding presence. His grief was a bright thread woven into the tapestry of the Khala, shimmering in its purity. Adun had loved Zoranis almost as an elder brother. More than any of the other templar, he grieved this loss. He looked over at Jake and their eyes met.

Ah, my old friend Vetraas, *came Adun's pain-filled thoughts,* I am glad you walk beside me. Your composure gives me strength.

There is no shame in deep grief, *Jake sent back.* To not mourn the dead is to dishonor them. But we must also be thankful for their lives.

I am, Vetraas. I am.

The walk took almost an entire day. They reached the temple at sunset, and it was Jake, adviser to Zoranis, and Adun, Zoranis's protégé, who had the honor of bathing and dressing the body and sitting with it. Traditionally this was done to protect the body from scavengers. Now the corpse was safely preserved in stasis until the moment of burial, but the ritual of lovingly protecting it lingered on.

Jake looked down at his old friend. Clad in robes of simple white as opposed to the armor in which he had spent most of his life, Zoranis looked at peace. The robes hid the horrific wounds that had claimed his life. The large eyes were closed, the flesh looking almost alive.

Jake wished he could speak with Zoranis one more time, tell him how well he had served his people. How greatly he would be missed. Instead, he contented himself with pressing the dead hands and thinking the traditional farewell: "Und lara khar. Anht zagatir nas": "Be at peace. The gods watch over you." *Night was falling on the last day of Zoranis's leadership. Before the sun rose, as tradition had it, there would be a new executor.*

The Templar caste, like any group whose members were finite, was not without its flaws, disagreements, and occasional corruption and infighting. This time, the templar would rise to the heights of which he knew it was capable, the heights of what Khas intended when he created the Khala. There was one among their number who exemplified all that was right and good with the templar. One whom everyone respected. One who, if he accepted it, would greet the dawn as executor.

And quite possibly, Adun himself was the only one who didn't know it.

Jake opened his eyes as he heard the slight hissing sound of the door irising open. "A highly successful run," Rosemary said. "Can you give me a hand with these?"

He turned to see her standing beside the door, behind her another nav frame. She was still in her suit, which was clearly too large for her. At her feet was an opened container filled with a variety of items, none of which Jake recognized and all of which he was glad he had very little to do with. He carefully took the piles of chips, plating, and wires and moved it into the main cabin.

"Not only were we able to ditch the tracking device," she told him as she emerged from the bulky suit, "it's now going to lead anyone who's latched onto its signal on a wild-goose chase. I've rigged it to engage from here. We'll want to beat a quick retreat once I activate it, though, just in case the movement attracts any attention." She hung up the suit and turned to Jake. "I'm certain that those Wraiths are in the area. Let's put you to work monitoring Dominion standard com channels while I hook all this stuff up."

She directed him into a seat and entered a rotational sequence in the com system. "Maybe they'll give their presence away and allow us to get a fix on their location." The minutes ticked by as Jake monitored and Rosemary tinkered. Annoyed, Jake finally began to suspect that she had given him this task to keep him out of the way and occupied. Finally, Rosemary emerged, looking grubby and tired. As she took her seat, she said, "So. Hey, Zamara, how do we get to Aiur from here?"

I will require an accurate map of the sector.

"Pull up a map and show her where we are," Jake said. Rosemary did.

"Zoom out," Jake said, again speaking for the alien intelligence inside his skull. "Again," he instructed. And a third time he asked her. She raised a raven brow.

That is sufficient for my needs. I shall enter the coordinates.

. . . Okay.

Jake leaned forward and relinquished control of his hands and watched, bemused, as they entered a series of digits. How did Zamara know how to program a—of course. Zamara had been linked with R. M. on a very deep level a few hours ago. She'd have the same knowledge the human woman did. Rosemary looked on with interest.

"Well, it's no day trip. Good thing I scrounged up some extra rations. Okay. We all set?"

Jake and Zamara nodded.

"All right. Getting in was fairly easy. Getting out won't be. Those Wraiths will scan for power sources and movement inside the debris field, so we need a little diversion. There's no way they won't come here looking for us, so we might as well make the most of it. Now. Watch that ship right there."

Rosemary pointed at a freighter. She lifted a small device and thumbed a button. Sure enough, after a few moments, the freighter powered to life and began to move steadily away from them.

"Nice job, Rosemary," Jake said.

"Thanks, Professor."

It was quite possibly the most pleasant exchange the two of them had ever had.

However, the good mood was short-lived. A few moments later, as R. M. was slowly and carefully steering them out of the debris field, she swore under her breath.

"Yep, looks like our decoy's stirred up a bit of interest. Buckle up, Jake. We might have to make a run for it, and it could get pretty bumpy."

He sat down at once, strapping himself in, and peered over at the screen. He could see a few blinking red dots, and knew by this point that red signified Dominion.

"You think they've found us?"

"Not sure yet." Both of them watched the screen intently. After a few seconds, the red dots began to converge on the decoy. Jake felt a quick stab of horror, relief, and then fresh worry in rapid succession. Rosemary's ploy had worked, but pursuit had found them much too quickly for comfort. It wouldn't take their pursuers long to determine that this was a trick. And then they would start looking around the ruins of this old battlefield to see where the real quarry was.

With perfect calm, Rosemary continued to move the system runner. Jake bit his lip nervously. The Dominion vessels closed in on the decoy freighter.

"Rosemary . . ." Jake said.

"Not yet," she murmured. Her face was focused, intent. Jake felt sweat break out beneath his arms.

The red dots stopped moving. The decoy freighter continued on.

"They figured it out," Rosemary said. She hit something, and the system runner surged forward. The red dots stirred to life and began to close in on them. Jake gripped the metal arms of his chair.

"Now!" Rosemary pressed the button. Space shimmered around them. There were no more small blinking red dots on the screen. Rosemary leaned back in her chair and laughed. "Piece of cake."

Jake smiled weakly.

"A decoy. I see."

Valerian's voice was cold with disapproval, and the woman on the screen looked dreadfully unhappy. He supposed he shouldn't be too surprised that, once again, the damnably clever Rosemary and Jake had slipped through his fingers. The handful of people set to guard what had essentially disintegrated into a space junkyard were hardly the best and the brightest the Dominion had to offer. He'd never have gotten even this close to finding the two fugitives—or was it three? Should he count the protoss intelligence in Jake's brain as a separate entity? How unfortunate that he did not know—had it not been for Devon Starke's knowledge of the tracking code.

"There, uh, is something," the woman was saying, shuffling papers with a rather frantic air. She was clearly going to do everything she could to make this not seem like the disaster it was.

"Oh?"

She nodded. "Yes. Security did report seeing another ship power up shortly after we caught up with the decoy. Now, Mr. V, you understand that that's not unusual. The wreckage is tempting to a variety of scroungers and we aren't sufficiently manned to patrol it as thoroughly as we would like."

He gave her a smile. "I understand. But please continue."

She seemed heartened. "Let me send you the documentation we have on it."

A few second later, Valerian and Starke were watching a poor-quality hologram. They watched in silence as the somewhat battered Wraiths followed the Valkyrie, took a scan, and listened to the two pilots express their annoyance in colorful words at having been tricked. More colorful words ensued as they realized another vessel was moving out of the debris field and into open space. The Wraiths turned to follow, but the system runner they were following had made it to a clear place and had subwarped to who knew where, and who really cared, and it was time for lunch anyway.

"I hope that was helpful, sir." The woman was slightly pink, realizing, as she knew he had to, that it hardly painted security in a particularly inspirational light.

"It may well be. Thank you."

Unable to continue smiling politely, Valerian thumbed off the switch and scowled. "We almost had them. If my father staffed these places with intelligent people rather than lazy buffoons, we would have."

Even as he said the words he knew they were unfair. A government that had the luxury of staffing remote space junkyards with top-notch staff by definition would have far fewer problems than the Dominion had.

He sighed and turned to Starke. "The question is, where would they go next? There are hundreds of places in this sector alone they could hide."

Starke nodded thoughtfully. "In the . . . the link, for want of a better word, I managed to sense a little something of this protoss that's using Professor Ramsey. Of course, it is much more adept at hiding its thoughts and feelings than even the best-trained ghost is, because it's a protoss. But one thing I did get was a trace of annoyance at the links being utilized, and a hint of concern. Dahl was right. The protoss didn't just force itself into Professor Ramsey's brain for amusement or as part of a normal cycle. It did it because it felt it had to. So, knowing this, my best guess is that the protoss would want to rejoin its people. And look at this."

Starke pressed the rewind button and again they watched the hologram. He paused it at one point. "Look at where the system runner is heading."

"It leaps, Devon; we can't follow it if we don't know its destination."

"True enough. But think about what we know of human nature. You've been discovered, you know where you are heading, you make a run for it—silly as it might sound, even if you're planning a jump—wouldn't your first instinct be to flee in the right direction?"

Valerian smiled slowly. "Yes. Yes, it would be." He called up a star chart of the galaxy and smiled. "Of course. They're heading for Aiur."

CHAPTER FIVE

AS JAKE HAD KNOWN IT WOULD, AIUR HAD PROSpered under Adun's guidance as the executor of the templar, which managed to be strong and yet not heavy-handed. Directing the templar to the will of the Conclave, Adun had overseen the settling of several colonies that were thriving and content. Any disputes with other races that had broken out had been quickly quelled with few casualties to the protoss. It was a good time to be alive.

Jake entered the executor's citadel, which was a small, private retreat that hovered gracefully above Antioch. He found Adun in deep contemplation, wearing the heavy purple, black, and white robes of his office, staring out onto the cityscape below. In the distance, the lush green and blue hues of the rain forest softened the line of the horizon.

Jake inclined his head deeply, respectfully. Adun turned from the view and repeated the gesture.

"You sent for me, Executor?"

Adun nodded. "Yes, Vetraas. I have been called in front of the Conclave. It seems they have some information they wish to impart."

Curiosity flickered in Jake, but was quickly hooded before Adun could pick up on it. Over two millennia ago, the great Khas, as he had become known—"He who brings order"—had rediscovered the profound link all protoss could have with one another. He had drafted a series of rules on how best to navigate this intimate space, and the collection of rules and the emotional and mental link itself had become known as the Khala. Jake knew that Khas had had another name, but it was lost to everyone but the preservers now, and besides, what Khas had done was more important than who he had been before such a significant discovery.

"I don't know that that's true," Jake said to Zamara. As before, when Jake had relived the memories of a protoss named Temlaa as if they were actually happening to him, Zamara was with him, guiding him through the process so he retained himself. "Savassan was a pretty remarkable fellow before he even found the first khaydarin crystal. It's a shame his name has been forgotten."

"The preservers know it. The preservers know all. Well, almost all. And that is what matters now. Khas he has become, and Khas he shall be, until the final protoss closes his eyes for the last time and all becomes lost to the stars."

Part of the dictates of the Khala had advised a caste system, with various tribes falling into one of the three castes of judicator, templar, and khalai. The vast majority of protoss tribes were collected under the khalai, who were the artisans, scientists, and builders of their people. This caste was as valued as the others, for without them, there would be no infrastructure, no development in culture and science and art. Their contributions were vital.

The templar, of which Adun and Jake were a part, was the warrior caste. The templar tribes were those who had great physical prowess or agility, or tended toward sound military insight and strategy. In the early days of the Khala, they fought to protect the newly unified protoss culture from those who did not agree with the tenets, or were too afraid to do so. It was, Jake mused, an indication of how relatively primitive the protoss were then. It did not take long for all the protoss to eventually realize that the only way to peace and prosperity was through the Khala. There could be no hatred then, for even if you disagreed with someone, you felt *him as yourself. Once this harmony was achieved, the protoss society flourished quickly and healthily, and the templar were free to focus on protecting their people, at first from the fearsome creatures who prowled Aiur, and later from hostile alien beings they encountered while settling their colonies.*

The third and final caste, the judicators, were the elders and statesmen, the governing body of the protoss. Their highest members were known as the Conclave. This was a select group of elders, chosen for their wisdom and knowledge of the Khala and a passionate adherence to its rules. Some of them were protoss whom Jake deeply admired and respected. Others were . . . not. Nonetheless, Adun and the other templar answered with unquestioning obedience to the Conclave. Which was why Jake was surprised to note Adun's discomfort at having been summoned to appear before them at the Great Forum, the Khor-shakal, the seat of Aiur's government.

"I would have you accompany me, Vetraas," Adun continued. "They have asked to speak with me alone, but I would prefer to have my most trusted adviser with me at such a meeting. There was something . . . well. Will you come?"

"Of course," Jake responded.

The Conclave, led by the elder Kortanul, was none too pleased that the executor had disobeyed their instructions and not come alone. Adun calmly and respectfully asked that Jake be included, and after some private discussion the Conclave agreed. While the thoughts they directed toward Jake were definitely not conciliatory, he was only amused and curious as to the need for such secrecy.

"Before we begin," said Kortanul, "it is imperative that you both swear that word of what transpires here goes no further."

Jake and Adun nodded. Kortanul stepped forward to Jake, holding up his hand, palm facing out. Jake mirrored him. A gentle glow began to pulse between them and easily, naturally, their minds merged. So linked, Kortanul asked for Jake's solemn promise. So linked, in a deep place within the Khala where he could not lie, where violation of this oath would result in swift punishment, Jake made the oath.

He watched, filled with apprehension, as Adun did likewise. Never before, in the centuries in which he had served, had anything like this been asked of him. He wondered what was so dire that the Conclave felt they had to resort to such measures to ensure loyalty from two whose loyalty had never once been questioned.

The members of the Conclave nodded, satisfied, and Jake and Adun were permitted to sit in the beautifully carved chairs that were usually reserved only for the Conclave. Jake noted that while they were lavish and opulent, set with crystals, inlaid with precious metals, and of a form pleasing to the eye, they were not very comfortable.

"We can either show you this information in a link or tell you," Kortanul continued. "It is your choice, Adun. Though I will advise you that if this is merely told, you may find it hard to believe."

"Speak," Adun said. "If this is as portentous as you say, I would hear reasoned thoughts about it, not the emotions you feel toward it."

Kortanul inclined his head. "As you wish, Executor." Despite his words, he seemed deeply reluctant to speak. Adun and Jake waited patiently.

"Impossible as it may seem, there are those among us who would destroy everything we have sought to build over the last millennium. They—"

"We're finally here," Rosemary said, shaking Jake awake. "But boy, Professor, I'd talk to your travel agent of a protoss. This place doesn't look at all like you described it to me."

Jake woke up with a start. He'd slept wrong and had a terrible headache. He went to rub his temples and winced; he'd forgotten about the bump on the head he'd taken not that long ago. It took a second for

Rosemary's words to register. He threw off the blanket and got to his feet, sitting down heavily and looking through the screen as Rosemary guided the ship into orbit around the homeworld of the protoss.

"Oh my God," he breathed.

He had come expecting the verdant lands of Temlaa and Savassan, a world of lush rain forests and oceans, of gleaming cities and mysterious temples. But the planet that filled the screen had been horribly brutalized. With a sickening feeling, Jake beheld mammoth patches of blackened, charred earth. Here and there were what struck him as being pathetically small patches of green rain forest, although his rational mind realized they must stretch for hundreds of kilometers. What lakes there were looked brown and unhealthy. The oceans alone seemed to have escaped. . . .

Jake's mind flashed back to the dinner conversation he had had with Rosemary and the late Ethan Stewart. Ethan had said something about Aiur—but Jake had been more than a little the worse (or better) for the alcohol and focused on the sorbet.

The sorbet is indeed made from the juice of the sammuro fruit of Aiur, Ethan had said. *Damned hard to find, even on the black market. This may be the only taste any terran may ever have of it.*

"So that's what Ethan meant," he said, grief closing his throat. It was not Temlaa's grief or Zamara's he felt now, but his own—a nauseous sensation of loss and anger and disappointment.

Zamara—what happened?

The zerg found our homeland. You can see the remains of their infestation from here.

So that was what that somewhat shiny, crusty gray material that covered huge clumps of what had once been a fertile planet was. Zerg "creep," humans called it. Jake thought he might throw up.

Why did you not tell me?

It was not necessary. Zamara seemed genuinely puzzled at his anger. *We were not coming here to behold my world's beauty. We came here because we need to enter the underground chambers to recover the lost technology.*

But I didn't understand this had happened. . . . I wasn't prepared to see this!

He realized that she would never understand why humans needed to be braced for something like this. It was yet another thing that reminded him just how alien Zamara was, even though they had grown to be fairly close. She was much more rational and logical than he, and doled out information on a "need to know" basis.

I share your pain, she said unexpectedly. *I was witness to much of this unfolding. That . . . I hope I do not have to share with you, but it might be necessary.*

Rosemary was looking at him with a hint of sympathy on her face. "Why didn't she tell you?"

"She didn't think I needed to know," he said, embarrassed at how bitter and angry he sounded.

Rosemary shrugged. "Whatever. I don't much like the idea of landing down there. I've heard a little bit about what happened, but not a lot. So are the zerg and the protoss all gone or what?"

My people were evacuated through a warp gate to a safe place.

Relieved, Jake sagged a little in his chair. *And the zerg?*

They obey their controller. They would have been recalled once their mission was accomplished. Aiur was attacked four years ago, there would be no reason for them to linger.

"She says there are no zerg left, and the protoss all made it to safety," Jake said to Rosemary.

"Good. Sounds like we go in, find what you need, and get out. I like that. Then what?"

Then what?

We take the technology to other protoss.

Where? And what is this crystal for, anyway? Why are you being so mysterious about this?

You do not need to concern yourself with that right now.

Zamara . . . this is really starting to get irritating. You know I trust you—and not just because I have no choice in the matter.

Her mental voice softened, became kinder. *This I know, Jacob. All will be revealed as needed.*

Jake sighed. "We go find other protoss and they help her out. And that's all she's telling me now."

"Doesn't tell you a lot, does she?"

"Well, you don't either." He regretted snapping at her but damn it, his head hurt.

Unexpectedly, Rosemary grinned. "Touché," she said. They spent several minutes in silence looking out at the shattered world of Aiur as Rosemary brought the ship into the atmosphere and began to scout for a good place to set down. "So no zerg, no protoss. Anything else we need to worry about?" She pointed at another screen readout that listed the chemical composition of the planet's atmosphere. "Can we breathe that stuff, Prof? Looks like there's still a lot of crap in the air from the fighting."

There is nothing in the air that would be harmful to you with short-term exposure. However, there could be residual radiation from the conflict. She should check for that. Any formerly inhabited area—

"—could be dangerous," Jake relayed as Zamara thought the information. "Unstable buildings and so on. We should be able to breathe just fine; we're not going to be here long. Looks like the atmosphere is slightly heavier than on most terran settlements, but we should be okay. Oh, and she says there's wildlife."

"Nothing a rifle won't blast to smithereens, I hope?"

Jake thought of the omhara, the giant predatory beast worshipped as a god by the early protoss. Huge, with three eyes and hooves and extremely sharp teeth. He thought of other creatures he had seen, from the small primate known as Little Hands to enormous, placid, burrowing creatures known as lombads, to the small and incredibly swift kal-taar, all glimpsed through the eyes of Temlaa, who was regarded as primitive but who had as bright a soul as anyone he'd ever met. R. M. regarded the animals of this place as an obstacle, and he supposed if they attacked, they would be.

It wasn't worth picking a fight over. "No," he said with a sigh. "Just animals."

He felt suddenly weary. The nap hadn't rested him much. And the headache was coming back, as it had during the last three days of traveling. He supposed it was to be expected. He wasn't cut out for this sort of thing. He missed the feeling of good ol' dirt between his fingers, of the thrill of the hard-won archeological discovery . . . the familiarity of friends and a job he knew and was good at. Jake supposed anyone would get a headache under the current circumstances.

He also was keenly interested in this mystery the Conclave was about to reveal and annoyed to have been awakened right when they were getting to the good part.

I select each memory I share with you for a purpose, Jacob. Much deliberation goes into what you see. They are all, as you put it, "good parts."

He chuckled softly at that, then continued briefing R. M. He gave her the coordinates for the underground chambers. She entered them and started their final descent.

Jake heard a sound he'd heard before, in the shipyard—a proximity alarm. Rosemary glanced at the console. "What the hell—"

No!

Zamara's mental cry was not so much a word as a gut-punch of a negative, an urgent sensation of not-wanting, and Jake doubled over. His head felt like it had had an ice pick driven through it and for a second everything went gray. He was glad he hadn't eaten because he was sure he'd vomit his guts out. *Stop! Don't land!*

"Don't land!" he said in a raspy voice.

R. M. turned, confused, but she'd halted their descent above the ground. "What's wrong?"

A dark shape suddenly appeared in front of the screen. "What the—" Rosemary shouted.

The ship suddenly rocked. Something yellow-white and gooey spattered over the shield, which immediately went opaque. Sparks chased each other along the console and smoke billowed out in black waves. Other alarm systems added their voices to the din. A sharp burning smell made them cough and Jake again came close to being sick as the reek of something acidic burned his nostrils. Jake and Rosemary unbuckled themselves and scrambled back. The ship rocked again, as if something enormous and hard had either struck it or landed on it.

"Hang on!" Rosemary shouted. Jake dropped to the floor, but there was nothing to hang on to. The ship, which had been hovering about ten meters over the ground, began to fall and crashed hard. Jake had the wind knocked out of him and couldn't breathe. What the hell was going on?

Zamara shouldered him aside in his own body. She forced his lungs to work, got him to his feet, had him fling open the weapons locker and grab a rifle.

I was in error. There are indeed still zerg on Aiur after all.

CHAPTER SIX

"WE RETURN, O QUEEN." THE VOICE IN HER MIND was harsh and rasping. Kerrigan turned her attention upon the overlord whose mission it had been to retrieve this latest prize.

"Show me what you have brought me."

The things chittered, mandibles and antennae and pincers moving. Four hydralisks came forward, the linked scythelike arms cradling a precious burden instead of ripping something to bloody bits. They slithered in front of their queen, and moving as one lowered the chrysalis to rest at her feet.

Kerrigan felt a wave of emotions wash through her, all powerful and some long-forgotten. She realized she felt . . . tenderness and affection toward the being encased in the sticky cocoon. Protective. There was a kinship between herself, the mighty Queen of Blades, and this nascent new life that even now writhed in torment inside the sludgy fluids of the cocoon. Surrendering to the emotions of the moment, feeling no shame or weakness at them, she knelt beside the softly glowing chrysalis.

"I know it hurts right now," she said to the being's mind. "Your body is being stretched, pulled, remade. You are being reborn. Your very cell structure is not what it was." She laid a long, clawed hand on the pulsing cocoon, wishing that she could offer the comfort of touch. Inside, what had once been a human man named Ethan Stewart kicked as best he could and sent forth a silent scream.

"But you will be glorious when it is all done," she murmured. "Glorious as your queen is. You will know power such as you have never tasted." She began to explore the mind that was being re-formed the same way his body was being re-formed. She was surprised to discover that Ethan had no latent psychic abilities. Still, his was a highly intelligent mind. Highly disciplined. But damaged. It would need to be repaired as much as possible, but some of the damage could be of use to her. She had seen through the eyes and mind of the zergling that had gazed first at the surgeon, then at the patient on the bed, then at the familiar, delicate filigree of wires that constituted a psi-screen. She had jumped to the conclusion that Ethan was, like herself, a ghost. She had thought that he was the originator of the strange ripples she had sensed so far away. Clearly, he wasn't capable of such things. But as she insinuated herself into his mind, she realized that while he himself was not responsible for the ripple, he knew . . . something. Something about protoss and terrans. Right now, the rage and paranoia rampaging through his brain was preventing her from accessing that information clearly. But the organic chemicals that were modifying his brain would help settle some of that.

Not all, but some. She was familiar with what overusage of a psi-screen did to a person. She'd been given a graphic demonstration during her training. She'd seen the loss of control, the rage, the cunning, the paranoia. Had quailed as her instructors had let the poor shattered ghost hurl herself against padded walls and scream epithets. Because he was not psionic, Ethan would have suffered less injury. But he'd still be damaged. Maybe even a bit insane.

She could work with that.

She had created him, in a sense; right now he was helpless, in agony, entirely dependent on her for his survival. She had put others through this process before, a matter of trial and error, learning more with each failure or mild success. Ethan would, she hoped, be the culmination of all she had learned through those experiments. If all went as she anticipated, he would be magnificent, though of course not as perfect as she herself. She had no intention of creating a rival. She hoped to create an ally, a general, a warrior.

She hoped to create a consort.

There was no time to suit up. There was no time to do anything but hit the switch, watch the door iris open, and fire point blank at the two four-legged monstrosities who charged at them. Bits of shattered chitin, blood, and flesh sprayed all over the cargo bay door, sprayed all over Rosemary and Jake.

"Hold them off!" Rosemary shouted to Jake. He obeyed, his will and Zamara's completely one and the same. He was almost numb with horror but kept the rifle leveled, squeezing it so hard his hand cramped. Another, smaller zerg came at him, mandibles snapping, chittering madly, its eyes black and shiny and focused on him. It crawled without hesitating over the still-twitching bodies of the fallen. Jake trained the rifle on it and blasted it to a pulp, hyperaware that more would be out there. He tried frantically to remember what he knew about zerg. It wasn't much that was helpful.

Rosemary dove for the lockers and emerged with a handful of small round things. "Get down!" she cried as she lobbed one toward the door.

Jake dropped, lying on his side, still somehow gripping the rifle, still firing. The third thing was dead. There was quite the nasty, foul-smelling pile accumulating. The puddle of sludgy blood was oozing toward him.

"Cover your head!"

He did so, and heard a terrible *boom*. Bits of dead zerg spattered his body with soft plopping sounds. The stench was appalling as the liquids started to seep into his shirt.

Inside him, Zamara sent calm to his brain and nervous system. It helped, a little. For about a second the door was clear of zerg—living ones, anyway.

But he could hear their awful sounds, and knew they were there. He propped himself on his elbows and prepared to resume firing. Sure enough, four zerglings began swarming in. They died like the rest of them had. Jake began to hope they might make it.

"How many are there?" he yelled to Rosemary over the din.

"No clue!" she shot back. Then she did something that appeared to be totally insane. She gathered up an armload of grenades and raced for the open door, leaping out gracefully.

"Rosemary!"

She'd never looked more beautiful to him than now, when he was suddenly convinced he was about to lose her. She stood with her feet planted firmly on Aiur soil, tendrils of short black hair clinging to her sweaty face, one arm cradling death conveniently packaged in handy fist-sized grenades, lobbing them one after another at something he could not see.

Explosions, four of them, hard on the heels of one another, shook the earth. He tried to get to his feet but slipped in the disgusting stew of zerg body parts. By the time he made it outside, ready to help, it was over. Rosemary shot him a triumphant grin.

"You did good, Professor."

He gave her a feeble smile. "I'm afraid you did most of it."

"Nah, you did fine."

"We get them all?"

"For the moment. But from what I remember

about zerg, they don't act alone. Reinforcements'll be in any minute. Take what we can carry and let's—"

Go. She'd been about to say "go." But go where? The ship was damaged beyond repair. What—

We must get to the chambers.

We're still miles away. We don't know—

The mental surge Zamara sent was the equivalent of a smack across the face. *Panic will serve nothing. We will take tools and supplies and weapons. It is the only choice we have, Jacob.*

"Yeah," he said aloud, both to Rosemary and to Zamara. "The chambers. We've still got to get there and, like you said, we've gotta get out of here fast. Might as well run toward something as away from something."

Rosemary nodded her head in acknowledgment and ducked back into the reeking charnel house that was the ruined system runner. He followed, fighting back nausea. With an efficiency he could only mutely admire, she searched quickly through the lockers. "We need to travel light and travel smart," she said. "Here." She tossed him a standard marine-issue pack and he quickly stuffed it full of whatever she threw toward him, doing his best not to drop food, weapons, or life-saving tools, including one of a pair of walkie-talkies, into the pools of zerg guts on the floor. Within five minutes both packs were loaded. He shouldered his and caught the rifle she tossed him.

"Ever seen one of these?" she asked, as she examined

a small rectangular device with a screen in the center and a keypad running along the bottom. He shook his head and half jumped, half slid out of the ruined ship. "It's called a Handheld Personal Information-Gathering and Navigation Unit. HPIGNU—"Pig" for short. It'll look for pretty much anything you need—where your enemies are, how far away your destination is and how to get there, what the terrain is like, stuff like that."

"Wow, that's useful."

"No kidding. No life of any notable size within scanning range." She touched the pad again. "And we're a mere five hundred and thirty-two kilometers from the chambers. Walk in the park."

"Rosemary—I'm sorry, Zamara had no idea—"

Rosemary waved off whatever he was about to say. "The Pig suggests two routes. One is circuitous and takes us through the rain forest. The other is a straight line, but it's over a stretch of blackened earth and we'll be totally exposed to the sun and any zerg that might be flying overhead. I vote for the jungle. Slower going for sure, but we're much more likely to get there alive. We'd have cover, water, and a better chance of getting food to supplement our rations."

"The zerg might be thinking the same thing."

"They might indeed. But it's still the smartest choice."

Into the rain forest they went. Jake was in pretty good shape, but they had landed in the morning and the day grew increasingly hotter and, with the moisture of the rain forest, steamier. They were soon both bright red and sweating, but Rosemary had been right: Water was plentiful and tested safe enough to drink, and the thick canopy protected them from the worst of the sun's rays. But the undergrowth was not insubstantial, and they had to forge a path through huge tree roots slick with moss, ferns bigger than the two of them, and vines as thick as Jake's arm. Jake's headache, which seemed ever-present these days, worsened as the day wore on. The loss of the ship, the slow going, and the perpetual tension of having to stay alert and ready to defend himself against everything from insects and snakes on the ground in front of him to gargantuan versions of the same that might pounce on them from the sky at any moment was wearing him down.

They stopped to rest beside a waterfall that under any other circumstances would have demanded his attention for its beauty and now demanded it because it was wet. Rosemary scanned the pool with the Pig and determined it was safe to drink from. Jake gulped down water along with a handful of pills from the medkit. Rosemary watched him.

"I'm told that two work as well as six," she said.

"Not when the headache's this bad," he muttered. "You think we can jump in for a minute? I'm so hot." He also reeked of vomit and zerg insides, the scent of which was not growing any pleasanter as the time passed. Rosemary glanced at the Pig and nodded.

"No sizeable water creatures. Some smaller things

like leeches and so on, I would imagine, but nothing too harmful."

"Thank God." Jake removed his boots, pack, weapon, and nothing else and strode in. He heard Rosemary chuckle, and she emulated him. The water was not cold, but it was cooler than the air around him, and he sighed in pleasure as he scrubbed at his stained clothing.

And then he felt a small hand on his head pushing down with surprising strength and he was underwater.

He came up sputtering to see Rosemary grinning at him, and the splashing battle began. It felt good, to do something silly and stupid and playful that had nothing to do with life or death or protoss or secrets. He'd just drawn his hand back, preparing to execute a particularly large splash, when the look on Rosemary's face stopped him.

"Damn it!" She surged out of the water and slogged up the slippery, muddy bank. Jake turned to see what had gotten her so agitated.

A small primate with red stripes peered at them with yellow eyes from its perch a good ten meters above them. For a second, all Jake knew was a surge of pleasure and recognition. It was a *kwah-kai*—"Little Hands" in the Khalani language—and for an instant Jake was again Temlaa, sitting with Savassan, regarding this same little creature and smiling at its curiosity and mischief.

Jake's smile faded. For in its little hands, the kwah-kai clutched the Pig.

Rosemary had seized a pistol and turned, dripping, to fire. But Little Hands was smart and fast, and before she could take aim it had chattered at her and fled, surrendering its prize and using all four limbs and tail to make good its escape.

The Pig tumbled down, seemingly in slow motion. Jake watched Rosemary scramble to catch it and knew she would be too late, knew that it would strike one of the gnarled and mossy roots and not soft earth; and as it did so with a sharp *crack* and bits and pieces of metal and plastic flew upward and twirled glinting in the few shafts of light that penetrated the canopy, Jake realized he might very well be watching their last chance of survival shatter before his eyes as well.

Rosemary's string of cursing would have impressed a marine, and sent several birds whirring away in flight. Jake stood in the water, sick with shock, as Rosemary picked up the pieces of the Pig and stared at them for a long moment.

"Do . . . you think you can fix it?"

She didn't answer at once. "Maybe. If I had the right tools. Right now, I don't."

Jake slogged out of the water. His headache was back, ten times as bad.

Jacob . . . the tool is useful, but I know how to navigate by the sun and the stars. And to a degree, I can sense the presence of the zerg.

Wearily, Jake told Rosemary what Zamara had said. She merely nodded. He didn't need to read her mind to know that she was swallowing her anger. "Well, that's better than nothing, I guess. You done with your swim, Professor?"

Jake thought about how good the water had felt when he'd plunged in. How pleasant it had been to just forget about their life-and-death struggle and simply play in the water and laugh for a bit. Now the wet clothing felt clammy and unpleasant, Rosemary's carefully composed face looked like it had never known a smile in her entire life, and a wave of hopelessness washed over him. He, an alien intelligence, and a woman who despised them both were all stuck on a hostile planet infested with hungry zerg, hundreds of kilometers from where they needed to be.

Do not despair, Jacob.

"Yeah," he said in answer to both Rosemary and Zamara. "Let's keep going."

Zamara was as good as her word. This was her world. She knew exactly where to take them, what was safe to walk through and what wasn't, where dangerous creatures, both tiny and toxic and large and threatening, lurked and how to avoid them. By the time they made camp, they'd learned how to expertly remove leeches and to recognize the telltale croon emitted by the poisonous *mai-lur* lizard, and had constructed and ridden a raft to take them miles down a swift-flowing river toward their goal.

Rosemary had remained dangerously silent throughout most of the seemingly interminable day, but toward sunset had seemed to relax slightly. When she said, "You know, we might make it to sunrise outside of a zerg's stomach," he was greatly cheered.

The rain that started in the late afternoon, however, did not do anything to keep that cheerfulness going. They created a makeshift shelter, propping several of the large ferns over the knobby roots of the enormous trees and flicking on an EmergeLite for illumination. The packs were watertight, but they rearranged some items so weapons were within easy reach if they were needed. The ferns were better than nothing, but unlike the packs were not watertight, so Jake and Rosemary were still soaked. The temperature was warm, even at night, so there was no risk of freezing. Just extreme discomfort.

Any sign of zerg, omhara, or anything else that might consider us a nice snack, Zamara?

I sense nothing, Jacob.

"I used to like rain," Rosemary said. "I don't think I like it much now."

"I spent three years in a desert," Jake said. Inside him, Zamara subsided, letting the two humans talk. "I can't bring myself to hate rain even tonight."

Rosemary grunted in an approximation of a chuckle and opened one of their rations. Cold, it was even more unappealing than it had been on the escape pod, sludgy and congealed. Rosemary sniffed at it.

"I think the zerg guts smelled better," she said.

It was an exaggeration, but only just. Jake peered

at the goop, trying to ascertain its true color in the off-white illumination provided by the EmergeLite. "Is it Beef Stroganoff or Chicken Supreme?"

"All I care about is if it's got peach cobbler." Rosemary began to peel away the foil that covered the dessert compartment. Hopeful despite everything, Jake watched with interest.

The first warning they had was the horrible tearing sound of trees crashing down and the now-familiar, blood-freezing chittering.

Zerg.

CHAPTER SEVEN

IN ONE SWIFT MOVEMENT, ROSEMARY SPRANG for the gun and dove out of the shelter. Jake went for the small box of grenades and followed. He was not a second too soon, for the moment he was clear of the shelter something large and snakelike crashed down on it with a large crack: the tail of a hydralisk, which now lifted its monstrous, cobralike head and reared back, poised to strike.

Without conscious thought, Jake drew his arm back and tossed a grenade at it. It was a lucky throw and went right down the creature's open gullet. A heartbeat later, Jake was showered by small bits of pulpy, reeking flesh.

He heard Rosemary shouting curses and the rapid fire of the gun and turned again to see her mowing down two zerglings. They screamed as their limbs flailed, not halting their approach until their lives were completely and thoroughly ended. Done with those two, Rosemary looked around, searching for the next wave of zerg. Jake could hear chittering, in the distance now, but coming closer.

There were too many of them.

He stared at Rosemary, his eyes wide with horror, grief, and guilt. Their gazes locked for a second, then she flashed a grin and turned to the sounds of their approaching doom.

Jake reached for Zamara, wondering if she could somehow pull another rabbit of her protoss hat, but she was silent inside him.

Zamara?

The sound of death came closer, but Zamara was not speaking to him. Somehow he thought she'd have last words or something, but apparently—

The by now too-familiar clacking, buzzing, angry insectlike sounds could still be heard, but the noises were now joined by a sound Jake had never heard before and could not put a name to. Groping for similarities, to make the unknown known and less horrific, Jake's mind incongruously went back to his childhood. When he was a kid, he used to love going to summer festivals on his homeworld of Tarsonis. They would often end with fireworks displays. Jake's mother always winced and covered her ears, but Jake, his little sister Kirsten, and their dad loved the high-pitched shriek of the fireworks racing up to the skies before exploding with a bone-shaking *boom* rather too much like that of the grenade Rosemary had just lobbed. The sounds outside sounded like those fireworks.

Now that odd screaming noise was joined by squeals and shrieks of zerg in torment. Confused, Jake risked a glance at Rosemary. She stood beside him, rifle at the ready. Every part of her petite, perfectly formed body was taut, frozen, except for her chest, which moved up and down rapidly as she drew in air, and the vein that beat wildly in her throat.

There was a sudden silence.

Jake didn't dare speak.

The moments ticked on.

Zamara was abruptly there, as if she had returned home to his mind after stepping outside. And she'd brought company.

Over a dozen voices suddenly began speaking in his head. They overlapped and echoed and their feelings caressed and assaulted him both. Jake cried out, dropping to his knees and letting the grenades spill to the earth, clutching his head as pain blossomed brightly. At once, Zamara put up a buffer between him and the—

"Protoss," Jake gasped. "There are still protoss left here!"

Rosemary lowered the rifle. Relief and irritation were both plain on her beautiful face. "Why didn't Zamara say anything?"

After that one excruciating moment, the pain began to ebb. Jake sat up cautiously and looked at the pile of dead zerg. His stomach roiled and this time he wasn't able to stop it. He got to his hands and knees and began to vomit, the contents of his stomach merging with the foul purplish-black blood and flesh of the dead zerg.

He sat down, wiped his hand across his mouth, and stared up into the curious eyes of several protoss as they stepped out of concealment among the huge trees.

Great. This is how I get to meet my first live protoss. Covered in zerg gore and puking my guts out.

He felt a rumble of amusement from Zamara. *They are much more interested in how I came to be inside your body than in said body's functions.*

Jake was not at all certain he found that reassuring.

"Hey, Zamara, tell them not to get in my head. Tell them that humans find it really offensive," R. M. said.

And again, and Jake could tell that this time Zamara was annoyed, *there are more important things my people have to worry about. Such as retreating before the zerg return with stronger numbers. They wish to aid us. We must hurry.*

"They want to help us," Jake told his traveling companion. "But there are more zerg out there."

Even in this moment of dire necessity and need for urgency, Jake knew a hint of wonder as he watched hands with two thumbs and two fingers reach toward him, helping him to his feet; saw large but also somehow slender bodies move in a way that was deeply familiar after "living" as Temlaa. One of them met his gaze, and though Zamara's barrier prevented the female from making telepathic contact, Jake knew from her body language that she was curious and pleased and intrigued, just as he was. In a species that had no voice, it seemed that telepathy was far from the only method of communication.

R. M. had darted back to the now-ruined shelter and retrieved their packs. She tossed one to a nearby protoss and shouldered the other one. "I hope these protoss have some way to get us off the planet."

They do not.

I'm not telling her that right now.

That is a wise decision.

Thirty seconds later, Jake, Zamara, Rosemary, and their rescuers and new best friends were hastening off toward safety.

If it hadn't been for the direness of the meeting and their current situation, Jake thought he might never have been happier. To finally meet a protoss! Because of the connection to Zamara, and the memories she had shared and was continuing to share, he felt a kinship with them. At the same time he was painfully reminded of how different they were from him, how . . . well . . . how alien.

He felt their presence skimming his consciousness and for the first time since joining with Zamara, Jake wanted to feel another's thoughts. But such a thing would have to be gradual. The pain he'd experienced the first time they'd all tried to talk to him without Zamara's intervention had been unbearable. It was even worse than when he'd attempted to read the minds of the drug addicts he and Rosemary had run across while in Paradise.

Therefore Zamara was acting as a translator. Even with the speed of thought it felt cumbersome to Jake, and he realized he was growing accustomed to communicating this way.

Maybe I won't make such a bad preserver after all.

. . . Perhaps not.

Her lack of enthusiasm stung a bit, but he pushed it aside.

At first, Jake had thought the protoss simply appeared as if by a miracle or the happiest of coincidences. After a few moments, though, when he caught glimpses of something metallic and gold glinting between the dark green fronds of the foliage, he realized that the protoss had a vessel. In his head, Zamara chuckled slightly.

We are far from divine beings, Jacob. We were detected long before I was even close enough to be in telepathic contact with them. But it is fortunate that they arrived when they did.

Rosemary looked at the ship admiringly. "I wouldn't want acid on that either," she said, acknowledging the reason the protoss had landed the ship here rather than closer to their shelter. It was a beautiful thing, even though Jake knew it was a simple atmospheric craft. Nothing, it seemed to him, was too simple or functional to not be beautiful as well. He wondered, not for the first time, how it was the khalai craftsmen managed to make things curve so effortlessly.

The door opened soundlessly and a small ramp was extended. Jake went in immediately. Rosemary hesitated for a second, then followed suit. The protoss swiftly entered once the two terrans had come aboard.

"Hey," Rosemary said, pointing at a pile of blankets, weapons, and other items, "that's our stuff!"

The protoss saw our vessel come under attack, Zamara explained. *By the time they reached it, we had moved on. They salvaged what they could—*

"—and then set out to find us," Jake said, relaying what Zamara had told him.

"I see. Hope they brought my tool kit—I might be able to fix the Pig."

"I hope so, too. Let's take a seat and get out of here before more zerg start sniffing around."

There were eight individual seats and a curved bench for the pilots. Jake and Rosemary eased into the chairs and Jake found his comfortable, if a bit large for his smaller human frame. Two protoss moved to the front bench and the rest took their seats, eerily motionless once they were settled. Jake knew that their minds were as perfectly still as their bodies. He wondered if this was part of the military training the templar underwent, that deep, profound stillness.

Most of those you see here are khalai, not templar. The only "training" they have had has been that which was necessitated by their situation here on Aiur, Zamara answered him. *Think of what you know of us already, Jake. The discipline that enables us to stay unstirring, in mind and in body, and then leap from that place into swift motion and thought kept us alive for many eons.*

In poetic contrast to the others, the two protoss pilots exchanged glances and gestures, although they kept their thoughts from Jake. Rosemary watched them keenly, as their long, four-fingered hands moved fluidly over a console. They did not actually touch anything; it seemed the motions alone were sufficient.

"Wonder if terrans could learn how to pilot these things," R. M. said softly. "This is one sweet little vessel."

Jake grimaced slightly. In the midst of all this awesome discovery, and, he admitted, sheer terror, Rosemary was thinking only about herself and what plunder she could take. Even as the thought brushed his mind, he chastised himself for it. He'd known Rosemary Dahl in the most intimate way possible—for a few brief moments, he'd been her. He knew why she was the way she was, what had shaped her. Like the ancient weapons Valerian so loved, she'd been tempered by the fires of experience. The anger dissipated, and all he could do was feel sorry for her that she was missing the real heart of what was happening around her.

There were no windows in the golden vessel except for the single large circular one in front of the pilots. Through this, Jake watched as the vessel climbed skyward so he could barely even feel it. The ship skimmed smoothly over first the thick, green canopy of the rain forest and then blackened, burned, and dead earth, heading toward a blackened, burned, and dead husk of a city. As they traveled, Zamara told Jake what had transpired here four short years ago. The preserver had relayed R. M.'s desire to keep her thoughts to herself and the other protoss had agreed, so Jake had to tell R. M. the old-fashoined way—with verbal speech.

"When the zerg attacked Aiur four years ago," Jake

told Rosemary, "it was absolute chaos. Hundreds of thousands were killed as all tried to get to the warp gate on the surface. The zerg were everywhere. You saw what they did to the planet."

"Yeah, that's why when Zamara said there weren't any protoss here I believed her. No offense or anything, but I figured that anyone who didn't make it off-planet didn't make it at all." Rosemary gestured to the ugly landscape over which they were flying.

He smiled a bit, at her, at Zamara, at the protoss who'd just saved their skins. "You underestimate them. They are survivors. Even the ones who aren't trained to be."

She scowled at him. "I don't know why you're so happy, Jake. This is a nice little ship, granted, but unless there's a nice *big* ship tucked away somewhere, we're stranded on this zerg-infested rock."

"We're alive. We've got friends. We'll be all right. Anyway, some of them weren't able to make it through the warp gate before the protoss disabled it."

She threw him a sharp glance. "Why the hell would they want to disable it?"

"Because it would take the zerg straight to the only haven the protoss really had left. And if enough zerg came through there, that would be the end of the protoss. All of them. Not just their world, and not those who had the bad luck to get left behind." He gestured to the protoss, who sat statuelike around them. "They understand that. Any of them—all of them—would gladly have died to protect their race."

The words were true, so far as they went, but Jake knew how inadequate those words were to the task of describing the protoss's love for their homeland and their people. It made any kind of terran nationalism seem trivial and petty. His head started aching again.

Zamara, this translating from thoughts to speech and back is getting tiresome. If I can convince Rosemary that the conversation will only go one way, can we let the protoss talk to us?

She hesitated.

Come on, I'm not that *bad at this.*

Very well.

Pleased, Jake turned his attention back to Rosemary. "It would be easier and more accurate to learn this directly from them. The protoss communicate telepathically; they don't even have mouths. They know what they're doing and they're . . . good people. They won't try to read your thoughts. Will you let them talk to you?"

She kept her eyes straight ahead, at the approaching ruined city of twisted metal, melted glass, and blackened crystals. Her Cupid's bow lips turned down in a slight frown. "It feels . . . weird, Jake." There was no cocksureness in her voice, no condescension. She was talking to him calmly and honestly. He was surprised but knew better than to comment on it. "I don't like it. You understand. You didn't like it any better than me at first."

"You're right. I've gotten used to it, though. It's a highly efficient method of communication."

She still didn't look at him. He let her mull in silence. "Okay," she said, finally.

Jake felt a presence inside his head, pouring over his thoughts like warm honey. "Thank you. We will be better able to understand one another now."

Beside him, he saw Rosemary jerk as if stung. She frowned slightly, an unguarded, completely natural gesture, then her normal mask descended. Jake thought that a shame. He turned to see one of the protoss clad in dinged golden armor gazing right at him. Jake smiled. The protoss inclined its head.

"I am Ladranix. I am the leader of one of the groups that remained. There is another, and I will speak of it later. First I will speak of what happened on those dark days. The terror, the fear—it was all so unexpected. And then when the warp gate was disabled, there was no place to go. We were left behind—we, the zerg, and the ruination that was once a beautiful world."

Jake got a vision, brief and tinged with sorrow like an old sepia photograph, of what Aiur had been like before it fell. Beautiful buildings reached skyward, sleek ships transported the inhabitants from one glorious city to another. The cityscapes were magnificent, incorporating nature and water and air and light, and the natural world was encroached upon only as needed. Jake's heart ached. Then the vision was gone, as if Ladranix regretted how powerfully the image had affected Jake and had drawn a curtain over it.

"I've heard about what the zerg can do—heck, I just had a demo. How is it that you're alive at all to even be telling us this?" Jake queried.

"The warp gate was disabled, so that there was no way for the majority of the zerg to follow. Many brave protoss voluntarily stayed behind to protect it as it was closed. They were accompanied by one of your own people, Jacob Jefferson Ramsey."

Jake glanced at Rosemary, shocked. She too looked surprised.

"His name was James Raynor." Again an image was shown to Jake, of a man with a shaved head that had begun to once again become dotted with stubble, of a close-cropped beard and mustache and eyes that he knew had once held laughter and now had seen too much. He was standing shoulder to shoulder with the protoss, obviously welcomed and accepted, obviously deeply concerned for their well-being.

"It is because of Raynor that we recognized your craft as being a terran vessel—possibly that of one who would be a friend. It is why when our observers spotted it, we came to your aid."

"Heh," said Rosemary, chuckling slightly. "If I ever meet this Raynor fellow, I'm gonna shake his hand and thank him for being such a good ambassador."

Jake shared her sentiment.

"We expected it to be a death sentence," Ladranix continued. "We were prepared to fall to the zerg and die as the proud people we are. And do not mistake me—many, many of us did. The zerg were well controlled and deadly. But Executor Tassadar saved his people by destroying the Overmind that controlled the zerg. It cost him his life, but he succeeded. The zerg were still mad to kill—but they were no longer directed in that goal. They fell upon themselves as readily as upon us. It bought us some time."

Jake recalled the attacks, unable to suppress a shiver of revulsion as he watched them unfold again in his mind. "But . . . they certainly seemed focused enough when they saw us."

Ladranix nodded. "Yes. Something changed sometime after the gate was closed. While the zerg no longer attacked quite so intently, nor with the same focus as they had while they were controlled by the Overmind, they were no longer mindless creatures. Something had shifted, somewhere. Certainly they were still dangerous. And still intelligent."

Jake got the impression of a predator toying with its prey. Cat and mouse, he thought, and sent the image.

Ladranix sent back an affirmative. "Yes. Once, the absolute obliteration of every protoss was their main concern. Now they wander about; they are tools that, while still functional, appear to have been largely discarded. Over the years we have managed to kill many zerg in this area, and as far as we can tell, no others have been bred to take their place. That gives us hope. Still, the zerg certainly do attack when they see us. And we knew they would head straight for your vessel, to determine if you were any kind of threat."

"Do you think they will pursue us?" Jake felt a sudden chill, despite the oppressive heat of the place.

"Unlikely. Your ship is ruined, and it was mere accident that they came across you a second time. We anticipate that you will become folded into our group, no more or no less a threat to them than we are. The weapons we recovered from your vessel will be useful to us."

Now they were navigating among what had been glorious spires and towers. Jake saw in his mind's eye, superimposed over what his true eyes beheld, what this view had once been like. The little golden ship, a firefly of a vessel, moved gracefully amid the ruins until it came to a blackened clearing. It looked like a bomb had gone off here once but that the area had now been at least somewhat reclaimed. To the north, he saw some debris that intrigued him, though he couldn't make sense of the jumble. The ship settled down easily, and the moment it alit, the protoss all rose in a movement timed so perfectly it might have been choreographed. The door opened and the elegant ramp extended, its delicacy at sharp odds with the ruination onto which it opened.

"Please, go first. You are expected."

Jake and Rosemary nodded. Rosemary went first, moving with her head held high and a lithe, in-control stride. Jake followed.

He immediately thought of a refugee camp. Dozens, maybe hundreds of protoss all turned as one to gaze at him. Large, lambent eyes looked him up and down, seemed to gaze into his very soul. The silence was the main thing that struck him. No cries of infants, no sobs or laughter, no murmurs of conversation—none of the things that one would expect of such a large gathering of people in one place. But then again, while the protoss were most certainly "people," they were not humans. He knew that if Zamara had not been providing a buffer, his mind would be awash in thoughts that dwarfed human sounds in their detail, their richness, their depth and complexity and interconnection.

They had erected shelter as best they could, a strange amalgamation of items they had brought in from nature and things that had been taken from the city. A shiny metal beam held up a roof of woven leaves; a second small atmospheric craft was protected by poles made from tree branches. Even in the starkness of their necessity, there was beauty. Doors were made of the fronds of different-colored plants, and the result was not merely functional but lovely. Some things had been painted, other things carved.

Attention quickly went from the newcomers to what they brought. The protoss who rescued Jake, Zamara, and R. M. placed what they had gotten from the now-defunct system runner on the black, uneven surface. The refugees scurried forward, elegant four-fingered hands taking up the weapons, the bedding, the tools, the precious medkit.

"They're taking everything!" Rosemary snapped, and started to move forward.

"They saved our lives," Jake reminded her. "A weapon in their hands can only help us. And others need medical supplies more than we do." At that moment his head throbbed. "Well, not all the supplies; they can't take any oral medication."

"Jake, listen, believe me when I say I'm delighted that we're not inside a zerg's belly at the moment. But this isn't an archeological expedition here. We've got to find a way to get off this planet." She was not looking at the protoss. She was looking at the wreckage that had once been a thriving city. She was looking for anything that might offer hope of a way out.

She's right, Jake thought to Zamara.

There may be a way. I must speak with the others first.

"Zamara's working on it," Jake said.

"Good." Rosemary looked edgy, and he supposed he could understand why. She was extremely competent in her own environment, but now they were surrounded by aliens that they had never beheld until a few moments ago. The technology with which she was so familiar and a master at manipulating had been melted to a puddle of acidic ooze, and she'd come within centimeters of being melted right along with it. They were stuck at the mercy of said aliens, on a strange planet. And she was watching her precious weaponry being examined and parceled out.

"It's all right, Rosemary," Jake said gently, feeling oddly protective. "I know you're worried and you feel out of place here. But it could be a lot worse."

She glared at him, blue eyes cold. "Reading my mind again, Professor? I thought we discussed that."

There was a time when her words would have stung. This time, he felt only compassion for her. "No. I just read your face."

She looked slightly embarrassed, then irritated, and then she turned away.

"We understand that humans need to feed upon plant and animal matter," said Ladranix. "We do not, so at this moment we have nothing to offer you. But we do have clean water for sterilizing instruments and will soon be able to provide you with what you require. Zamara has experienced . . . sharing a meal with you, Jacob. We will do our best to emulate this food."

"We brought rations with us," Jake sent back to Ladranix, looking him full in his glowing blue eyes. "We do not wish to inconvenience you any further than we already have."

The protoss leader half closed his eyes and tilted his head in the way that Jake knew meant laughter. He knew it even before Ladranix's warm mirth washed over him, coaxing his own lips to turn up at the corners in the human version of a smile.

"You bring us weapons and medicine. A few fruits from the trees and the flesh of beasts is nothing in comparison. You and Rosemary Dahl and Zamara are welcome here, Jacob Jefferson Ramsey. More than welcome."

Jake felt, in a very strange but very real way, that, in a sense, he had come home.

CHAPTER EIGHT

THE WATER THEY WERE GIVEN WAS STALE AND warm, but it was wet, and Jake drank thirstily. He felt about as stale and warm and wet as the water. The heat coming off the ruins of the city as it baked underneath a sullen sun was almost unbearable. The protoss did not appear to be affected by it, but that was to be expected. They had evolved on this tropical world of sun and humidity. Jake's and R. M.'s discomfort was noticed and after a short discussion, they were led inward into a jumble of metal and some sort of concrete that provided at least a bit of relief from the heat. It looked strangely familiar to Jake. He glanced around, sipping a second gourdful of the water. Ladranix came to stand beside him.

"Do you recognize this place?" Ladranix asked quietly.

"Sort of. But it's so damaged I can't place it." Jake walked up to the wreckage of a chair, ran his hand along it. Like everything else the protoss made, it had been beautiful once. So had this place been beautiful—and huge; he remembered seeing what looked like a shattered tower and the ruinations of a landscape atop a huge circular disc.

"There are places elsewhere in the city that are not habitable. We were fortunate to find this shelter as intact as it is. What you behold now is the ruin of what was once known as the Executor's Citadel. Since before the time of Adun, the leaders of the templar dwelt here."

Jake's gut twisted. Superimposed on this pathetic wreckage was the image of Adun standing and looking down on Antioch. He had perhaps sat in this very chair. Jake found his hand tightening on the back of the chair, as if he could hold on to the past.

"We like to think that even now, Adun somehow is watching over us," Ladranix said gently. He touched the broken remains of the chair with a long, four-fingered hand, seemed to recover himself from his emotions, and faced Jake.

"I have sent our best scouts to find you food," Ladranix said. "It is not without risks, but we are more familiar with how to evade the zerg than you. Night will fall soon. While the heat will not diminish greatly, the winds pick up at night. You will find it cooler."

"That sounds great," Rosemary said. Perspiration sheened her face, and heat had reddened it. Jake thought back to when he had first met her, calm and in control in the shadow of the *Gray Tiger.* He thought of how stunning she had looked by candlelight in Ethan Stewart's decadent enclave, her hair perfect, her dress cut down to *there* at the neck and up to *here* at the thigh. Right now she was grimy, sweaty, sunburned, and didn't smell all that good. And she seemed more real, more . . . human . . . than he'd ever seen her.

He felt a gentle mirth in his head and mentally scowled. It was tiring having every thought of hunger, irritation, weakness, lust, or boredom being read. For a moment he wondered, if this "mission" of Zamara's was successful and he indeed survived long enough to be a preserver, if all these thoughts would be available to every future preserver who cared to read them. It was an alarming concept and he quickly pushed it out of his mind.

"Please continue, Ladranix. What happened after the gate was shut down?"

The protoss leader inclined his head. "We scattered when the gate closed. Even the most rigorously trained among us knew a dreadful sense of abandonment when we realized that we had been left behind. Although we understood the reasoning—we few were the sacrifice to keep the others alive—it still hit hard. Most of the templar fell while distracting the zerg as the others fled."

"Wait—what's a templar?" Rosemary was confused.

Ladranix turned to her and gazed at her for a long moment. This was a private conversation between them, so Jake had no idea what was being said. But in a few seconds Rosemary nodded. "I see. A caste system. Seems a little—I don't know—intolerant for a society in which all are supposedly equal."

Jake realized that Ladranix was giving R. M. only the basics. The protoss was respecting her boundaries, conveying only words in his thoughts, not feelings.

"It's not as intolerant as it might sound, Rosemary," Jake piped up. "Protoss aren't quite like us. As I told you, before the Khala, they were separated into tribes. Each tribe had a definite proclivity, a—a strength, a *feel* to it. When the protoss turned to the Khala, the tribes fit pretty easily into three separate categories. But no one caste is better than the others."

Zamara sent an affirmative. *The caste system was originally created to better utilize the abilities of the whole, yes. To take our different strengths and use them to unite us rather than divide us. And for a thousand years it stayed thus. But even among the protoss, even in a place where we are so tightly bound to one another in an intimacy you are just beginning to glimpse, there are those who aspire to better only themselves. We are not angels or gods, Jake. We are just beings like yourself.*

. . . Hardly.

Zamara chuckled.

"The templar are the warriors," Ladranix explained. "Our job is to protect our people, defend them, give our lives for them if necessary. We are trained from earliest youth to harness fear, to make it work for us. For of course, we do feel it. All thinking, feeling beings do. But protecting the Conclave and their wisdom, and the khalai and their skills and talents—that is what we do. And on those long, dark days, that is what we did.

"More than the few of us you see here were stranded on Aiur that day. There were thousands. Hundreds of thousands. I am proud to say that the majority of those who died were templar, fighting to the death to save the others. The drawback is that now, while we face death every day still, most of those who are left alive are khalai. There are few trained warriors to defend them now."

"No judicators?" Jake asked.

"Not here, not among the Shel'na Kryhas."

The term was apparently untranslatable, for Jake saw his confused expression mirrored on Rosemary's face. Ladranix chuckled and sent an image: stoic, resolute, weathering what will come.

"Those Who Endure," Jake said quietly. Ladranix nodded.

"Yes. The words are but the crudest comprehension of what we are, but they will have to do."

Rosemary snorted.

"Those first few days, it was simple, pure survival. Protoss fled, alone, in pairs, or in small family groups. They found shelter if they could, and died if they could not. Much of the rain forests had been destroyed, as were our once-beautiful cities. I fully expected death to find all of us shortly, for I did not understand what had happened to the zerg. It is a blessing that the zerg never regained the unified intensity they had while under the

Overmind's control. Even so, they slay us when they find us, and they obviously felt it was necessary to investigate your ship when you were about to land. But whereas they were once single-minded of purpose to hunt us down and slaughter us, now that has changed. Perhaps they are merely waiting for us to feel a certain sense of safety before they decide upon our extinction.

"Whatever the zerg's plans—if there is indeed anything so complex as to be called such—it has given us time. Time to find each other again. Time to return to our poor, blasted cities and do what we can to make them homes. Time to find weapons with which to fight these abominable creatures, and to craft new weapons. I would not go so far as to say the Shel'na Kryhas are creating a new society here on the remnants of our world, but we are doing what we can. And now, we have a preserver among us. We are grateful to you for bringing her to us."

"I am no savior, Ladranix," and Jake saw Rosemary's china blue eyes widen slightly as she felt Zamara's mind touch hers. "I cannot stay to help you overlong. I have a mission of dire importance to the survival of our people."

"You are still wiser than any of us, for you have the memories of all who have gone before." Ladranix's mental words were tinted with awe. "We are grateful for anything you can do for us."

Something was bothering Jake, but he couldn't quite put his finger on it. There was something that was being left unsaid, unshared.

"I cannot help until I know all," said Zamara. She, too, had been sensing something amiss.

Protoss didn't breathe, at least not the way humans did, but Jake got the distinct impression of a heavy sigh as Ladranix spoke.

"We are the Shel'na Kryhas. We are Those Who Endure. We have gravitated back to what remains of our best and most noble creations, our cities. We have stayed true to the protoss ideals. We understand why we were left, and feel confident that when it is once again safe for our brethren to return to Aiur to retrieve us, they will. We rely as much if not more upon the Khala as ever, and the bond that unites us all. Not . . . all of those who were left behind that day feel the way we do."

Ladranix hesitated. "May I . . . show this? The telling . . . it is a hard thing to convey with just words."

"I do not think that is best," said Zamara, unexpectedly. Jake focused his thoughts toward her.

Zamara, why not? It's exactly what you have been doing to me with the memories of Temlaa and Vetraas this whole time!

Yes, she replied, keeping her thoughts for his mind alone. *And I am giving you that which I believe you need to understand in order for me to carry out my mission. Nothing more and nothing less. Words are easier for your brain to manage. I see no point in taxing you or, indeed, Rosemary further than is absolutely necessary from that perspective.*

The headache was coming back, no doubt due to Jake's sudden surge of exasperation. *Look, you picked me, I didn't sign up for this. And I think that all things considered I've been a damn good sport about it all.*

You have indeed, Jacob. Better than I dared hope the first time my mind met yours.

And whether I like it or not I'm going to be the next preserver. So I'd better get used to having my mind stretched in this way, hadn't I?

When she did not reply, Jake took it as a yes and said, "If it's all right with Rosemary, I'd be okay with your showing us." He glanced over at his traveling companion. She looked wary, but finally nodded.

"Yeah, you can do it if you have to. But no prying into my thoughts. I hate that."

Ladranix inclined his head. Almost immediately Jake felt a chill that had nothing to do with the temperature and everything to do with the protoss he beheld in his mind's eye. They did not look any different from the ones he now sat with in the physical reality. But . . . they *felt* different.

They shared the same worry, the same fear, the same anger as the Shel'na Kryhas. However, instead of gathering strength from adversity they had almost . . . embraced it. Emanating from them was something akin to a mental stench, something ancient and primitive, and Jake's heart suddenly lurched as he realized it was dreadfully familiar.

Suddenly he was again that ancient protoss, watching as the xel'naga abandoned them. *Up it went, the home that flew, bearing the* Ihan-rii, *the Great Teachers, the Makers, the Guardians away, away, forever away. Dozens of lithe, purple-blue-gray shapes sprang into the air in futile pursuit, clinging to starkly beautiful crystals that had edges sharp as shikmas. The home that flew continued to ascend, its inhabitants unmoved by the begging and pleading of those they forsook. Hands now slicked with blood lost their grip and the panicked beings fell to the earth, fell too far to survive, striking the ground with a thudding sound that was drowned out by the overwhelming noise of the departing vessel and the excruciating mental din that threatened to tear Jake's head apart, just as the pain in his heart threatened to rip his mind apart.*

No, no, they mustn't go, they were everything, everything—

Overcome with despair, Jake fell to the ground as well, thrashing, his dark blue skin mottled and heated with blinding, smothering fear and fury. What would they do? How could they go on? Alone, alone, so alone—

"Hey, you okay there, Prof?" Rosemary asked. Jake blinked, coming back to the present, back to Jacob Jefferson Ramsey and not that long-ago, terrified protoss whose sense of abandonment would know no ease. He was shaking and gasping, and when Ladranix handed him a gourd filled with the metallic, warm water he gulped it down thirstily.

"You all felt that, I know you did," Jake managed, his throat still somehow dry despite the water he had just drunk. "It's like a—a racial memory." He hesitated, then said softly, "A racial wound."

Ladranix nodded. "Only a fraction of our people are born preservers, but they are merely the ultimate expression of something latent in our people.

The abandonment of the protoss by the xel'naga is deeply ingrained in our psyches. That dark day when the gate was closed and we realized we were stranded—were alone—was a powerful echo of the day when we were forsaken so many eons in the past. For some, it was too traumatic an event from which to recover."

Again the "other" protoss came into Jake's mind. He steeled himself for the emotions pouring off them and this time it wasn't as overwhelming. He sensed a darkness, a wildness about them. It was as if the blow of abandonment had struck both groups of protoss hard, metaphorically knocking them down, but only one had risen. These others were ruled by anger and fear, not calm and enlightenment. He sensed a name—Tal'darim, "the Forged"—but did not understand why the name resonated, not yet. Just as Jake recognized the Shel'na Kryhas as being spiritual brethren to the likes of Adun and Vetraas and Temlaa and Savassan, he realized that these protoss had been so traumatized that they had reached back in time for a mind-set that would permit them to continue to exist. Instead of faith in the advancements that the race had made, they were returning to the primal, angry, powerful beings from which they had evolved.

"The schism happened slowly, but it came to a head in one angry night. There was no fighting, but there was . . . much rage. Their leader, Felanis, had been acting strangely for some time. He and I had never been close, but we had been united in our need for survival. He turned to a dear friend of mine, a fellow templar, Alzadar. We had trained together, stood together in many a battle, but no longer. My old friend began shutting me and others out. Turning inward, becoming solitary, sharing thoughts only for the most basic necessities. Felanis was the one he turned to now. Finally Felanis called us fools and idealists, and struck off for the wilds, Alzadar and others at his side. We tried to pursue, to stop them—it was madness, certain death, to venture forth from the cities—but Alzadar and the others insisted on going with him. We are a free people. We live and die by the choices we made. We could not force them to stay. And so the protoss on Aiur were a divided people from that moment forward."

"But Felanis, Alzadar, and the rest of the Forged—they're still alive?" Rosemary asked. Ladranix turned his glowing, pale blue eyes to hers.

"They are. They found an unexpected sanctuary. There are cave systems beneath the surface. Some of them are vast. Many are still unexplored. It is there that the Tal'darim find shelter, coming up only to take nourishment from the starlight. Faint though that light is, it is enough to keep them alive."

Rosemary and Jake exchanged glances. He was starting to get a bad feeling about this. "By any chance . . . do the Tal'darim live near the area where our ship was planning to land?"

Ladranix moved his head and arms in a way that Jake recognized as surprise with a hint of confusion. "They do indeed."

Despite his curiosity, Ladranix was as good as his word. He had not read Jake's or Rosemary's thoughts, and it was clear now to Jake that Zamara had kept her own thoughts on this matter well hidden.

Rosemary threw up her own hands in exasperation. "Well, isn't *this* just great! The one place in this whole blasted planet we need to get to and half the protoss are going to fight us to get there!"

Zamara sighed in Jake's mind. She was a preserver. Her knowledge was for her people, but it was nonetheless not knowledge that was intended to be commonplace. Jake did not doubt that had the situation been different, Zamara would have felt no need to share it even with Ladranix and the other Shel'na Kryhas. But Rosemary had summed up the situation accurately, if bluntly. They would require aid to penetrate the chambers to obtain what they had come here for, and the protoss, even though they honored their preservers, would insist on knowing before lending assistance in attacking their own, if it came down to it.

Thoughts, Zamara's and Jake's, intertwined, interconnected now, flowed gently into Ladranix's mind. His pale blue eyes widened as Zamara showed him the barest fragment of what Jake—a terran, an alien, not even a protoss—had seen in rich and powerful detail.

"We . . . did not know," Ladranix managed. He was stunned. "All this time . . . such treasures sat beneath the surface."

"Treasures, true, and dangers as well," Zamara said. "We are protoss. We might be the children of the xel'naga, but we are not them, and their treasures would not be our treasures. So the Conclave ruled long ago, after a brief initial investigation of the caverns."

"But now, what was hidden away . . . what was dark . . . has come to light," Ladranix said. "First the dark templar, an ancient and shameful secret, have reappeared in our lives. And now this. Can you reveal yet more to us, Zamara? Can you tell us why you must find this technology and take it to our brethren?"

Jake had yet to master the fine art of censoring his thoughts, and what escaped was: *Good luck with that.* He sensed astonishment, affront, and humor in rapid succession from the protoss, and blushed.

"In due time, it will have to be shared," Zamara said. "But first . . . we must do what we came here to do. And that will mean somehow entering the chambers beneath the earth where the Tal'darim live. In the meantime, we will join with you and help you as we are able."

CHAPTER NINE

VALERIAN LOWERED THE SWORD, FOR THE FIRST time ever voluntarily pausing during his training. He realized he could not bring his attention to focus on the stance, the whirling of the blade, could not drop into his body. The thought concerned him. *Or maybe,* he mused with a hint of humor as he respectfully put away the sword and reached for a towel to wipe his face, *I'm learning what it means to actually be in command.*

His father, God knew, certainly had distractions. Valerian had played enough chess and drunk enough port with the man to know that. But Arcturus had never possessed anything like Valerian had with his swordwork—something in which he could wholly lose himself and that belonged to him and no one else; in which all that mattered was being fully in the moment and striving for his personal best. Now, Valerian was starting to understand why. It was damned difficult to balance the two.

He'd been almost giddy at first, when he realized exactly where Jake and Rosemary had been heading. They were going to Aiur. He would follow. It had seemed simple enough in that first moment, but reality had soon set in.

Whittier had haltingly informed his employer that he was very, very sorry, sir, very sorry indeed, but there were no appropriate ships in that sector that Valerian could commandeer for this purpose. Well, that wasn't entirely true, the *Gray Tiger* was in that area, but she was hardly fit for action anymore, was she? Well, yes, there are several Dominion vessels, but His Excellency was utilizing those, and it was Whittier's understanding that the Heir Apparent had no desire to attract his father's attention any more than was absolutely necessary. Was Whittier misinformed as to this delicate issue? No? Well then, it would take some time to get any vessels at—*how* many did Valerian require? Oh my, that would take a bit of doing. . . .

Valerian growled in the back of his throat at the recollection of the conversation. The delay was excruciatingly frustrating. Every hour that ticked by meant Jake and the protoss in his head were that much closer to escaping. Still, Valerian was not about to sacrifice Jake to his father's whim by misplaying his hand. This had to be done correctly, or all would fall to disaster. He did not need a handful of vessels, he needed as close to a fleet as he could manage. Who knew what kind of state Aiur was in? The last information he had been able to obtain had indicated that the planet was crawling with zerg.

Valerian would not make the mistake his father had of underestimating Kerrigan. While he did not understand quite how the former ghost managed her abominable troops, he was not about to assume that once Jake landed on the planet, Kerrigan would be unaware of so unique a presence. And even if she was foolish enough to not recognize the opportunity, well . . . Jake devoured by zerg was as bad as Jake captured by Kerrigan or Jake tortured to death by Arcturus.

It was a delicate mission, one requiring care . . . and one that needed to have started days ago.

Valerian grit his teeth and again drew the sword from the scabbard.

Arcturus might not be able to balance running an empire with perfecting the Stance of the Stalking Panther. But Valerian was not his father. He would surpass his father as the sun surpassed the moon. And he would begin now.

Kortanul inclined his head. "As you wish, Executor." Despite his words, he seemed deeply reluctant to speak. Adun and Jake waited patiently.

"Impossible as it may seem, there are those among us who would destroy everything we have sought to build over the last millennium. They question the Khala. They maintain that the right of the individual takes priority over the good of the whole. Some have even resorted to the extreme measure of self-mutilation in order to sever their connection to the Khala."

Even though he spoke in words rather than a more intimate connection, Kortanul could not entirely conceal his revulsion. Jake and Adun shared it.

"This cannot be!" Adun cried. "What do they hope to accomplish? Hurtle us backward thousands of years to when we were no better than the beasts of the jungles—worse, because we had self-awareness. They know that the Khala was the greatest boon the protoss have ever had! Why would they wish to ruin our salvation?"

The Conclave members exchanged glances. "Would you wish to ask them such a thing yourself?"

Jake started. They had some of these . . . these heretics present?

Adun was very still for a moment, with that deep stillness that all protoss had but that was lifted almost to an art form with the templar. "Yes," he said at last. "Yes. I would know why one of these . . . renegades . . . thinks and feels as he does."

A soft murmur of approval flitted across Jake's mind. Such a mind-set was so inconceivable, so wrong, that even he would be concerned about brushing the mind that held those thoughts. And yet Adun stepped forward boldly. He was, as Jake and all the others had known, a true defender of his people. Not only did he have the skill and training to protect the protoss from outside threats, Adun had the deeper strength to protect them from this insidious, hitherto unimaginable attack from within.

Kortanul nodded to one of the Khalen'ri who stood immobile as a statue by the oval doorway. The guard bowed deeply, and then a moment later returned with one of the heretics.

Jake had been expecting a raving lunatic, a madman, powerful, perhaps not actually thrashing about but at least posing an obvious danger. When they brought in the adolescent girl, her body slender and frail-looking but her head held high, Jake was hard put to conceal his astonishment.

Her skin was pallid, and the unhealthy hue told Jake that she had been imprisoned too far away from the life-giving rays of the sun, moon, or stars. The Conclave would not have let her starve to death, of course. But they clearly had permitted her the barest minimum of nourishment. Her mind was shuttered from Jake's, but he imagined she had to be experiencing some level of fear as she was brought out, her slender wrists shackled with glowing, charged crystals, before the executor.

Adun was on his feet, staring raptly at the girl. She met his gaze coolly.

"This is the heretic?" Adun asked.

"Do not let her appearance fool you, Executor," Kortanul said. "She is stronger than she seems."

Adun nodded absently, his powerful attention completely focused on the girl.

"Speak, child," he said gently. "I would hear what you have to say."

She responded with a thought of annoyance so great that Jake blinked. "You will hear, but you will not listen. You will not understand."

"There is nothing to understand about lies and heresy!" snapped one of the Conclave, unable or, more likely, unwilling to conceal his thoughts.

Adun held up a hand. "You asked me to speak with her. Let me do so."

The girl kept her thoughts and feelings well masked. She had great control, for one so young and so . . . ill-treated. Reluctantly Jake discovered a sneaking admiration for her, despite the fact that she was a heretic and, worse, a fool. The Khala was the way of survival for the protoss. In unity, there was strength. In unity, there was compassion. To espouse or worse yet to actually believe anything other than that would be tantamount to wishing to doom the entire race. Was that what this was about then? Was this some kind of—of strange organization that found solace in the thought of the race's extinction? He would have to ask Adun, when he was done speaking with the girl.

Adun lifted his hands and turned the palms out. The girl didn't move for a long moment, and then, finally, slowly, she mirrored the executor's gesture. A glow formed between their hands, and they stood unmoving for a surprisingly long time. At last, Adun lowered his hands and nodded. One of the guards came and silently took the girl away. She left the vast, intimidating chamber the same way she had entered it, head high, dignity intact.

"Now, you understand the full depths of the dangers we face, Executor," Kortanul said. Adun nodded. His thoughts were hidden, even from Jake.

"What they believe cannot be permitted to spread," Adun said.

The Conclave looked at one another and Jake knew they were communicating quickly and privately. Kortanul turned back to Adun.

"Our past is rich and beautiful in many respects. There is much to be proud of. And . . . much not to be," he said qui-

etly. "It is through the unity of the Khala, staying on the path Khas showed us without wavering, that we can continue to have a beautiful and rich future. There is nothing that can be permitted to damage that. Not even other protoss."

Adun waited expectantly.

"This is a threat, like any other threat. It is worse in a way, for it is not a hungry omhara, or a strange, hostile alien being, but one of our own I am asking you to fight. But ideas are sometimes more deadly than blades. This idea is a sickness that must be vigorously cut out, lest it poison the whole. There are more than a handful who feel this way, but thus far, only those of us in this room know of their existence. It must remain so. Your task, Executor, is for you and your templar to find them. And when you find them—"

He hesitated. "When you find them, you must destroy them."

For a moment Jake was stunned, and then he spoke out. "Kill fellow protoss? Judicator, we have not done such a thing since Khas gave us the Khala! We know it to be the wrong path. It was Khas who taught us that hating or slaying another was akin to hating or slaying ourselves."

"Exactly!" Jake exclaimed to Zamara. "Good for you, Vetraas. That's exactly what the Khala's all about. Even if they're not preservers, even if they don't have the actual memories of how awful the Aeon of Strife was, they must know that they came close to killing themselves. And . . . I felt it. Even with humans. That closeness—how can they ask Adun to do that? He's a good person. He's going to refuse. Isn't he?"

Jake did not at all like the idea that he was living in the body of a mass murderer's best friend and trusted adviser.

"Hush, Jacob. It will unfold as it must."

"That is a truth with which I do not argue," said Kortanul. "But they have renounced the Khala. They have removed themselves from its dictates, its guidance, its protection. Worse, they seek to actively destroy it. They have chosen to withdraw from what it means to be protoss. They are the enemy, and they seek to undermine all that makes us what and who we are. They must be destroyed."

Adun nodded. "I must protect my people," he said. "You may trust that I will do everything I can to that end, Judicator. But how am I to go about this?"

"We have certain information we will share with you. Find them. Seek them out. That they exist at all is shocking. That they exist in such numbers is horrific. But they must and will die, one by one. Their ideology will not save them from the diligence of the templar."

*Adun inclined his head. "*En taro Khas, *Judicator."*

*Kortanul was pleased. "*En taro Khas, *Executor." Relief colored his thoughts. Jake realized now that Kortanul had been worried that Adun would refuse. But Jake was still concerned that this was not what Khas had envisioned those many centuries ago when he proposed complete unity and harmony among the protoss.*

"The girl?" Jake could not help himself.

Kortanul turned to regard him. "What of her?"

Before Jake could reply, Adun spoke. "Send her to my citadel. I would have all the high templar understand what it is they are undertaking."

"For a time," Kortanul cautioned. "We would have word of her execution swiftly."

Jake shuttered his thoughts quickly. He did not want Kortanul to see his pain at the thought of the young protoss, so proud and steady and vibrant, lying limp and lifeless. If the Conclave decreed it, it would happen. The templar were ever-obedient. The child would soon be the vanguard of slaughter, the first of these separatists to fall for their ideals.

"Oh damn it. Damn it. Zamara, must I really watch mass murder unfold? I get that it's a dark time in protoss history, but—even the different tribes' attacking each other was at least an honest mistake. This is . . ." Jake watched, his head aching even in his sleep, as Adun and Vetraas left the Khor-shakal.

"I show you nothing that is not necessary." There was an edge to Zamara's voice. "Be silent, Jacob."

They walked in silence for a while. Finally, Adun said, "Even without our minds being linked, I know that this troubles you, my old friend."

"It does. I am merely grateful the decision is not mine to make."

"The girl . . . she was not evil. She was not even truly misguided. There was an odd . . . merit to what she believed, although it seems at first to be directly against all we know to

be right. I need to know more. We, the high templar, need to know more. The Conclave wishes the threat removed, and I agree with that. The Conclave truly believes this is the only way. But perhaps these heretics can be reasoned with. Perhaps they can be reminded of what it means to be protoss. If they have concerns, perhaps I can allay them."

"What if you cannot?"

"It may come to that, Vetraas. It may come to eliminating them one by one, with my own hands, silently so that no one ever knows this threat. The Conclave is right about one thing: It is an alarming development and must be dealt with swiftly and quietly. We agree on that."

He threw Jake a glance. "Never before have I disobeyed the Conclave. The Conclave need not fear that I will stay my hand for squeamishness. But before I act, I must know.

"Do you wish to accompany me, Vetraas?"

Jake blinked. "Do you wish to accompany us, Jacob?" Ladranix repeated in his mind. The powerful images that had filled Jake's mind were gone. Rosemary nudged him and smothered a grin.

"I'm sorry," Jake mumbled, "can you repeat that?" He wondered if Ladranix knew what had been going on in his dreams. His head throbbed, and he rubbed his temples. He was probably dehydrated, he thought as he gulped thirstily at the water Ladranix offered. It was, as always, metallic and warm, but it helped some. His stomach growled. Ladranix seemed startled. Rosemary laughed, and Jake blushed.

"It is cooler now. A better time for movement. We were able to find you some nourishment, though it is paltry. We are going to scout further, perhaps hunt some prey. If we supply you flesh, can you prepare it for consumption? Until then, this must suffice." He extended his hands, each one holding something spherical and dark, with a ridged skin.

Sammuro fruit.

Jake stared at it. He recalled Ethan's comment, recalled tasting the sorbet made from its juice. His tongue tingled at the memory, and over that memory, his own, was that of a protoss who had died long ago—the memory of holding the fruit and slicing it open, to give as an offering. But now here one was, in reality. It was not as large or as attractive as the one he "remembered." Nothing here was as clean, as verdant, as it had been in the past. Everything that lived here was hanging on by its fingernails, and this little piece of fruit was no exception. Hungry as his growling stomach had proclaimed him to be, he took a moment to run his fingers over the knobby surface of the fruit, the skin thick and hard like an avocado's. He took the knife Ladranix handed him and began to peel the sammuro. The scent was just as he . . . remembered . . . it, and his mouth watered. The flesh of the fruit was shiny and purple and dripped with juice, and he bit deep.

"Wow, these are good," Rosemary said beside him, peeling and eating her own sammuro fruit. Jake ate in reverent silence, deeply aware that this act connected the past and the present in a profound way. Inside him, he knew Zamara approved.

"I am sorry there is not more," Ladranix apologized. "It is dangerous to venture too far without a great deal of preparation. We risk drawing the attention of the zerg if we do. But later, we will mount a foraging party for you."

"We have lots of rations," Jake said. "We'll be all right."

He sensed unhappiness from the protoss, something deeper than a host's regret at not being able to supply more food for hungry guests. Jake frowned at Ladranix. "What's wrong?"

"Three more of our number are gone."

"Dead?" Rosemary asked, taking another bite.

"Not dead. They have deserted."

Rosemary paused in mid-chew. "Where the hell are they going to run? This is the only game in town."

"No, it is not. There are the Tal'darim. This . . . has happened before. The safety they offer against zerg attacks is much greater than anything we can provide. And before we disagreed, Felanis and Alzadar were well respected." The unhappiness Jake was sensing from Ladranix grew. "Our numbers were far greater in the beginning. The Forged were initially a few malcontents speaking out against our established way of life out of fear. But over time it has become apparent that we were losing more to the zerg than they."

"Why didn't you all go down to the chambers right away?" Rosemary asked.

"It has traditionally been forbidden to us. So the Conclave declared it, and we obeyed. And truly, it is not our first instinct, to be hidden away in the earth, away from the life-giving rays of the cosmos. It was not the first thing we thought of when we were seeking shelter. Our homes, our cities—what was left of them; what was left of being protoss—that is where my mind turned. I . . . was foolish. Now not only do we not have the safety of this underground place, but our numbers are dwindling."

"Let's roust the Forged then," R. M. said, brutally practical. "Kill them, get to whatever technology Zamara's dragged us out here to find, and kill two birds with one stone: We get what we came here for and you get a safer spot to escape the zerg. Then I guess we try to figure out how to get out of here."

Ladranix shook his head. "Even if they did not have the superior numbers, Rosemary, we would not do such a thing. Protoss has not attacked protoss in a long, long time."

Jake thought of Temlaa, lithe and feral and powerful, running through the prehistoric forests of this world. And he thought of Adun, ordered to slaughter every dark templar he could find, and balking at the order even as he seemed to be agreeing with it. It was obvious that Ladranix believed what he said. It was equally obvious that while the protoss history was not quite as bloody in the past millennium as terran history, it wasn't as idealistic as the templar liked to think.

That understanding must be a hard burden for you to bear, Zamara . . . you and the other preservers.

. . . It is. But we bear it, because it is our duty. There are many things we must do because it is our duty.

"Can they be reasoned with?" Jake asked, feeling Zamara's sorrow as his own although he didn't quite understand it.

Ladranix shook his head. "No. We have tried. I had hoped to be able to reach a fellow templar, but . . . they shutter their thoughts against us and turn away. They are unreachable, determined to stay apart from their brothers and sisters. They even sound mad sometimes, when they hurl mental attacks at us, speaking of new power and mysterious benefactors. They have no wish to rejoin the fold."

"Why don't you join them?" Rosemary asked.

"Unthinkable." Ladranix's mental voice was rigid on this issue. There would be no swaying him, and frankly, Jake agreed with him.

"Then it seems we're at an impasse," said R. M. "We're never going to get down there if it's guarded as heavily as you say."

Jake blinked. Why hadn't they thought of this before?

Zamara knew his thoughts as they occurred to him, and she approved. "Unless," he said slowly, "we know exactly what we're getting into."

CHAPTER TEN

IT TOOK ROSEMARY ABOUT A NANOSECOND TO figure out what Jake was getting at. She laughed.

"They'll sense me coming from a kilometer away. Besides, why send a human? Can't one of you protoss do it?"

They can shutter their minds, and they can move quietly, Zamara said. *But this is a place that has long been forbidden to my people. It is doubtful they would be able to concentrate fully on the task at hand.*

Jake relayed Zamara's comments. Rosemary looked at him, clearly expecting him to say something more. He felt heat wash over him. "Um . . . and, well, you kind of have more experience at this sort of thing than they do."

"At breaking, entering, and sneaking around? You raise a good point. You all have agreed to not read my mind, even though I know you can do so easily." She looked a little uncomfortable. "I, uh . . . appreciate that. But what's to stop the Tal'darim from detecting me? You can't tell me they wouldn't pick up on a human."

If she will let me, I can put up a screen, Zamara told Jake.

"Zamara can put up a screen, to shield your presence from them."

Rosemary's blue eyes hardened. In recent days, Jake thought he had seen a bit of a softening, a sense of opening and maybe even trust . . . maybe even liking . . . from the beautiful assassin. Now, she looked just like the woman who had had no compunctions about pointing the business end of a rifle at him.

"Like hell," she said.

As Zamara spoke in his mind, Jake relayed the information. "She won't need to do any . . . rewiring to you. And it won't last very long . . . just a few hours. Just long enough for you to get in, check it out, and get back to us."

She didn't reply immediately. Jake took that as a good sign and continued. "Zamara has an eidetic memory. We can sketch out a detailed map of the inside of the chambers. Zamara knows exactly where you need to go."

A muscle worked in Rosemary's jaw. Zamara began to speak again, calmly laying out her plan and providing logical reasons that Rosemary should attempt the endeavor. Jake stayed silent. Zamara paused, and he sensed her confusion and irritation, then understanding as she read his thoughts before he could even form them into words.

Rosemary would have the final word on this. And her decision would not come from persuasion, or logic, or sound plans. If she agreed, then all those things would come into play, of course, and would be vital to the success of the mission. But first, Rosemary Dahl, assassin, black marketer, victim and victimizer, would have to make the decision to put herself in a position of vulnerability for the good of all of them.

That choice had to come from her. And so Jake waited.

"I go in well armed," she said at last. "And at the first sign of trouble I either open fire or turn tail. I'm not going to be a hero for you."

Jake felt the smile spreading across his face. "Do what you have to do to get back safely."

Her eyes flitted to his, and she nodded. "All right. So, let's get cracking on this map."

Like Temlaa and Savassan before them, Zamara and Jake had to rely on nontraditional materials to draw the map. With their finely honed mental communication abilities, the protoss had had no need recently to write anything down. Each day was about simple survival. Gone for the most part were the luxuries of art and records and literature. There had been some attempt to make this makeshift refugee camp a place of beauty amid the ruins, but no one had any writing instruments of any sort. That night, a small party ventured forth into the closest forested area in search of wood for fires and beasts for food for the humans. Rosemary and Jake went with them. Ladranix had been reluctant to permit Jake to accompany them, hesitant to risk the precious preserver he bore, but Jake had insisted.

They took a small vessel and navigated to an area that was relatively clear of zerg. The protoss disembarked in silence, their eyes glowing in the darkness, their movements lithe as Temlaa's on the hunt but with a more elegant bearing, carrying terran rifles instead of spears. Ladranix and the other templar in particular Jake found compelling to watch. Their telepathy enabled them to hunt in almost total silence as they spread out in groups of two, searching for traces of *kal-taar* or the more obvious burrows of the lombads. They employed technology, but also their ancient senses of sound and smell and sight and telepathy, and after about an hour it became apparent that there were no prey animals readily available.

They turned their attention to gathering wood, moving deep beneath the canopy to find pockets that were still dry. Quickly they found the dead trees and began to hack off dry limbs.

One of the females suddenly started. "Zerg," she said.

Jake knew what she knew—a small band of zerg, eight of them, their thoughts manic and bestial, were milling about a short way away. "They do not seem to have noticed us," she said, "but we should go. Now."

Jake thought about the two encounters he'd had with the things and agreed wholeheartedly. They hurried back the way they had come, their scout monitoring the erratic thoughts of the beast the whole time. Suddenly she shouted in his mind.

"They have sensed us."

Rosemary swore under her breath and broke into a dead run. The protoss swiftly outpaced the humans, but Ladranix hung back, guarding them, ready to die for the preserver he so revered. They raced out onto the flat, charred surface, out from under the canopy, and Jake saw the beautiful, golden craft floating to the ground. He thought he'd never seen anything so gorgeous, and as the ramp extended, he raced aboard. Three seconds later everyone was in and the ship took off.

They'd made it. This time.

Jake didn't know how the protoss managed to stay so damn serene.

An hour later, after he'd rested and gotten a good fire going, Jake felt almost spooked as he did exactly what Temlaa had done over two millennia ago—took a slender stick and held it into the fire until it charred; and then, on a piece of gleaming metal that had once been part of a beautiful building, he began to draw the map.

The protoss crowded around him, having no difficulty seeing. Jake wished that he'd been gifted with an eidetic memory ere now—it was a damn handy thing to have. The night wore on, with Jake grimly and intricately drawing a detailed map of the subterranean caverns, telling the awestruck protoss what was located where.

"So much . . . right here . . . literally beneath our feet. And we did not know," breathed Ladranix.

"Yeah," said Rosemary. "Makes me wonder what the Tal'darim have found in there. Found to use against the zerg—or against us." She was sitting next to Jake, her thigh pressing against his, leaning in to look at the map. Her bobbed black hair swung forward to frame her face, once porcelain-pale and now reddened from the sun. He found her terribly distracting and forced himself to concentrate on the excellent point she had raised rather than the curve of her lips, pursed now in a pensive gesture.

"I think if they had found anything particularly unusual or dangerous, we would have seen evidence of it by this point," Ladranix said. "We would have seen what happened to the zerg remains."

Rosemary tilted her head to give him an arch look. "Would we? I'm guessing the zerg eat their fallen comrades. Fresh meat's fresh meat, I would think."

"They do," Ladranix agreed, "but there would be evidence. Residual radiation perhaps, or strange energy fluctuations, or marks on nearby vegetation or rocks."

Rosemary nodded in a yeah-I-get-that gesture. "Fair enough." Jake noticed that despite her initial reluctance to get involved, she seemed to have stepped up to the task with enthusiasm. He'd even have gone so far as to say "excitement." She'd assumed the role of leader and planner, and Zamara had gracefully yielded that position to her.

Jake couldn't even pretend to know why Rosemary was so apparently pleased to be doing this. Once her worries about thought violation had been assuaged, she'd plunged in with gusto. Perhaps it was a chance to do something instead of sitting around waiting. Perhaps it was a chance to help instead of harm. Perhaps it was a chance to—

"The technology in there might give us a way to get off this damn rock," Rosemary said. Turning to Ladranix, she said, "No offense, but that's really all it is now."

"I do not disagree with you," Ladranix said. "It is not the nurturing homeland it once was. Shakuras is our new home now—if we can ever get there."

When this is over, and we have what we have come for, I will ask them to take me to the gate. It is possible I can repair it. Zamara's voice was cool and clear in Jake's mind.

What—you—why don't we do it now?

We do not have what we need. And I do not wish to plant false hope. Right now, we need one thing from the chambers, and then we will be able to investigate this opportunity. If I cannot repair the warp gate, we will be forced to revisit the chambers. We will then have to attack our brethren, a prospect I do not relish. That must be a last resort. I do not like turning against my own, nor do I like jeopardizing the mission. But I will if I must. For now, the less risk incurred, the better.

"That's a possibility," Jake heard himself saying. "But let's take it one step at a time."

Rosemary narrowed her eyes at him for a moment, as if she knew he knew something she did not, then she nodded. "So I've got a good idea of what the inside of this place looks like. I go in, scout around, and don't get caught. I come back and report on what I see, and we plan the next step."

Jake sighed. She made it sound so easy.

Rosemary was impatient to be off, but dawn was approaching. "Like us, the Tal'darim will be inside during the day. They come out at night for nourishment," Ladranix said.

"Aren't the zerg active at night as well?" Jake asked.

Ladranix turned to him. "They have no set periods of inactivity. They are organic beings, yes, who need to eat and sleep, but they do not require extended hours of rest. Night or day is equally dangerous."

"Great," said Rosemary.

Jake did not sleep well. For one thing, it was almost as if the zerg knew something was afoot. He heard their cries in the night, something he had not heard before. He wondered if they were really the unorganized creatures Ladranix claimed, or if they were just waiting until the Shel'na Kryhas got complacent. Or—and this thought kept him awake for hours—what if the Tal'darim had found a way to control them? He muttered to himself and rolled over, kicking the blanket off, steaming to doneness in the humid heat. Zamara did not give him any more memories wrapped in the blanket of a dream, and the sleep he did get was fitful. He was already awake by the time Ladranix and several others gently shook him.

Rosemary was up and already prepared. She looked more like the woman he remembered from their initial encounter: poised, cool, with weapons hanging from her slim hips. Moonlight was good to Rosemary Dahl, casting highlights on her seal-sleek black hair and illuminating her pale face. She was a creature used to the darkness, after all; not an eagle, hunting in the golden sun, but a panther, a shadow hunter, who viewed stealth and silence as weapons just like any other.

Towering over her were three protoss clad in gleaming armor. It made for an odd picture. He rubbed the sleep out of his eyes, frowning. There was something wrong about it—

There used to be another templar, Zamara said. Sorrow and a hint of judgment was in her mental voice.

. . . *Yeah, there was. She was the one who deserted then?*

It would appear so.

Jake looked around. There were now only three trained warriors in this entire encampment of hundreds. The rest of them were khalai—craftsmen, artists, scientists. He felt slightly sick.

How could a templar abandon them?

I do not know. You would have to ask her.

Disheartened, Jake got to his feet and moved to join Rosemary. She glanced up at him. Jake wanted to say something, tell her he realized how dangerous this was, how he admired her for being willing to go. But he knew she'd shrug off the words or else make fun of them, so he merely smiled at her. She grinned back, her eyes sparkling. She was more than ready for anything that lay ahead.

"I feel sorry for the Tal'darim if they run into you," he said.

"Me too," she replied, finding a fresh ammo clip and sliding it into place. "Let's do this thing."

Jake and Rosemary accompanied Ladranix and two others into the small scouting vessel that had ferried them here. Again he marveled at the beauty and grace of the little craft. As they rose slowly and moved carefully out of the obstacle course that was the ruination of a city, a question occurred to Jake.

"I know some of the zerg can fly, and some of them can even travel in space. Are there no flying ones here?"

"We targeted them first," Ladranix said. "They were by far the greatest nearby threat. Not only could they attack from the air, they would be able to direct other, land-confined zerg to us. Fortunately, there seem to be no spawning sites in the vicinity to create more."

That was a break, then. At least this part of Aiur would be free of zerg flyers. No hideous, nightmare-based creature spewing acid or launching tiny little symbiotic things at them while they flew. Jake wondered how many protoss had given their lives to eradicate the airborne zerg. The thought gave him a headache.

Absently he rubbed his temple, peering out as the planet surface unfolded beneath them. He saw kilometer after kilometer of scorched earth, of twisted and melted cities, offset by the life-affirming sign of areas of undamaged rain forest still managing to hang on. Nature was tough to defeat, though the zerg had tried. It still made him sick to think about the violations that had been visited upon this poor world.

Would they even be able to find what Zamara so desperately wanted? What if the crystals had been destroyed somehow? Or uprooted and carted away by the Tal'darim?

Then we will find another alternative, Zamara soothed inside him. *We know this is where the technology is secreted away. That is the important thing.*

Yeah, but "another alternative" would be protoss-on-protoss violence, and no one here wants that.

Of course not.

But . . . you'd advocate that if it was necessary, wouldn't you?

. . . I would, yes. For this information . . . many of them would gladly sacrifice their lives.

Jake placed his aching head in his hands for a moment. He thought about his friends, dying in the icy cold of space aboard the *Gray Tiger* at the hands of a madman he'd been used to unleash. He thought of the woman Leeza who'd tried to double-cross them in the rough town of Paradise, and how her face exploded right in front of his eyes as Rosemary fired at her. He thought of watching from inside his own body as Zamara used it to kill Phillip Randall.

I've had so much of death already, Zamara.

Her response was more tender than any he had had from her, and he felt a brush of pain and worry. *I know this, Jacob.*

"We are approaching the area you showed us, Jacob," Ladranix said. Jake sat up, tensing. This was it then.

The earth had fallen away from the entrance, after more than two thousand years. It looked almost burrowlike, and he wondered if perhaps the huge, burrowing marsupials known as lombads had been responsible for uncovering the great chambers of the xel'naga. Even so, it was a nondescript hole in the earth, and nothing about it hinted at the secrets it contained. Perhaps indeed the Tal'darim had found nothing of import at all.

The small craft began its descent, slowly drifting downward to settle on the uneven, rocky surface. Even though it was an uninviting place, the fact that it had not been melted by blaster fire or covered with creep made it seem positively beautiful to Jake's eyes. They disembarked, and Jake felt a shiver of anticipation run through him. The protoss who moved up behind him looked around, their gestures betraying their unease.

Rosemary was the last to step beside Jake. "Any sign of the Tal'darim or zerg?" she asked.

"No," Ladranix said. "Varloris will let me know immediately if they appear." Ladranix nodded to the comparatively small khalai, who straightened proudly under his leader's acknowledgment and bowed deeply. "We would have time to depart before we would be sensed." He turned to Jake, half closing his eyes and tilting his head just so in a smile.

"Okay," said Rosemary, breaking the spell. "Glad you guys are monitoring, but the sooner I get in there, the sooner I'm out." She double-checked her weapons, the invaluable Pig she had indeed been able to repair, and one of the walkie-talkies they'd found in the system runner. Jake had the other one. No one was certain if they would be able to stay in touch once she entered the chambers; it was possible there was something that could dampen communications. But it was the best chance they had. She turned to Jake.

"Okay, Prof—have Zamara do her whammy on me. I don't like her poking around in my head, but it's better than having a bunch of hostile protoss doing it."

Jake nodded and moved toward her. He held out his hand. She hesitated, then took it. Not for the first time, he marveled at how small her hands were, to do the things they did. He didn't need to be touching her to enable Zamara to make mental contact, but he wanted to—not just because he found he liked the feel of her hand in his, but because he wanted to reassure her with that most ancient of comforts, the human touch.

Zamara was in and out of Rosemary's mind so quickly the two terrans barely had time to register anything. Rosemary blinked.

"That it?"

It is accomplished, Zamara replied. *Her presence is effectively blocked.*

Rosemary nodded. "I might just have you keep it up, Zamara," she said, looking into Jake's eyes but speaking not to him, but to the alien intelligence that had taken up residence there.

"Just to go over the plan," Jake began. She interrupted him.

"I got it, Prof. I go in, have a look around, you all meet me back here tomorrow night at this same time. If I get into any trouble I'll contact you." Without further ado she turned and began to stride into the gaping hole in the earth.

"Be careful," Jake added impulsively, and winced at how worried he sounded.

Rosemary Dahl paused. She looked back at him, a slow grin spreading over her face.

"I'm always careful, Professor," she said, and gave him a wink before her small form was swallowed entirely by the darkness.

CHAPTER ELEVEN

THE DARKNESS INCREASED AS ROSEMARY MOVED steadily, stealthily, downward. She had come prepared for that; infrared goggles and the Pig would keep her well clear of any of the troublesome Tal'darim. She hoped.

Actually, she was rather relieved to be clear of the protoss in general. Shel'na Kryhas or Tal'darim, it didn't matter much to her—she felt uncomfortable around all of them. She hadn't liked the idea of Zamara's tinkering around with her brain, but everything else about this little plan suited her ideally.

It was good to be on her own again. Rosemary functioned best by herself, second best as leader of a well-trained and trusted team. This new role she'd been forced to adopt, a tag-along on some epic "mission" that Zamara didn't see fit to tell even Jake about—it wasn't at all what she was used to.

And yet—part of her was enjoying it, she mused as she stepped forward carefully. She'd had a bad moment when she had realized that Ethan was planning on turning her over to Valerian. But she'd recovered. Blowing a hole in the center of her former lover had cheered her greatly, and she'd been riding an adrenaline high through most of the rest of what had happened. True, Rosemary was indeed more or less along for the ride, but Jake and the protoss inside him had definitely needed her. She'd helped Jake off the *Gray Tiger* before the nut job Jake had turned loose on it had decided to have them for dinner. She'd gotten him to Ethan, which had seemed safe, and then away from Ethan, which had actually *been* safe. While Jake had done something—she still wasn't sure what—involving a sort of human version of the Khala to allow them to escape Valerian at the last minute, it had been Rosemary who'd fixed the battered ship after the bad jump.

And now, when they needed someone to go scout out to make sure it was safe, they'd turned to the one person who wouldn't screw it up. Rosemary Dahl.

Because she wasn't stupid, she also realized that she was the one person they all thought was expendable at this point. And she could live with that. She also was well aware that no one liked her, and that bothered her not at all. At least . . . it didn't use to. Recently, though, she found herself enjoying the moments when she and Jake got along. She wasn't trusted by him or Zamara or any of the other protoss, and she understood why. But they all had the same agenda now—get off the planet. They could trust her for that, and right now, that was all that mattered.

She tried to remember everything Jake had told her about this place. As he'd said, the walls were smooth at first, as she had started to descend. Too, once the natural light from the entrance began to fade, other light—crystals embedded in the walls—provided gentle but serviceable illumination. She noticed that the texture of the walls changed the deeper she went, and spared a quick glance to look at the colors as they appeared to her in the faint light of the glowing crystals. Black and silver and gray, with threads of something that looked like veins running through them.

The temperature dropped as Rosemary went deeper into the earth. She paused at one point and strained to listen. She could hear it now, the faint pulsating sound. Her lips curved in a smile. It was like a heartbeat, just like Jake had described. No wonder Temlaa and Savassan had been rattled when they heard it.

The stairway turned and abruptly Rosemary found herself staring down into darkness. There were no more crystals to provide light after this point. Air swirled up from the huge cavern she couldn't see, but knew waited below.

Rosemary reached the end of the stairway and fished out the Pig, checking to see if she was still as alone as she thought. Perfect. From what Jake had said, once she entered the rooms down here, lights would come up and she would, for all intents and purposes, shout her presence to anyone nearby.

She dropped the Pig back into her pocket and stepped forward.

Sure enough, up came the lights, glowing a soft white in contrast to the more tinted, gemlike hues that had provided illumination on the way in. The area the light displayed to her was even bigger than she'd thought. She took it in with a practiced eye: flat, clearly artificially leveled floor, a ceiling inlaid with gems that provided the light, all perfectly preserved.

Jake would have a field day.

She looked at a rectangle of gems on a stone pillar, and knew that if she touched them in that Golden Mean order Jake was so fascinated with a door would appear on the far wall. When Temlaa had touched the gems so, long ago, a platform had emerged. A platform upon which had lain six desiccated protoss bodies. The sight had given poor Temlaa a bad scare. Idly, Rosemary wondered if they were still there. But she had no real interest; she was here to see if the Tal'darim had penetrated this far into the chambers.

Rosemary looked at the map and nodded. There were the five oval doorways in the walls, just as Jake had drawn them, that led out into five different directions. She put her finger on the map over the door Temlaa had chosen as the one that best fit the Golden Mean ratio. She walked forward, and then paused. A slow smile spread over her face.

On the wall next to the door was a small black mark.

Despite herself, Rosemary felt a shiver as she lifted a hand to touch the mark that Temlaa had made, some two thousand years ago. In this place where there was no weathering, no water or wind or oils from human or protoss flesh to erase it, the charcoal mark had stayed in almost perfect condition. She was suddenly very sorry that she had seen this first, not Jake. She shook off the unusually soft sentiment and stepped into the corridor.

This place was much, much larger than it had seemed. Would she even get anywhere near the chamber they sought? She wished she had a vulture hoverbike right about now, but she supposed the walk would do her good. If she didn't get far enough in a single twenty-four-hour mission to learn anything useful, well, she'd have to come back. It certainly seemed as though it was going well. Ladranix had assured them that there were no protoss or zerg spying on them, and she believed him. The Tal'darim could mask their thoughts, but little red dots on the Pig's small but accurate computer screen were good old-fashioned hard technology and so far Rosemary had seen none of those. So far.

Not for the first time, she wondered if as she saw, she was also being seen. She'd asked that question, if there was any comparable protoss technology that would expose her. Ladranix had assured her that such a thing was not necessary, at least not short-range.

"We can sense another's presence, as you know," he said, sounding confused.

"Yeah, but you also said that these guys are shielding their thoughts from you. And that sounds like something protoss have been able to do for a while," Rosemary replied.

"True," Ladranix admitted. "But never for stealth, not from each other. We are all touching one another to some degree in the Khala."

Jake had seemed a bit troubled and followed up on Rosemary's point. "When I was reliving the memories of Temlaa, that's how they were able to sneak up on each other to attack. The attackers would shield their thoughts and presence."

"And now, what goes around comes around," Rosemary said. "You're right back where you started."

"Rosemary—" Jake said warningly.

Ladranix had lifted a hand. "She is correct. Now, since the fall of our world, we have again turned against one another. Or rather, the Tal'darim have turned against us. We do shield our thoughts, to protect ourselves. For they will attack us. But this happened recently. Before the warp gate was shut down, there was no need to hide ourselves from one another. So therefore, no technology was created to overcome such an obstacle."

It made sense to Rosemary. She was a very practical woman, and this all sounded practical to her.

But she was heading down into a place that was apparently crammed to the gills with ancient technology that was as advanced as it was forgotten. If the Tal'darim had been down here for a while, and it sounded like they had, might they not have uncovered some of the xel'naga secrets? No one seemed concerned about this but her. Well, she mused as she continued to move slowly inward to the heart of the place, that might be because she was the one putting her ass on the line.

As she walked, constantly checking her map and the Pig to make sure she was not getting lost and not having company, she became increasingly grateful for the map. Wandering on her own would have been far too dangerous. Jake had told her the place was huge, but she hadn't realized just how big. After several hours, she sat and ate some fruit and drank some water and rested for a while. She couldn't risk sleep, and she'd stayed awake for longer than twenty-four hours at a stretch many, many times.

Her constant companion on this exploration was the deep, thrumming heartbeat sound. She knew she was on the right track because with each turn she took, each corridor that led her inward and downward, the noise increased. That sound, and the marks that the protoss whose memories Jake now kept in his brain had made were her guideposts.

Rosemary was mildly annoyed with Temlaa. The way Jake remembered it, it hadn't taken all that long to get to the room where the crystal was. Maybe Jake didn't get every memory of every second of every protoss's life. Hell, she didn't remember every second of her own life. Which was actually a blessing. Maybe it was just the important things Jake remembered.

Or maybe the protoss moved faster. Also, she was coming in a different way than Temlaa and Savassan had. While she was obviously on the right track, it might take longer to reach the same place the protoss had.

Regardless, she knew that several long hours had passed. She hoped she was getting close to the damned thing.

Jake tried not to worry about Rosemary, and failed utterly. He told himself that she was about a thousand times tougher than he was, and was more than able to handle herself in any situation she might encounter. She was also smart, and not likely to get herself into trouble. The word "trouble" reminded him of Ethan Stewart, who used to call her that, and he thought of what he'd last seen of Ethan, and told himself that Rosemary could defend herself very well, thank you very much, even if she did startle some of these Forged protoss.

"If she's found out—do you think they'll kill her?" he asked Ladranix as they returned to the city.

Ladranix hesitated, and Jake's heart sank. "I do not know," he said, and Jake knew he spoke the truth. "We would not, but we are not the Forged. Protoss do not kill protoss." Unspoken were the words, *But protoss might kill Rosemary.*

He couldn't help it. He had to know. He took out the walkie-talkie and thumbed it. It would make no sound or light that might put Rosemary in danger; instead it would vibrate to let her know they were trying to get in touch with her. If it was safe, she'd reply.

There was no response.

Jacob—you must not make an assumption. Any number of things could be happening at this moment with Rosemary. She could not be in a safe place to respond, true. Or the device could have malfunctioned. Or perhaps there is interference from the technology below the surface. Any or these could be the reason she is not responding.

I know, he said, and ran a hand through his hair. The worry was making his headache return. *But . . . I'm going to worry about her until she gets back. That's just how humans are, Zamara.*

So I am observing. I knew that I would have many experiences as a preserver. I never expected dwelling inside an alien body and mind to be among them.

Some ride, huh?

Her mental voice was hauntingly tender. *It has been . . . "some ride," as you put it, yes.*

I wish I could stop worrying about her. I wish—I wish I could stop caring *about her.*

I cannot change these things, Jacob, nor would I attempt to even if I could. I have demanded and taken enough from you. I would not take that also.

A sudden thought struck him. He'd wondered this before, but hadn't let himself follow that line of thinking. Now, he did. *Preservers have all the thoughts and feelings and memories of all protoss, right?*

Correct.

And since I'm now a preserver—as much as a human can be—all my thoughts and feelings and memories . . . oh boy.

They will be added to the whole. Future generations will remember all of this.

Jake turned a bright shade of red, and it wasn't from the sunburn.

You should not be unduly distressed. Future preservers will not probe for such base and common things as sexual desire or petty jealousies.

Oh thank you, that makes me feel so much better.

If it is any comfort, Jacob, what you will likely be preserved for are your moments of greatness and insight and heroism.

That did make him feel a little bit better.

Since I cannot alleviate your worry, perhaps I can distract you. You need to know what happened with Adun, and the renegade protoss who eventually became known as the dark templar.

Zamara was right; it would do no good to worry. There was no way of knowing what was going on with Rosemary until he saw her again. It wouldn't be that long, he told himself. And in the meantime, he would find out more about the protoss and their history, and that was always a worthwhile thing.

The girl, shackled as if she were as dangerous as a trained templar fully equipped for battle, was brought before the high templar. A second meeting with her did nothing to convince Jake that the Conclave was correct in its desire to have her executed. This time, he shared thoughts with her, questioned her, and listened, as did the other templar. The unease grew inside him. Adun watched and observed the other tem-

plar as they, too, interrogated the girl—Raszagal was her name. Finally, she was led away, head still high.

Adun spoke to his fellow templar. "Always, we templar have obeyed the will of the Conclave, for always, they have done what is right and just to protect us all. It is they who keep pure the tenets of the Khala, which has been and continues to be our salvation."

Jake said nothing, observing the other templar, listening quietly to their thoughts. They, too, wondered where this was leading.

"They have found heretics, like Raszagal. They have asked us to hunt down the others, and execute them quietly, so that their very existence remains a secret. They fear that if word spread that there were those who rejected the Khala, it would lead to panic. And that panic might hurtle us back to another Aeon of Strife."

Everyone in the room reacted with instinctive dread. Adun continued. "They are right not to want to replay those dreadful times. They are right to want all to be in the Khala."

And then he hesitated. "But . . . protoss do not kill protoss. And if we go down this path . . . perhaps this *is what will eventually lead to another Aeon of Strife. You have spoken with Raszagal. We will find others, and we will speak with them too before we summarily execute them. In my heart . . . Raszagal is not a threat. I have questioned her—extensively. Nothing in her desires revolution, or disharmony. She merely wishes to keep herself to herself. Is that worthy of death?"*

No one answered. Jake felt their indecision tear at him; felt his own indecision heavy in his soul. He liked Raszagal. He admired her. And Adun was right. She was no threat.

"She is only one," Jake said slowly. "She may not think like the others."

"What my old friend Vetraas says is true," Adun replied. "And thus we must know more before we obey the Conclave. Or . . . before we do not."

Startlement rippled through the assembled templar. "You would disobey a direct order from the Conclave?"

"I have always obeyed," Adun said, and such was true. "Because always, they have acted with wisdom. But they are not Khas. They want to protect us, but they are also fearful of what Raszagal represents. I am a warrior, and proud to fight for my people. All *of my people," he said. "Perhaps you too now deem me a heretic. Who here, then, wishes the honor of slaying young Raszagal?"*

No one replied. No one wanted to be the first to walk down a path from which there was no turning back—slaying the blood of one of his own people for the first time since Khas brought the Khala to them and ended the slaughter.

Adun nodded, slowly. "We will learn more."

Jake had expected that the heretics would come largely from one or two tribes, but he was wrong. According to the information given to them by the Conclave, members from several different tribes had quietly simply refused to join the Khala. And while the Khala was constant, one's involvement in it did not need to be, and indeed, it would be difficult to live every moment in such a state of unity with others. But Jake and Adun went to be nourished by the rich contact many times each day and emerged refreshed and invigorated by this sacred, special immersion. So did the other templar, and the judicators, and many of the khalai.

It would be easy to locate someone in the Khala. But how to find one who never came to this place for nourishment was the problem. The Conclave had a list, however, and quietly, with no fanfare, templar found and took prisoner those on the list. Each one they interviewed unsettled Jake, Adun, and the other templar further. For like Raszagal, they were calm and reasoned, and their arguments . . . had merit.

But which course of action represented following the Khala—refraining from killing protoss whose hearts held no true threat, or exterminating those who did not wish to merge so deeply with others?

Jake was glad the responsibility was Adun's, not his. And after several days, Adun called them together.

"I have reached a decision," he said quietly. He looked at each of them in turn. "I will spare the prisoners."

A flicker of relief ran through those assembled, along with concern. Jake voiced what they were all thinking.

"It is well that their blood is not on our hands, Executor. But I was there when you were given your orders. The Conclave believes it is right on this issue. They will insist on the deaths of these . . . these 'dark templar.' "

Adun had been looking at his hands. Now he lifted his glowing eyes to his old friend. "I have . . . an idea."

Rosemary decided it was time to risk contacting Jake and the others. She was feeling pretty confident that she wouldn't run across any Tal'darim here. The place was enormous, Jake had told her. It was a veritable underground city, and it was fairly obvious that all the protoss were clustered in one spot. If this had been a forbidden area until recently, they were probably too frightened to do much exploring. She took out the walkie-talkie and thumbed it.

"Yo, Professor," she said quietly.

There was no response. She frowned and checked it. It was definitely working, but something was preventing the signal from getting through. It figured. She sighed, replaced it in her small pack, and continued on.

The heartbeat sound increased. After all this walking, she was finally getting close. She hurried forward, then broke into a quick trot, realizing that she was excited to see this thing of which Jake had spoken so raptly and a little annoyed at herself for being so excited. Through several more corridors, each marked by Temlaa's ancient symbol. It was there, right there, and—

They sprang up before her like living shadows, and as she skidded to a halt and drew out her rifle, she realized that she was surrounded.

The psionic attack stabbed her like an ice pick driven through her brain, and Rosemary collapsed. She didn't have time to fire even a single shot.

CHAPTER TWELVE

ROSEMARY AWOKE AND FOR A LONG, LONG moment thought she was still deep in the nightmare. The nightmare of searing pain, of a hunger that refused to be sated, of being helpless before both other people and her own cravings. Then she realized that the pain of a body twisted too long in an unnatural position and the itch of blood drying on her wrists and ankles were indeed very real.

"Shit," she said, and drowned out the rising fear with irritation at herself for getting into this predicament.

She was lying on the cold stone floor. Her wrists were bound behind her back with some kind of cord. Cautious, exploratory movement revealed that her legs, bent behind her, were also bound, and something attached ankles to wrists, so she was effectively well trussed up. That she'd been in this position for some time was evidenced by the screaming pain of her muscles. She was no longer where she had been attacked; they'd taken her somewhere else, some dimly lit niche somewhere in this vast underground city. Rosemary lifted her head to look around. Were her captors here or had she been left alone?

"So, you are awake," came a voice in her mind. "Good. I was worried that Alzadar here might have permanently damaged you."

One question answered, then: Her captors, the templar-turned-Forged Alzadar among them, were most definitely present.

"Well, wouldn't want that, would we?" she shot back cheerfully. There was no point in plotting an escape when you were surrounded by people who could read your mind. The block Zamara had erected had prevented the Tal'darim from detecting her; it would be of no protection if she was stupid enough to literally stumble across them. And besides, it had worn off by this point, as Zamara had said it would, which meant they probably knew everything she knew now. She tried not to think about it and couldn't, just, she realized, like the old, tired saw that if someone said "Don't think about a purple elephant," all you saw in your mind's eye was a lavender pachyderm. Instantly, of course, she *did* think about a purple elephant, and she got a brief and satisfying jolt of pleasure at the confusion the image presented to her captors.

"Only temporarily damaged, I can deal with," she continued. "You didn't kill me outright, so that means you want something."

Long, cool hands closed on her body and she was positioned so she could see. She bit her lip to keep from crying out, from giving them the satisfaction of knowing how it hurt her, and then thought, *That was stupid,* because of course they could read her mind. God, she was really starting to get pissed off at this whole mind-reading business. She clung to the anger.

She looked around at the protoss. Most of them hung back, but two stood gazing down at her. Overall they looked pretty much like the Shel'na Kryhas. There was certainly no immediate visible difference between the two factions. They were various colors, ranging from purple to gray to blue, and they had a variety of ridges and shapes to their faces. No doubt to each other they looked completely different, just as human faces looked individualistic to other humans. But to Rosemary Dahl, they all looked like . . . protoss.

Apparently, that was the wrong thing to think. The eyes of the protoss who was most likely their leader—Felanis, she recalled—narrowed and darkened, and he hunched slightly. The other, whom Rosemary assumed was Alzadar, stayed almost frighteningly calm as he stared at her with unblinking eyes.

"We are completely different from the Shel'na Kryhas!" Felanis cried. "They are unenlightened fools, clinging stubbornly to the flawed past, the very past that led us to disaster. We were deserted once before, long, long ago, by the beings we loved and trusted. But this desertion is far worse. This was abandonment by our own people!"

More thoughts bombarded Rosemary. But she did not feel their emotions; perhaps they kept them rigidly in check. She was glad of it. Their thoughts alone were hard enough for her mind to handle.

Felanis began to pace. Alzadar continued to regard her with almost unnatural calm. Rosemary glared back, defiantly.

"Our only comfort is that those who fled Aiur and left us behind are likely dead now," said Felanis. "The dark templar cannot be trusted. Only we survive—the Tal'darim, the Forged. Only *we* were deemed worthy to be called here, to the ancient places of our people. Our Benefactor looks after us. He keeps us safe and whole and teaches us how to defend ourselves against the zerg."

There were mental murmurs of agreement. Rosemary looked around, remembering now that the Forged numbers grew while the Shel'na Kryhas numbers dwindled, not just because of zerg attacks, but by desertion.

"Speaking of turning your backs and abandoning things, which of you are the deserters?" she said.

Several of them turned their heads sharply to look at her. "You judge what you do not understand, human," one of them said. Rosemary still had trouble distinguishing between individual protoss, but she was pretty sure she recognized one of the Shel'na Kryhas who had rescued her and then left soon after.

"So do you," she shot back.

Felanis waved a dismissive hand. "We understand you well enough," he said. "As you have surmised, we have read your thoughts."

"Then why do you need to keep me alive if you know everything I know?" She tried to move her hands and feet slightly, to bring circulation back to them, but the pain was too intense, and she gasped.

"Felanis, this is ridiculous," said one of the protoss. "Alzadar's idea will not work. She is too different from us. We should offer her to the Benefactor. Perhaps he can find an appropriate use for her. Or kill her ourselves and send the body back for her traitorous allies to stumble upon."

"Silence," ordered Felanis. "If the plan does not work, there will be time enough to offer her to the Xava'tor." He turned lambent blue eyes back to Rosemary. "We have kept you alive because they trust you. Particularly the other terran."

She actually laughed at that one. "You want me to spy for you?"

"It is in your interest, human."

"How the hell do you figure that? Other than the obvious." She thought about being able to move her limbs.

Felanis half closed his eyes and tilted his head. Laughter, dry as scudding leaves across dead earth, filled her mind. "Is not the obvious sufficient?"

He had her there. Only once before had Rosemary professed loyalty to anyone and really meant it.

That was to Ethan Stewart, whom she was now starting to realize she had loved. She frowned to herself. She was getting soft. That mind whammy Jake had done to her had really messed her up. Or maybe it was just that the pain was starting to wear her down. She wasn't sure. It was obvious what would happen if she didn't cooperate. She'd be served up to this Benefactor, whoever he was, or have her throat slit and be tossed out like yesterday's garbage. Still . . .

"Zamara's a preserver. I thought even the Forged respected such things."

"Once, we did. But our heritage means nothing to us now. Only our future, only what the Xava'tor can give us. What you attempted to do—what Zamara and Jake and Ladranix want to do—is against his wishes. You may not enter the chambers. We will not permit this to happen. And—the Xava'tor desires the preserver."

"And you're gonna use me to lure Zamara to him? Listen, buddy, if you've read my mind as well as you think you have, you know one thing for damn sure: I want to get off this rock. Zamara says she can do that. There's no way I'm turning against her." With humans, she would have tried to bluff. There was no point in attempting it with the protoss. She wasn't schooled enough in mental disciplines to bluff a mind reader.

"Perhaps Zamara is lying."

"Zamara hasn't trussed me up like an animal and mentally tortured me. Guess who I'm gonna trust first."

Felanis and Alzadar looked at one another. "You will have no choice in the matter," Felanis said. Alzadar moved to the side and returned with a large jar. A mental murmur went up among the protoss and they all leaned forward eagerly. Despite her pain, Rosemary felt a flicker of curiosity. What the hell was in that jar?

"You will become one of us. Our cause will become yours. Our goals will become yours. It is an honor, Rosemary Dahl."

For one moment, the desire to struggle blindly like a mindless beast struck Rosemary very hard. She ignored it with the will she'd developed through years of discipline. But she couldn't control the sudden racing of her heart.

Alzadar shook his head and spoke for the first time. His mental voice was rich and in control, the voice of one who was well disciplined and had no need to rage and shout as Felanis did; no need to even speak unless he decided it was necessary.

"No, my brothers and sisters, it is not time for us yet. This is for our guest's benefit." He stepped forward, tattered robes flowing, and lifted the lid off the jar.

A sweet, cloying scent tickled Rosemary's nose, and she coughed violently. The movement sent pain shooting along her imprisoned limbs and the cough twisted into a sharp cry. Sweat suddenly dewed her body, and she looked to see what was in the jar. It was an ointment of some kind, dark gold in color, and as she watched, Alzadar scooped some of it out on his long-fingered hands and stepped toward her.

Rosemary couldn't read minds. But she didn't have to to know somewhere deep in her soul that if this pretty-looking stuff touched her, she'd be in real trouble. So even though she almost blacked out from the white-hot agony that shot through her at her sudden movement, she tried to scoot back. It was foolish, and futile, but she could no more stop the instinct than she could stop her heart from beating.

"Hold her," Alzadar said almost dispassionately. Cool fingers closed like manacles on her legs, shoulders, waist, and arms.

"No!" Rosemary shrieked, fury and a nameless dread lending her energy. But the delicacy of the hands that held her was misleading, and her writhing was useless. Effortlessly they flipped her on her stomach. A wave of pain so intense she almost blacked out shot through her. Alzadar bore down on her, smearing the ointment first onto the inside of her wrists and then clutching her hair, yanking her head back, and rubbing the unguent onto her throat area.

Rosemary had the incongruous thought that these were the same places she'd apply perfume—on her throat and wrists, on the pulse points of her body. Manic laughter welled up inside her and she forced it down. The ointment felt warm against her skin. Soothing. And pleasurable.

"No!" she screamed again, and put all the power of her will behind it. It startled them, she could tell, but it was too late, had been too late the moment she had taken the first step down into this hellish pit. For a fraction of an instant, Rosemary understood what was happening, and with all that was in her rejected it. She did not want to become that person again, that slave, that needy, captive thing. She did not want the pleasure, the peace, the calm, because she knew it was all a lie and that soon enough, too soon, it would end and she'd need more. Have to have more. Would do unspeakable, degrading things for more.

And then all resistance, all fear, all refusal was gone. Even the pain in her bound, twisted limbs was gone. Rosemary's head lolled and she closed her eyes, almost purring with contentment.

"You were right, Alzadar," Felanis said. "The gift of the Xava'tor works on the terrans as well."

"This one is particularly susceptible, but yes, the way terran skin works has similarities to our own. Although it is much more primitive. The Sundrop has reached her. We can release her. She is ours now."

The hands came again, cradling her body as they cut the bonds that held her. More of the pleasure-giving salve was rubbed onto her neck and wrists, and this time Rosemary Dahl, eager for more of the bliss, assisted them, reaching her own hands along her skin and massaging the soothing, slippery stuff in with a soft, relaxed sigh.

Sundrop. She liked the word.

Rosemary screamed.

For the last several languid, drifting, hazy hours—she had no idea how long it had been—she hadn't cared. She had slipped in and out of consciousness, her dreams soft and sweet as her reality, as the topically applied Sundrop wound through her system. But it had started to fade an hour ago, the euphoria dwindling bit by bit until it had mutated into discomfort, then pain, and now the wrenching and horrifically familiar agony of withdrawal.

The others had departed, off to do whatever it was they did when they were not capturing strangers and getting them addicted. Alzadar alone had stayed, talking in his cool, in-absolute-control mental voice about the Benefactor as she babbled through the ecstasy and staying almost gleefully silent as she started to come out of it. She knew he knew how badly she craved another dose.

She huddled shivering in the corner, trying to find a dollop of the Sundrop that hadn't been properly spread over her skin. She failed. It was all gone, absorbed long ago. Her skin erupted with gooseflesh and she fought back yet another wave of nausea. Even in the midst of her misery she wondered how she could keep being sick when there was nothing left in her body to vomit up.

"Tell me you want more, and you shall have it, Rosemary Dahl," Alzadar said, sounding infinitely reasonable. "Right now, that is all I need to hear. Your mind is screaming it. Simply choose to form the words and your agony will cease."

She shut her eyes. Tears poured from them. She huddled against the wall, pressing her hot face against the cool, curving stone. She didn't want to give this bastard the satisfaction of begging for the drug. Besides, if they wanted her to be effective, they'd give her another dose sooner or later. They'd have to.

"True," Alzadar said. "But that will not be for some time. How much longer can you offer resistance? You can end your suffering with but a word. I must say, the Sundrop seems to affect humans more severely than protoss. I envy you your ecstasy, but not this. Are you quite certain you do not desire more?"

Oh, God, she did. She wanted it more than anything she could ever remember wanting in her life. Rosemary closed her eyes, and for the next hour stayed silent by the sheer power of her will.

Eventually, as she had known would be the case, Alzadar applied more, and she basked in the pleasure for a while. He fed her, he gave her water, and she ate and drank and dozed.

The cycle began again. The pain came, deep and shattering and worse than before, a lower low from a higher high, and Rosemary sobbed openly this time.

"Tell me you want more, and I shall give it to you." Alzadar rose and padded over to her, crouching down, his mouthless face centimeters from hers. "I shall see that you are cleansed, and given a soft place to sleep, and more Sundrop is applied to your wanting skin. Only ask for it, and it shall be done."

She turned her face and stared at the former templar, into his pale blue eyes.

Go to hell, was what she wanted to say. Was what she fully intended to say.

What escaped dry, cracked lips was "Please . . . give me more. I'll do whatever you want."

Alzadar nodded, pleased, and his hands, full of succoring ointment, came up and stroked her outstretched wrists like one might stroke a beloved pet. And as the comfort came and the pain ceased, Rosemary despised herself, and knew herself to be utterly lost.

CHAPTER THIRTEEN

KERRIGAN FELT ALMOST . . . HUMAN IN HER excitement.

The change was complete. The cocoon was glowing, pulsing, and the shape inside was moving more and more vigorously. She was not certain what sort of changes her creation would display. He was undergoing the same process by which she herself had been created, been made anew, and she knew that the reborn Ethan would not be identical to herself. But the details would be a fascinating surprise, just as such things were to any mother, and her wings folded and unfolded in eager anticipation as she watched and waited.

The instinct was to hasten the birth along, but Kerrigan did not want to steal Ethan's triumph from him. Let him fight his own way out of the cocoon, as she had. Let him be the instrument of his own birth. It would be his first act to claiming what was his—what she had bequeathed to him.

In his cocoon, Ethan struggled. If he did not break

free soon, rip and claw and tear his way into this new life, he would not be able to survive much longer in the fluids that encased him. He would die unborn, and her experiment would be a failure. Kerrigan was content with that knowledge, and the thought did not move her to action. The Queen of Blades wanted no one at her side who could not find his own way into this new incarnation.

Her eyes were bright as she watched. Lumps formed and receded in the elastic surface of the cocoon as Ethan's fist punched here, his knee thrust there. Another two limbs entirely distended the membranous cocoon. Her heart fluttered to see it. So he, like she, would be augmented. It was good.

A sharp spike pierced the cocoon and glinted in the dim lighting. It looked like a blade, but not like hers—her talons and claws and spikes were stilettos. This was a scythe, a hook, a masculine counterpart to her more feminine knife. A smile curved her too-wide mouth.

The wickedly sharp spike slashed downward, almost the length of the cocoon. Hands, dark green and powerful but devoid of the claws that graced her own, seized the edges and ripped with inhuman strength. Two other limbs, not quite arms, similar to the scythelike pincers of the hydralisks, extended almost as if in prayer. No wings for him, then, but these extra limbs, sharp and lethal and ready to kill for her. A head, sleek and smooth as a dolphin's, thrust upward. Ethan tilted his head back and opened his mouth. For a moment she thought he was shouting his birth to the universe, but instead a sludgy, luminous green fluid poured from his mouth as he coughed.

Now he did fill his lungs and cry out. Kerrigan smiled. Everything about him pleased her, from the color of his skin, a browner green than her gray-green; to the shape of his body, fit and toned; to the limbs that did not challenge her own graceful bone-wings but complemented them. Beautiful . . . he was beautiful. She had chosen well, and had manipulated his genetic redesign masterfully. He opened his eyes, a glowing green hue, and looked down at his new form. She watched, her smile widening, as her child-consort beheld himself. He ran his fingers along his sleek, hard skin, turned his head to examine the new blades protruding from his sides, and stepped free of the cocoon. Moisture, once so vital and now superfluous, flowed along the floor. He lifted his head to her, taller now than he had been, a little taller than she. But only a little. He seemed startled to see her, and frowned.

"You—you are the one who has done this?" It was a statement, not a question. The content of it did not surprise her, but what did startle her was his voice. Ethan Stewart's vocal cords had been altered not at all by his transformation. His voice was totally and completely human, although he obviously was not, and she delighted in its smooth richness.

"I am," she said, her own voice reverberating and strong and changed by her own transformation. "I am

Kerrigan, the Queen of Blades. I have made you to serve me and be my companion."

She touched his mind briefly, giving him the barest taste of her mental power. She was not surprised to find more than a hint of insanity lurking in his brain. Psi-screens did that.

She'd touched mad minds before. When she was human—when she was weak—she had found such contact to be abhorrent. Traumatic. Now, in this form, she found it intriguing. Parts of Ethan's brain had been permanently ruined, but there was enough there for her to control and to manipulate. She would dispatch him with no compunction if he proved of no use to her, and she let him know that as well.

He regarded her thoughtfully, his twin scythe arms flexing and unflexing. For a moment, she sensed a possible hint of a challenge.

She let him *see* how she would dispatch him.

Anger, then humor, then respect.

She walked to him then, slowly, remembering how to use her body to its best advantage, and his eyes flickered over her. She knew he found her beautiful. Kerrigan stood beside him, a breath away, and reached to touch his face with the claw of her index finger.

"You have wanted to excel," she murmured. "You have wanted power. Your body is superior to that of any human male, and if you serve me well and loyally, I will give you power beyond your wildest dreams."

"I should warn you that my dreams," he said in that rich, silky voice, "can be rather wild indeed."

Kerrigan smiled. "I looked into your mind. I know. Perhaps I should put it another way. Serve me or die."

She felt only the faintest flicker of fear. Already, now that he understood her, he trusted her. "I will serve you with my life. What would you have me do first, my queen?"

Kerrigan smiled, well pleased. "Tell me everything you know about Professor Jacob Ramsey."

Something had gone wrong.

Jake had suspected something, but had let himself be reassured by Zamara and her . . . well, her logic. But it had now been two days since they were supposed to rendezvous with Rosemary, and he was almost frantic with worry.

"I shouldn't have let her go down there by herself," he said for the umpteenth time. They were heading back to the burrowlike entrance to the chambers where they had last seen her, walking down into the darkness with a sure stride and a quick grin. He feared now that he would never see her again.

"Jacob," Ladranix said gently in his mind, "there was no other choice. We must get into those chambers; Zamara has made that very clear. We needed to know if it was safe to proceed. Rosemary has the most experience in such matters."

At least the protoss hadn't used the past tense. Jake buried his head in his hands, rubbing at his aching temples. It seemed the headaches were increasing in frequency, becoming chronic rather than intermitent.

Further compounding his worry, they were risking discovery. They had been very lucky indeed that it hadn't happened ere now. Jake knew that soon the protoss would give up hope altogether; it would be too risky to come back every night as they had done twice now.

And they would consign Rosemary to her fate.

Jake had always found the woman attractive. They had begun their relationship in mild conflict. When Rosemary had betrayed him and his team to Valerian, Jake had despised her. But he'd developed a grudging respect for the assassin as time went on, and when he had brushed her mind in an experience which was the closest human beings had ever come to the Khala, he'd been staggered by her will and sheer gutsiness. He knew he could never hate her again after that, no matter what she did. Since that moment, she'd proved trustworthy. And now that she might be dead because of something he'd put her up to, he realized that he had come to care for her very much. A word that began with L and wasn't "loathe" danced around the edge of his mind.

It is entirely possible that you are falling in love with her, yes, Zamara agreed as Jake practically leaped out of the vessel and hastened to the entrance.

Jake winced. *I was trying not to think that.*

You all but shout it, Jacob, she said, not unkindly. *I too hope she is unharmed. But if she is not, understand that she sacrificed her life for something very important.*

Anger, fueled by worry and guilt and the now-constant headache, flared inside him. *Damn it, Zamara, you keep hinting and hinting and never saying anything. I might feel the way you do if I knew what the hell you were—*

Jacob. She approaches.

Sure enough, Jake reached out and sensed Rosemary's presence. *Rosemary, are you all right?*

I thought I told you to stay the hell out of my thoughts, and I'm fine. I'll be right there.

He laughed aloud at that. Yes, if the biggest worry she had was him poking around in her brain, he didn't need to worry about her. The relief was almost overwhelming. Jake started down the steps two at a time, and almost collided with Rosemary halfway down.

"Hey," he said lamely. "We were worried about you."

She looked tired, but otherwise well. "Yeah, for a while I was worried about me too," she said as they ascended. "The walkie-talkie stopped working pretty much once I got past the doorway. I tried to contact you and got nothing."

"We tried to contact you too," Jake said. "When we didn't hear anything—I got worried."

She gave him a quick glance with those blue eyes and made an annoyed sound. "Your confidence is overwhelming. I've been completely fine."

"Then why did you miss the rendezvous two nights in a row?" he countered, a bit stung that his concern had been met with such obvious scorn.

"I got cut off from the entrance. A whole bunch of the Tal'darim came and squatted there for a while. I have no idea what was going on, but I had to hide in a corridor for some time. After a while they moved on and I was able to continue investigating." They had reached the top now, and she made a beeline for the vessel.

"What did you learn?" Ladranix inquired.

She didn't answer immediately, instead hopped lithely into the ship and settled into the seat. Ladranix did not press, but Jake, curious, couldn't hold his tongue. "Rosemary?"

Rosemary sighed and folded her arms across her chest. "It's guarded. Heavily. Don't know that they quite understand what it is they're guarding, but there's no way you're getting in without a fight. A big one."

She spoke without looking at them at first, then turned her blue gaze to Jake. "Is there some other way Zamara can get us out of here?"

I do not need to access the innermost chambers to escape this world, Zamara told Jake. *You know this. There is another reason entirely.*

One which you're not going to share with me, Jake thought. He was both resigned and irritated, but whether with Rosemary or Zamara, he couldn't tell.

True. But you must understand, Jacob, that it is of vital importance. What is in those caverns is as important to me as rendering the warp gate functional.

There was no mistaking the sincerity in her thoughts, nor the urgency that tinged it. Jake blinked a little bit.

Okay then . . . but what do we do now?

I . . . do not know. We must question Rosemary more thoroughly. It is imperative that I—that you—enter the chambers as soon as possible.

We'll talk to her, but not until after she's had a chance to rest, Jake said, surprising himself at the vehemence of the thought.

Agreed, said Zamara unexpectedly. *If she has been forced to hide as she says she has, then she is weary. She has been trained well, she will not forget details upon sleep. Rest may indeed sharpen her recall.*

"Is there anything to eat or drink?" Rosemary said, fighting a yawn. She leaned her head back against the seat, closing her eyes briefly. Blue veins were clearly visible on her eyelids, and there were dark smudges under her eyes. She definitely did look tired, Jake thought. Tired and almost fragile. He had a sudden very strong urge to pull her into his arms and let her rest her head on his chest while she slept. He turned pink, knowing that Zamara was reading his thoughts and wondering if the other protoss were too.

What's the rush to get in there, Zamara? I mean, I don't want to be a zerg snack any more than anyone else does, and this is hardly a romp in the park, but has something changed?

There is nothing you need to worry about, Jacob. I have it all under control. But I must get in, and soon.

Ladranix gestured, and some sammuro fruit was brought forward as the ship quickly lifted off. Jake nudged Rosemary, and she started. He realized that she'd drifted off in that short period of time.

"No water, but the fruit is juicy," he said, offering it to her. She smiled tiredly and took it, fishing for a knife to peel it.

"Thanks," she said. She lifted her gaze to his and held it for a moment. "You've been good to me, Jake. Better than I expected, considering . . . well, everything."

His heart turned over, and he gave her a lopsided smile.

Her own smile widened and she turned her attention to the fruit, peeling it quickly and popping some of the moist purple flesh into her mouth. "Oh God, that's good," she said. "I had the rations, but . . . well, you know."

He did, recalling the days they had spent together eating nothing but military-issue rations while they eluded Valerian's net. It was then that he'd started to shed some of his mistrust and hatred of her, and begun to share some of what he was experiencing with Zamara. To his surprise, he found he recalled those days with a hint of nostalgia.

She offered him a slice of the fruit, dripping with dark purple juice, but he waved it off, happier in her delight of the sammuro than he would have been in eating it himself. A thin trickle of purple fluid escaped her Cupid's bow lips, and Rosemary wiped it away with a forefinger, sucking the moisture. Jake watched, mesmerized.

Be careful in this, Jacob, Zamara said in his mind. But he knew, and therefore she knew, that any warning of this sort was coming far too late.

CHAPTER FOURTEEN

THEY PERMITTED ROSEMARY SOME SLEEP, AND then the planning began in earnest. Maps were drawn, most of them from Zamara's memory, detailed and perfect and precisely to scale. Despite everything she'd already seen them do, Rosemary marveled at it. She watched and listened closely, observing Jake closest of all. She wished she knew what to look for in a protoss, but although she was a skilled student and a keen observer of human nature, she hadn't been trained to analyze aliens. Just terrans.

Jake had changed a great deal since the first time she'd met him on the *Gray Tiger,* and not for the worse, either. She'd not been overly impressed with him then, and not for some time. Rosemary had been a bit surprised when he'd cracked the code and figured out a way into the temple's heart, and her respect for him had gone up several notches. He'd weathered the melding of an alien intelligence with his own shockingly well. She didn't think she'd have adjusted so smoothly. He hadn't liked what Zamara had done with Marcus back on the ship, though, and it was at that point that she realized that she could respect and understand the protoss inside him as well as the man who housed it. Zamara had done what needed doing, and hadn't been squeamish about it. And when Zamara and Jake had combined to dispatch Randall so handily—well, she hadn't been displeased to have him at her back. Him. Zamara. Them. Damn, it got confusing.

Rosemary suddenly shuddered, and sweat broke out all over her. She felt cold and clammy, even in the humid warmth of the Aiur afternoon. Jake/Zamara was talking earnestly to Ladranix, pointing at a spot on the map he had sketched in the earth. Ladranix was hunched close to the terran, his luminous eyes following Jake's pointing finger.

Thank God, or any listening deity, or just her own stubbornness, that she had made it clear that they were never to read her mind uninvited.

She needed another fix.

She had promised to bring Jake to the rendezvous point in six hours. She would not do so. When she had made that promise, her body taut and racked with a pain that hitherto she had never even imagined, she had not lied. She had promised to deliver Jake, and via him Zamara, to their mysterious Benefactor, and she'd meant every single word of that promise. And Alzadar had believed her truthfulness, and granted her the mercy of the Sundrop on her aching skin, and let her go.

The plan had been to say that the way was clear. To tell Jake and Ladranix and the others that they could proceed unchallenged. "You are one of us now, a sister of the Sundrop, Rosemary Dahl," Alzadar had assured her, rubbing the salve into her wrists as she wept with relief and ecstasy. "The Xava'tor is merciful. He has no reason to harm one who aids him. Who knows but that a terran might prove useful again in the future? Bring us the preserver and her allies, and the Sundrop will be yours to partake of freely."

But despite the pleasure that still hummed along her skin and in her blood, the words that left Rosemary Dahl's lips upon her "rescue" were not the ones she had agreed to speak. She'd warned them away from attempting to enter the cavern.

Now she mentally cursed the impulse to protect Jake and Zamara. Ethan wouldn't have done it.

The thought of Ethan made her frown. For so long, she'd admired and respected him. Ethan's lack of loyalties had amused and delighted her, until that lack of loyalty had been turned on her like a searchlight upon an escaping convict. Maybe that was why she'd impulsively decided not to betray Jake. That had to be it. Regardless, right now she wished the words back, and would have done anything if Alzadar had miraculously appeared with a palmful of Sundrop.

She excused herself, claiming the need to empty her bladder, and instead wandered off and threw up.

She wiped her mouth with the back of her hand and surrendered to the shaking for one moment, and then tried to think.

Rosemary was supposed to meet with Alzadar tonight. She was supposed to not show up alone. She'd have to think of something to delay Alzadar with, and pray that the story was good enough so that he'd give her another dose.

A slave—she was a slave to that drug the same way the slaves in the den at Paradise had been. The same way she had been a slave to stims, to turk and bog and fireweed and to everything else she'd injected, swallowed, or sniffed the four long years she'd been an addict. Whatever Ethan had done to her the last time they'd met, he'd helped her kick that, at least.

Until now.

Rosemary took a deep breath, spat, and returned to the gathering.

She arrived at the site after checking to make sure it was zerg-free, and for a minute that was both excruciating and glorious thought that Alzadar had either forgotten about the rendezvous or else had been caught. A slight brush of her thoughts dispelled the notion at once, and she turned to see him standing in a puddle of moonlight. The light fell upon his form, tall and imposing, his eyes gleaming as bright as the moon's radiant glow. A shadow pooled ominously and starkly beneath him.

"You are late," he said.

Rosemary stood as straight as she could. "It's not easy to get away, you know."

"Did they believe you?"

Rosemary was smart. She had a mind that was, if not as disciplined as Ethan's, definitely under her control for the most part. She formed the thoughts as she spoke.

"No. I told them the story we agreed on. But they don't trust me. Jake in particular doesn't trust me after I was willing to turn him over to Valerian. I warned you about that."

The lambent eyes narrowed. "Go on."

"I'll need a few days to persuade them. In the meantime, if you give me some of the Sundrop, you won't need to risk discovery by meeting with me. I'll meet you here again in a few days. By then I'll—"

His shoulders trembled and she felt his laughter, dry and frightening, rush through her.

"Foolish little girl," he said. "You think those barriers will stop me, a trained templar? It was a brave try, and better than I expected from someone who is not a protoss. But it was in vain."

She swallowed hard and clenched her fists. God, she wanted the stuff. And he knew it.

"If you betray us," he said calmly, "you will not have it again, and the lack of it will kill you."

"I've quit tougher drugs."

"No, you have not. Your stims, as you call them, are paltry things compared to the Sundrop."

"If it's so bad, why don't you quit it yourself?" Rosemary challenged frantically.

"Why should we? It is a gift from the Xava'tor. The withdrawal, while painful, does not damage us. And the ecstasy is—well. You know." He closed his eyes and tilted his head in a manner that Rosemary was starting to understand conveyed a smile.

"What shall I do with you, Rosemary Dahl?" he mused. "I've no real wish to kill you, but our Xava'tor must be satisfied. I cannot return to him and say that I have failed him. So what do we do?"

"Give me another chance," she said. She'd tried to lie. She'd tried to do the right thing and been caught out at it. What were Jacob Jefferson Ramsey and Zamara the preserver to her anyway, in the end? All they had done was make her into someone on the run. She owed them nothing. Maybe this Benefactor could get her off Aiur. At the very least, Alzadar could give her enough Sundrop so that she wouldn't give a rat's ass at being stuck here for the rest of her life.

A spasm of pain shook her, and worse than the pain was the wanting of the pleasure.

"Yes," said Alzadar, satisfied. She knew he'd read her thoughts. "There is still time yet." He opened a sack he had slung over his back and withdrew a small pot. Rosemary's heart leaped, and as he removed the lid on the pot and the familiar scent wafted out, tears formed in her eyes.

He extended the jar to her. As she reached eagerly for it he drew back, laughing, teasing, cruel.

"Tell me again what you will do."

She hated him in that moment. Hated herself worse.

"I'll bring him, I promise." The note of pleading in her voice disgusted her.

"Tell me how."

She'd been fixated on the little pot of salve, but now her blue eyes flashed to his. The violence and loathing in her thoughts was powerful, but Alzadar seemed completely unperturbed. Her anger sputtered and subsided beneath that icy gaze.

"It will be easy enough to get him alone. I will bring him out here. You can take him then, and do whatever the hell it is your Xava'tor wants done to him and Zamara, I don't care. Just take me back with you and give me access to the Sundrop."

He nodded, satisfied. This time when he extended his hand, he didn't take it back. Rosemary snatched the little jar, scooped out a fingerful of the stuff, smeared it on her throat, and exhaled in relief.

They were waiting for her when she came back. She forced herself to appear calm.

"I miss a meeting?" she asked lightly, reaching for a waterskin and drinking thirstily. She wondered if they could detect the sweet smell of the Sundrop. Alzadar assured her that the scent dissipated beyond protoss sensing after only a moment on the skin, but she wasn't sure. If even one of them made the slightest effort to read her thoughts, they'd know it all.

"No," Jake said. "Not really. We were going to go do some scouting and some foraging, and you weren't around. I . . . got worried."

She smiled at him. "Don't worry, I know better than to go too far. Just sometimes—you want a little privacy. To think about things."

Rosemary felt Ladranix's searching gaze upon her. "What things?"

Rosemary shrugged. "You spend three days hiding from your enemies, you start thinking about things. Humans do, anyway. I don't know about protoss."

Ladranix nodded. "Yes . . . we do as well. We have thought much."

Rosemary let her gaze flit back to Jake long enough to meet his gaze, allowed it to linger, then looked away quickly. His eyes widened slightly and even in the dim light she could see that his cheeks darkened. It was almost too easy.

"Zamara had been reconsidering," Jake said. "She originally thought we'd get what we needed from the chambers and then see what she could do to open the warp gate. She's considering reversing the order."

What? They'd been that close to escaping? "I thought Zamara needed whatever was in the chambers in order to open the gate!"

Jake looked uncomfortable. "She wasn't very clear on any of that, not even with me. But we've got to defeat the Forged first, regardless, to get either goal achieved." He smiled at her. "But thanks to you, we know what we're getting into now."

She forced a smile, forced herself to look relieved. "Yeah. Glad I and my unique talents could be of some help."

"The Tal'darim would have been shielding themselves from detection," Ladranix said. "If, as I fear, they are prepared to be hostile toward us—we would have been slaughtered. Now, we will not be caught off guard."

She went on the scouting mission with them. She helped refill the water bottles and find food to supplement her and Jake's rations. She looked serious when she was supposed to, smiled when it was expected of her, and all the while moved forward on her new plan.

When day came, she slept closer to Jake than usual. And when night came, before it had a chance to be filled with planning and recons and other things that would eventually come to nothing, Rosemary stood next to Jake and said, quietly, "Walk with me?"

"Um . . . yeah, sure. Everything okay?" he asked as he fell into step with her.

Rosemary hesitated. "Mostly," she said. "I . . . need to talk to you. Far enough away so the others can't hear." She wished she could blush at will, but contented herself with quickly averting her gaze.

"They won't read your thoughts," he said, still not quite understanding what was going on.

"They'll read yours," she said, and gave him a quick grin. It faded almost as quickly and she repeated,

"Please. I know there's a ton of stuff we're supposed to be doing, but . . ."

She let her voice trail off. She wasn't looking at him but she was pretty sure he'd swallowed. Certainly he cleared his throat. "Let me tell Ladranix," he said.

"Okay," she agreed. No harm in that. By the time Ladranix and the others realized what was going on it would be too late for them to do anything about it. Jake would be captive or dead and she'd be luxuriating in the most exquisite high she'd ever known, one that would enable her to forget what she'd done. Jake hurried away, then returned, smiling.

"Lead on," he said. They both were familiar with the surrounding area at this point, even out of the remains of the city, and once they'd double-checked for zerg he followed her willingly, completely clueless. He didn't press her for conversation, and she imagined he was glad for the chance to be quiet as well. At last, they were almost there. She slowed. The meeting place was not much farther, only half a kilometer or so away. She wanted Jake completely unaware, so she came to a stop.

They stood there for a moment, the moon dim upon them. *Now,* she thought. *Say the words, do what you need to do, and lure him in with a promise.*

"Jake?" She turned her face up to his and stepped closer to him. Now and then she wished she were taller, given her line of work, but her diminutive height always, always worked to her advantage when she had to play helpless.

Jake stepped back, every line of his body relaying his uncertainty. "Rosemary—what's going on? What's wrong? Why did you need to take me so far from the camp to talk to me?"

She laughed, and this time she didn't have to feign its shakiness. The mild discomfort was starting to turn into pain. "I—well, what I have to tell you—protoss may like to share everything in the Khala, but this is just for you and me."

"Of course," he said. He reached as if to put a reassuring hand on her shoulder, then stopped himself. Rosemary followed his hand with her gaze, then took it in hers. She curled her fingers around his, entwined them. He didn't protest, but he was obviously utterly confused.

"Rosemary?"

"I hated that name," she said, and that was the truth. "That's why I went by R. M."

He grinned, relaxing slightly. "When I first read your mind and learned it, the only thing I could think of was how incongruous a name it was for—well, a traitor and an assassin."

That was not the line of thought she wanted from him now, and she squeezed his hand. "Yeah. But Jake—you know I'm not that person anymore. Well, not entirely; you can't change who you are overnight. But . . . so much has happened. It seems like a lifetime ago that I was that woman."

Again, the truth. The woman who'd gone by the moniker R. M. was someone who was in control.

She'd kicked her addiction and knew her role and her place in the universe. The woman standing in front of Jake Ramsey, her hand in his, her gut clenching and her body shivering with addictive need, was not that creature.

"I know what you mean. So much *has* happened, hasn't it? But it's all right. I . . . I got to know you. When we were in the Khala—I touched you." His voice was soft.

Perfect. "You're touching me now."

He nodded, looking very boyish and uncertain in the moonlight. A few more lines and he'd be hers. He'd—

—be killed. Or tortured. They wanted Zamara, and they would have to go through Jake to get her. Unbidden, unwanted, Rosemary too thought of the moment when she had been so intimately joined with so many, when all that had been her had been seen and touched and known.

He lifted his other hand and brushed the bangs from her forehead. "I won't say that I misjudged you, because we both know I didn't. But—I sure as hell didn't know everything."

Something snapped inside her.

"I can't do this."

He blinked. "What?"

"I can't do it. I can't. Not to you, not now. Damn it, let's go, just—"

She dropped his hand, whirled, and fled back the way they had come. A second later, he was following, grabbing her arm. "Rosemary, what is it, what—"

"Let go of me! We have to get back!"

With practiced ease she shook him off and kept running, as if some part of her truly believed that she could run away from her choices, her need, the siren song of the Sundrop as the pain intensified.

He grabbed at her again, confused and worried and angry because of it. "Damn it, what's going on?"

She whirled and struck out at him. It was testimony to how badly the withdrawal was crippling her that the blow went wild.

"Don't you understand? *I was going to give you to them*!"

"You—"

She'd seen that look on the face of those she'd betrayed dozens of times, and never before had it rattled her. Seeing it on Jake's face—again—suddenly devastated her.

"They caught me," she said, and to her shame her voice was raw with pain. "They got me addicted to this stuff they smeared on my body—" Her hands went to her arms and clasped them hard, fighting to control the shivering. "They want Zamara. They said they'd give me more stuff if I—but I couldn't do it to you. I couldn't. I—"

Jake's arms went around her, and his embrace shocked her, made her go stiff. In some part of her mind that wasn't screaming in agony, she noted that his arms were surprisingly strong and sure. "Let me in, please," he whispered in her ear.

She nodded, dumbly.

Help me, Jake—I don't want to be this anymore.

I'll help you, Rosemary. I promise. You don't have to do this alone.

She felt him—them—racing through her thoughts, laying bare all her plotting, her pain, her shame, every unkind thought, every selfish whim, every moment when she lay vulnerable and exposed before the Tal'darim and their damned Sundrop and the awed mental whispers about their Benefactor. Her knees buckled as a fresh wave of pain hit her.

Her eyes rolled back in her head. He caught her as she fell. Dimly she felt herself being swept up in his arms, her head being cradled against his shoulder, and then merciful blackness descended.

CHAPTER FIFTEEN

IN HIS PRIVATE QUARTERS—A LUXURY ON THE battlecruiser—Devon Starke closed his eyes and cleared his mind. It was both easier and harder now than it had been during his days as a ghost, but he would have it no other way. Valerian Mengsk had saved him, and if he had merely traded one form of servitude for another, Devon was fully aware that in this version, he served as himself.

It had taken Valerian time—perhaps, the young emperor-to-be had feared, too much time—to assemble even this skeleton fleet that now traveled as fast as possible toward Aiur and archeologist Jacob Ramsey. The "fleet" consisted of a single battlecruiser, six Valkyries, and eight Wraiths. Their cargo was made up of marines, siege tanks, and dropships. All this effort to capture one human male. Well, that wasn't quite true. Starke was uncertain if Ramsey could be called "human" anymore.

Starke opened his eyes and stared up at the ceiling. Again and again, his thoughts drifted back to that remarkable moment in time where his mind—no, more than his mind; his essence, his . . . soul?—had connected so profoundly with so many others.

What the *hell* had Ramsey done?

It had been—beautiful. Glorious. And Devon Starke ached for it again. He hoped that somehow, some way, Valerian would be able to experience this. The younger Mengsk was both like and unlike his father. He was disciplined, he was smart, and he was ambitious. But the younger man still had ideals and hopes. He still found beauty in the arts and sciences. He still had compassion. Devon didn't fool himself that Valerian had saved his life for anything other than his own purposes, but even so, he knew his employer genuinely liked and respected him.

If Valerian could grasp this, this union—could understand it, as Devon felt he was starting, with all the power of an untrained child, to understand it—then this mission to find Jacob Ramsey could have consequences that might shake the foundations of human existence.

Rosemary awoke sometime later. She had been bathed and was wrapped in a blanket from the system runner. For a second, her head was clear, and she wondered who had taken care of her. Then nausea struck and she rolled over and retched. Nothing came out; she'd apparently thrown up everything in her stomach.

Gentle, nonhuman hands closed on her bare shoulders. "The Sundrop had permeated your clothing,"

Ladranix said. "When you have fully cleansed your system, we will give you new clothes to wear."

She nodded her understanding. Jake knelt next to her. She couldn't meet his eyes.

"Ladranix isn't familiar with this topical drug they hooked you on, Rosemary," Jake said. "He thinks it's something completely artificial, manufactured by this Benefactor to keep the Forged under his sway." He took her hand. She gripped it like a lifeline.

"You can beat this," Jake said quietly. "I know you can. You've beaten drugs before."

Tears filled her eyes, scalded them, slipped down her face. "Nothing like this. Believe me."

"Zamara and I can help you, but we can't do it for you."

"Wouldn't want you to," she said, her teeth chattering.

He grinned, suddenly and unexpectedly. "That's the Rosemary I know."

Her skin prickled, as though a thousand ants were crawling on it. She spasmed, slapping at her skin. Gentle but insistent hands gripped her, preventing her from injuring herself.

"I'm coming to join you," Jake said. "We'll get through this together. Like we've gotten through everything so far."

And then he was there, in her mind, sitting next to her mentally just as he was to her physically. Exhausted despite having just woken, Rosemary closed her eyes.

She was on a hill back on Nemaka. The sky above them was blue from the light of the atmospheric field generators. Jake sat next to her, wearing his customary dig outfit. She was clad in her old familiar jumpsuit.

"Not the most scenic of places, but one we both know," he said, grinning at her.

"Why conjure up a fake landscape anyway?" Rosemary asked.

Jake sobered. "I thought it would be a good anchor for you. Because the protoss seem to think that your withdrawal will cause hallucinations."

The earth shivered. Rosemary's hands splayed out to steady herself. Jake's arm went around her. At the foot of the little hill, the earth caved in, and then *things* began to crawl out in a thick blanket.

"Like these," Jake said with a sigh.

Rosemary leaped to her feet, reaching for her weapon. The rifle was cool and familiar in her hands, until it turned into a zerg pincer. She dropped it. It snapped, writhing, then grew six legs and began crawling up her leg. Red-hot agony shot through her.

"It's not real," Jake said in her ear. "Not the gun, not the zerg leg. Stand still."

"Easy for you to say," she growled, but fought to obey. The pain increased. It felt as though white-hot needles lanced her, but she summoned her fierce will and didn't move. The pain increased and she bit back a scream, and then it was gone.

Until the next hallucination came.

* * *

Jake's heart broke for Rosemary.

It was easy enough to analyze it intellectually. This Sundrop, whatever the hell it was, produced euphoria in its users. That meant that the brain's pleasure center, the nucleus accumbens, was being flooded with dopamine. Sundrop appeared to be particularly malicious, as a cursory reading of Rosemary's thoughts had revealed that while the first high had been ecstatic, each subsequent one had been less so, and the withdrawal worse. Rosemary would not have lasted long, even if the Tal'darim had indeed welcomed her into their fold. Eventually, the withdrawal would have killed her.

He wasn't at all sure it wasn't killing her now.

She is battling this, but she needs your strength, Jacob.

Our strength, he corrected Zamara.

No, she mused, *it is my skills that will help. But you are more effective. She trusts you.*

Jake stared down at the shivering woman in the blanket, surprised.

I don't think . . . I could have endured what she has.

Few could, Zamara agreed. *She is strong, and has retained herself.*

It was no wonder Rosemary had become so cynical and self-serving. The wonder—and Jake stood in awe of it—was that there was a place in her that hadn't let her bitterness destroy her.

I can't help her with this! Jake cried to Zamara. They had done what they could with the technology they had on hand, but they hadn't dared use any medication.

She will have to ride this out on her own, Zamara agreed. *Her determination and will to survive will either carry her through or not.*

But at least she knows she is being watched over. She knows there's something to come back to. I wish I could take on her pain for her. She's so wrung out after fighting it for so long.

Not even in the Khala can we take on another's pain, Zamara said, gently. *We can know of it, and feel it as our own, but we cannot eliminate it for another. The dark templar have said they fear losing themselves in the Khala, but it is not so, not in the way they think. We remain who we are. And we, in the end, every one of us, must face our torment alone.*

Jake bit his lower lip and sent a thought to Rosemary.

Come back, Rosemary. Get through this, and come back.

Her face, drawn with pain but still perfect in its porcelain beauty, showed no sign that she had heard.

Rosemary blinked sleepily. The scents of smoke and cooking wafted to her nostrils, and she sniffed. She was suddenly ravenous. For a long moment, her mind was a blank. Something was missing. . . .

Oh, yes. Excruciating torment. That was what was missing.

"I'm hungry," she announced, turning her head and seeing Jake, as she had known she would.

He smiled down at her, running a hand along her hair with a familiarity that told her he'd done it a lot over the last . . . however long it had been. She let him do it. She found it comforting. "I thought you might be. We've got some real food. Come on."

He helped her sit up, and she frowned. "Weak as a damned kitten," she muttered, clutching the blanket around her and letting him assist her.

"Stay right there," he said, and grinned. Surprised, she smiled back.

"Smart-ass," she said, her voice warm. He returned momentarily with a plate of some kind of roasted meat. She speared it on the knife he gave her and bit into it hungrily. It was charred on the outside, raw in the middle, and was the best thing she'd ever tasted.

"Roasted *kal-taar.* Don't gobble it down too fast—you haven't eaten in days," Jake said soberly. "The drug took away your appetite. You didn't even realize you were hungry."

Rosemary nodded and swallowed. "Yeah . . . I ate because you all expected me to. Would have blown my cover. And then—well, it never stayed down for long once the withdrawal kicked in."

"Are you well enough that we may speak with you?" The mental voice in Rosemary's head belonged to Ladranix, of course. She made a slight face and nodded.

"Yes. I'll tell you everything I know. There's not a lot that's useful, though, I'm afraid." She took another bite.

"Uh, about that," Jake said, and scratched the back of his neck sheepishly. "We already know a lot.

To help you we had to go in pretty deep. Even into your subconscious."

"I'm not surprised," Rosemary said, her mouth full. "You did what you had to do. What I asked you to do," she corrected.

They looked at one another a moment. Both of them knew what he and Zamara had found there. To her surprise there was no trace of disgust in Jake's blue eyes, only admiration and empathy. And for the first time in a long time, Rosemary was ashamed of how she'd treated someone.

Jake cleared his throat. "Anyway, the good news is, you knew more than you thought you did. While you were, uh, high on this Sundrop, the Forged spoke freely to one another, including you in the loop."

"Really? Anything useful?"

"A lot," Jake said. "By what they said, Zamara was able to identify this Benefactor of theirs."

Rosemary was instantly alert. She hungered for information—for ways to fix the damage she'd caused—even more than she did food right now. "Who is it?"

Jake looked around at the gathering of Those Who Endure. "He goes by the name Ulrezaj. He's something called a dark archon."

A mental murmur rippled through the Shel'na Kryhas. "A *dark* archon? We know what an archon is. . . ."

"I don't," said Rosemary.

A mental image filled her mind: glowing, swirling energy, a sense of tremendous psionic power radiating from it. She also understood that this was a sacrifice—that templar had assumed this form, in order to aid their brethren with their very lives.

"Oh," she said.

"There are few more powerful weapons among the protoss," Ladranix said.

"It gives literal meaning to our terran slang 'going out in a blaze of glory,'" Jake said. "Two templar sacrifice themselves to achieve this power for a brief time. The dark templar can create archons as well."

"Has Zamara seen them?" Rosemary asked.

"I—better let her handle this," Jake said. Rosemary watched as Zamara stepped to the fore. Jake's expression changed, became calmer, more reserved. Even so, there was less of a difference than there had been earlier. Jake was starting to become more and more like Zamara. She wondered what he thought about that, wondered if he even realized it.

"The dark templar do not have preservers," Zamara said, speaking with Jake's voice. "When they decided to withdraw from the communal link that is the Khala, they forfeited the ability to create preservers. The Khala is vital to a preserver; it is only through that link that we are able to access the memories." Jake/Zamara smiled as he saw the confusion on Rosemary's face. "It is complex for terrans to grasp, and you need not fully understand. All that matters is that you understand that I have no memories within me of any dark templar once they left Aiur. Thus, I have not seen a dark archon—save one, which I saw only through reading the mind of the assassin it sent to kill me."

Zamara looked gravely at those assembled. "What I know is that this dark archon—Ulrezaj is his name—wants to keep me silent. He is more than a mere dark archon. Whereas archons are comprised of two joined souls, this entity contains the psychic and spiritual energy of seven dark templar."

"Seven?" Ladranix's shock rolled over Rosemary. "How is such a thing even possible?"

"Likely that knowledge lies only in Ulrezaj himself, and it is doubtful he would ever share it," Zamara said dryly. "He is powerful beyond anything I have ever encountered, and my being a preserver, that is a considerable statement. His assassin was sent to execute me and all other preservers, to ensure that the protoss would never know what we know, and be crippled without us to rely upon. When I read this dark templar's mind . . ."

Zamara hesitated. "Based upon what I learned, I am one of the last surviving preservers. And if I die, all hope for our people—for this entire galaxy—dies with me."

CHAPTER SIXTEEN

INSIDE HIS OWN BODY, BUT NOT IN CONTROL OF it, the essence that was Jake Ramsey turned to Zamara with horror. *You're one of the last? Why didn't you tell me?*

What purpose would your knowing this have served, other than to further alarm you?

Zamara, you have to stop this not telling me things. You're in my body. You're running the show much of the time. I deserved to know this.

Well . . . now you do.

"I do not know what Ulrezaj's ultimate plan is," Zamara continued, as if she had not just dropped the equivalent of a nuclear bomb on them all, as if she were merely passing the time in idle chitchat. "But he needs assistants. He must, or else he would not need the Forged. He has created this drug to addict and enslave them. One other thing I have learned from Rosemary's subconscious is that this Sundrop does not permit them to touch one another's hearts the way the Khala does. It may do even more that they do not even know about, affecting them on very deep levels. They have become angrier, more primal; they could well be changing in other ways also."

Rosemary nodded. "Yeah—they all seemed . . . less reasonable, I guess. Much more inclined to fly off the handle, except for Alzadar. I don't have a whole lot of experience with telepathy, but I did notice that I didn't get any emotional hits from them. It was kind of like . . . words spoken in a flat voice, if you know what I mean."

Ladranix nodded. "That was the gift of Khas and the Khala. Not just a touching of minds, but a touching of souls, of hearts. This intimacy is what the dark templar have turned their backs on."

"The Forged would be unaccustomed to not being in the Khala. They would be alone, and fearful, and ashamed to admit that they could not connect. Thus, their loyalty and dependency on their Benefactor—on Ulrezaj—would increase," continued Zamara. Jake knew that most of this was for Rosemary's benefit; the protoss wouldn't have needed it spelled out like this.

Thanks for including her, Zamara.

She has endured much. She has earned trust. It would have been easy to deliver us into the hands of our enemies, but Rosemary chose not to.

Jake looked again at the woman sitting wrapped in a blanket, her shoulders bare, her face worn. He was pretty sure he was falling in love with her.

I am quite certain of it. But this is no time for romance.

Jake was glad Zamara was in control of his body at this particular moment.

"I believe that most—perhaps all—of the Forged do not understand that they are enslaved. They do not know what monster it is they serve. We must enlighten them. And whatever happens, I must not be allowed to fall under Ulrezaj's control. He will either slay me or use me. Both are unacceptable."

"So how do we do that?" Rosemary asked. "They outnumber us, and they've got a big old dark archon running the show."

Zamara thought. "Jake and Rosemary did not get within telepathic range of Alzadar," he said. "Which means he does not know that Rosemary changed her mind about allying with the Forged. I think you should meet him again, Rosemary, but this time, we will all be waiting for him."

She grinned slowly. "A trap. I like that. I want to be the one to blow his head off, though."

"No, no, we wouldn't kill him!" Jake shouldered past Zamara in his body, fully inhabiting it once again. Zamara relinquished control with a hint of amusement. "We'd capture him and find out how much he knows about the Benefactor's real identity. Rosemary, these are protoss. They're not evil; they've just been lied to and addicted to a horrible drug. You know what it did to you. If it did half as much to them, they're in bad shape. Maybe—maybe worse, if it really cut them off from the Khala, as Zamara believes. They need to know what kind of creature they've been duped into serving. My guess is that once they know, they'll be as appalled as we were."

"We didn't come here to save the protoss, Jake. We came here to find whatever it is Zamara needs in that chamber and to get away as soon as possible."

Jake heard the reluctance in her voice, and was heartened by it.

"Even that goal will be served," said Ladranix, choosing, in typical protoss fashion, to react to her concern rather than her somewhat callous comments about his people. "If they are our allies, they will not stop us from entering the chamber. And we can all stand together as we attempt to escape the zerg and flee Aiur."

His mental voice held a hint of sorrow. Jake realized that even now, when his homeworld was crawling with monsters and his own people had gone nuts, Ladranix—and indeed all the other Shel'na Kryhas—felt pain at the thought of finally and fully abandoning Aiur.

"You're right," Rosemary said. "But you can't expect me to not want to give Alzadar a good punch for what he did to me."

Ladranix's eyes half closed and he tilted his head in amusement. "No, Rosemary Dahl, no one would expect you not to want that. But we do expect you to refrain, in the interests of the greater good."

"Yeah, yeah," she said, a smile tugging at the corner of her lips. "Whatever it is we end up doing, though, let's get on with it."

* * *

Rosemary hunched and shivered as she hurried toward the rendezvous spot. The moon was full and she knew that Alzadar would see her clearly. She had to convince him that she was still under control of the drug. Her mind was shielded from his; he'd have questions about that, but it was better than his outright knowing exactly what the plan was. At least it would buy them some time.

Two seconds later, the question slammed into her mind: "Why do you hide your thoughts from me?"

She couldn't reply, couldn't even speak, because although she knew protoss could hear, they didn't understand terran. They were able to communicate only with thoughts, and hers were sealed from Alzadar. Instead she shook her head violently and kept running toward him, kept making gestures indicating she had been very, very sick, and was desperate for the drug he offered, and was still his ally.

He was arrogant, and that was his undoing. He was so firmly convinced that she was in his thrall because of the Sundrop that he hesitated, confused, for just a few seconds too long. That was all it took.

She could see Alzadar now, his eyes blazing in the shadow of the trees. And a heartbeat later, she saw Those Who Endure emerge from the jungle and descend on him.

Rosemary abandoned all pretense and pulled out her pistol. She desperately wanted to empty it into Alzadar's midsection, but she refrained, running as surely now as she had been uncertain before toward the fight.

Damn, but they were beautiful as they fought. She knew some martial arts, mainly enough to get free if anyone managed to get a hold of her—which was very rare—but she'd watched Ethan practice for many years. She knew that he was proud of his grace and accuracy and power, and wished fiercely that he could see this display of protoss in combat. It might teach him some humility.

Templar against templar, they fought, Ladranix in his dented, damaged armor, still clinging to his heritage, and Alzadar in long, flowing robes. She had thought it would be an uneven battle, having seen Ladranix in combat, but this was his friend, his equal in skill, and although Alzadar had no armor, it seemed that he did not need it. Each attack, each thrust from Ladranix was either met with Alzadar's own psi-blades or dodged so deftly it was a blur to Rosemary's eyes. Too, Ladranix was at a disadvantage in that he had no desire to injure or slay his old friend. Alzadar had no such compunctions.

Light pulsed from glowing daggers of psionic energy, moving so swiftly that they seemed ribbons of light rather than blades. Alzadar ducked and leaped up, blades flashing perilously close to Ladranix's unprotected face, but the other templar brought his armored arms up just in time. He sprang over his former friend, somersaulting in the air to land deftly behind Alzadar. Long, powerful legs kicked out. Still pivoting to keep his foe in front of him, Alzadar was vulnerable. The kick struck home and Alzadar staggered back—back into the sudden rush of untrained khalai who, with no real knowledge of combat and heedless of their own safety, simply hurled themselves upon the templar and knocked him to the earth. Then Ladranix was there, pinning his friend with a psi-blade to his throat that, Rosemary knew, he had no desire to use.

Jake was there too now, dropping to his knees beside the struggling Forged. Rosemary heard Zamara's thoughts in her mind as she slowed and stopped, watching, her pistol at the ready.

"We can help you," Zamara said.

"Help?" If protoss had mouths, Rosemary got the distinct impression that Alzadar would have spat. "You are as good as dead, preserver. You will soon be able to help no one."

"Listen to yourself," Zamara urged. "You are a templar—you have sworn to protect and defend other protoss. And yet you insist you desire to slay a preserver. That is contrary to everything you are."

"I am one of the Forged!" Alzadar gave a sudden violent twist and almost, but not quite, broke free of Ladranix's paristeel grip.

"His enslavement to the drug is strong," Zamara said. "This . . . will take some time."

It did.

While the initial purging of the drug from Alzadar's system was accomplished swiftly—Jake recalled how easily Zamara had cleared his system of alcohol when he had had dinner with Ethan and Rosemary—the actual detoxification took many hours. Alzadar shivered, the color of his body becoming mottled and sickly as they removed the drug that had given him so much pleasure, and for a surprisingly long time, considering the physical and physiological pain that racked his body, he resisted bonding with them. The Shel'na Kryhas continued to reach out to him, mental tendrils of compassion and understanding and lack of judgment twining gently in Alzadar's paranoid, angry mind. With the Sundrop cleared from his system, Alzadar was once again able to step forward into the Khala. He refused at first, claiming it was a trap. Zamara was deeply pained at the mistrust, but when, eventually, Alzadar tentatively entered the Khala, where all knew there could be no lies, no deceptions, he understood.

"It is the Sundrop that has kept you from us, my old friend," Ladranix said in that place of deep connection. "You are not at fault. It is not a punishment. The Khala is and always has been here, part of our birthright."

"I . . . I thought I was the only one . . . that something had happened. That I was . . . flawed." Jake felt the fear, the isolation, felt it softening and thawing like ice under a warm and blessing sun. His heart ached with it.

"You were deceived and betrayed indeed. But not by us. We welcome you back, brother. Together, we can defeat this murderer, this obscenity, who has so warped and violated the Forged with his lies. Do you know why he has done this?"

Jake felt Alzadar's trust flicker.

"I know you do not lie in telling me what you believe," Alzadar said. "But you may be wrong. The Xava'tor—the Benefactor—may not be this abomination of which you speak. He has cared for the Forged—he has kept us safe. He gave us hope—made us proud, again, to be who we are. You cannot argue with that."

"No," Zamara agreed. Jake tasted the concern that all the surviving Aiur protoss had had upon realizing they had been left behind while their brethren fled to the safety of Shakuras. He understood how easily it had turned to resentment, then hatred, cold and implacable. He felt the hope rekindled as Alzadar shared with them the memory of the Xava'tor's arrival. Suddenly, they had worth, and purpose, and value. "But it is my firm belief, based upon all I have learned—which you know is vast—that he has deceived you. He kept you safe, but for his own ends. As for making you proud of who you are—you are a templar. What is more—you are protoss. Such is your birthright as much as immersion in the Khala."

Jake thought of Rosemary. Was this universal, then, this need to matter? To be held of value? To have a direction and a goal to strive for? She had needed it, and when it had been given to her, she had turned her back on treachery. So too, now, did Alzadar.

"He keeps us safe from the zerg," Alzadar said, repeating himself as a hint of doubt began to color his thoughts. "He is stronger than they are. He teaches us how to trap them and bring them to him. The Sundrop . . . pleases so very greatly. And when he asks for one of us, now and then, to go to safety with him, it is always so joyful, although the rest of us are sad not to be chosen. Some, he calls the Hands of the Benefactor—the Xava'kai—and he takes them to perform special tasks, and we envy them."

"Tell us how you came to follow him," Zamara said, trying another approach.

"The Xava'tor began by speaking only to Felanis, telling him about the place beneath the surface where he and those who followed him would be kept safe from the zerg," Alzadar said. "Then . . . he spoke to me. Such a powerful mental presence."

"But you have never seen him?"

"No. Only been touched by his mind and will."

"You said he has tasks for you—what are they?"

Alzadar twitched slightly. Rosemary, watching apart from the mental link, frowned a little as she munched a sammuro. "Careful," she cautioned. "Whatever you're saying to him is starting to freak him out."

"Most of the tasks, we do not know," Alzadar said. "Such are deep secrets, revealed only to the ones he selects to become Xava'kai."

"He lives in the chambers?" Zamara pressed.

"I do not believe so. Zamara, he has been good to us. I do not wish to believe that we have been serving such a thing as you say!"

Zamara, in Jake's body, nodded. "I can well believe that. You have not fallen into evil, Alzadar. You have only been angry and afraid—as the Shel'na Kryhas are. As any sentient being would have been. And when you saw hope—you followed it."

"You must come with us," Jake said suddenly, pushing past Zamara as he had done on a few occasions before. "Come with us to find the crystal. See for yourself what's in the chambers. The protoss really are one people. They want you with them."

He was the first to think it, to feel it, and he sensed the surprise and admiration from the others as they agreed. Too, he sensed a slight shame in them, that it had been a mere terran to offer such evidence of forgiveness and acceptance, and for the first time he, Jacob Jefferson Ramsey, felt as welcomed into this sacred space as Zamara.

"Yes," said Ladranix. "Yes, come, my brother . . . we will share this with you . . . ," came other mental voices.

"It is . . . a forbidden area," said Alzadar. "The Xava'tor has ordered us on pain of death not to go there."

"Aren't you curious as to why a so-called benefactor would issue such a statement? Don't you want to know why he takes some of you and you never return? Or what the Xava'kai are doing? And why he demands that you slay a preserver, the pride of the protoss race, one of our most precious treasures?" Ladranix continued.

And of course, Alzadar was curious—he was a protoss, he was of the race that begat Temlaa and Khas and Vetraas and Adun. He hesitated, and Jake felt his indecision. Then, finally, "Yes. I would know if we have been cherished or betrayed. And if I am convinced that it is the latter . . . I am not without influence in the Forged. I will join you, and convince others to come with me. I was once a templar, trained from birth to protect my people. I pray I have the chance to do so again."

He turned to Jake, and inclined his head slowly. Zamara's thought was for Jake alone, proud and oddly wistful. *Well done, Jacob. Well done.*

Jake stood in his formal robes beside Adun as they spoke with Kortanul. "It is done," Adun said heavily, "and my heart is heavy with the doing."

"You are a templar protecting the protoss from an enemy. Your heart should not be heavy, but soar with righteousness. I have been shown the recorded images you sent. The young female Raszagal was a very real danger. Her proud thoughts as she died angered many of us."

"Stay your anger; she is dead and can harm the protoss no further. We are continuing with the purging, as you requested. We will send documentation for each one as executions are performed," Jake said. He did not like how Adun looked; the executor seemed close to losing his composure.

Kortanul softened a bit. "I know this is hard," he said gently. "I know it seems wrong. But it is to preserve the Khala—our way of life, everything that it is to be protoss. Adun, you must trust in our wisdom. This is truly the right thing to do. Keep me apprised."

The screen went dark and Adun dropped his head and closed his eyes.

"You did not need to be quite so inflammatory on your deathbed, Raszagal," Jake said wryly.

Raszagal, wearing a long robe, her arms free from the crystal bindings, stepped smoothly out of the alcove where she had listened, undetected, to the entire exchange. "I am sorry," she said, ducking her head and raising her shoulders in a smile. "But I could not resist. Besides, it distracted them. They were so angry they did not see that the wounds you made were false."

"Still, it was risky," Adun rebuked. "And we cannot afford to take risks. Are you and the others ready?"

Raszagal sobered. "We are," she said quietly. "And there is not a one among us who does not speak your name without honor, gratitude, and . . . well, to say truly—disbelief."

Jake shared that disbelief. For the last several days, templar had been quietly dispatched to various locations on Aiur. They had sought out places where these "dark templar" could safely be relocated, to live in peace until such a time as the Conclave was of a mind-set to discuss their reintegration. The templar were not without contacts among the khalai, contacts who could be trusted with a venture of this magnitude. Not even Adun would know where all of the dark templar were when this came to an end. No one would know the whole picture. That way, it was hoped, the Conclave would not know it either.

"An underground railroad," Jake said. "Just like back on Earth, before slavery was abolished in one of the major countries. Something that went against the law of the land—but that was the right thing to do. I have to say, though, I never would have expected Adun to come up with that kind of solution."

"There is a quote among humans I have learned," Zamara replied. "'Desperate times call for desperate measures.' Adun was faced with a terrible choice. Kill his own kind, or lie and hide in order to protect them. It tormented him until he chose, but he was at peace with his decision."

"I know," Jake said softly. "I felt it."

Raszagal turned to Jake, her eyes bright with humor that he could not sense but nonetheless beheld in her body language.

"You do not approve of this course of action, Vetraas," she said boldly.

"I approve of Adun. I approve of staying my hand when it came to taking your lives. Templar though I am, when it comes to my own people, I believe talking and understanding is always better than slaughter, young Raszagal."

Adun seemed lost in thought. "Your final destination will be unknown to me," he told Raszagal after a moment. "I will have a way to contact you, though. You understand why this must be?"

"Of course. If the Conclave read your thoughts, you can only betray part of the puzzle."

He nodded. "But when you are at the first . . . station, I suppose . . . I would come to you and teach you."

Both Raszagal and Jake stared at the executor. "What?" Jake managed.

"We can take all the precautions we like," Adun said, "but there is still the chance they will be discovered. I cannot permit that to happen. The . . . the fugitives need to be able to cover themselves. To . . . hide."

The word was enveloped with distaste. The templar were noble. They fought well, and proudly, and openly. Falsifying deaths in the first place was bad enough. Hiding the dark templar was difficult to rationalize. But teaching them mental disciplines that they might better avoid detections . . .

"They could use such skills as weapons," Jake pointed out, his thoughts directed solely at Adun. "They could become a great danger!"

"Vetraas, my old friend," Adun replied, including both Vetraas and Raszagal in his thoughts, "if I believed for a moment that they would be a danger, Raszagal would be lying on the floor. If we would help them, we must trust them."

Raszagal's eyes were wide with astonishment. Then, to Jake's surprise, she strode up to the tall, powerful executor and dropped gracefully to one knee. She lifted the hem of his robe and pressed it to her forehead.

"Such compassion—I will never, ever forget. I will be a diligent student. And I will do as you ask, noble executor, as I am certain we all will. We will put our knowledge toward

keeping ourselves safe. To merging with the shadows, unseen. And when the time is right, we will joyfully reunite with our brethren, for it was never our will to be in opposition to them."

Jake woke up from the dream of Adun to find himself drenched in sweat and shaking. It was the heat, surely, that and the stress of dealing with Alzadar and Rosemary. The dream itself had been profoundly moving. He had had no idea that Adun had had such an elaborate plan to deal with the dark templar. But he was too hot to integrate it, to mull over it. He sat up and groped for a waterskin, taking care not to disturb Rosemary, who slept deeply beside him.

Pain throbbed in his head, and for a moment he thought he was going to be sick. Inside his thoughts, he felt Zamara stir uneasily. Overheated, shaking, faint, in pain, Jake mentally cornered the protoss with whom he shared a body and demanded, *I've had enough of this, Zamara. What the* hell *is going on?*

For a long moment, she did not reply. He clutched at his head, wishing for just a nanosecond that he could tear it off. The pain from that would have to have been less.

Oh, Jacob, and there was an infinite tenderness as she brushed his thoughts, like a mother with a beloved child. Fear rose in him. *I am so, so sorry. I had hoped . . . I was wrong.*

Tell me.

Again, that awful, terrifying hesitation, that dreadful compassion and affection.

I did everything I could, when I reshaped your brain to handle the memories a preserver must manage. I did only what was absolutely necessary, in the least invasive way possible. I had thought there was a way to do so that would grant harmony to both of our presences in your body. It is not something that preservers know how to do. It is not something . . . any protoss has ever done. I used the energies of the temple to aid me, and I thought I had succeeded.

Jake waited, his body tense, not daring to breathe, praying she wasn't going to say what he knew she would. Beside him, Rosemary stirred, stretched, and sat up, knuckling sleep out of her eyes and regarding him curiously.

But . . . I was wrong. Your brain is able to bear these burdens only so long. Unless somehow my presence is removed and the strain eliminated. . . .

"I'm going to die," Jake finished.

CHAPTER SEVENTEEN

"WHAT?" ROSEMARY'S OUTBURST WAS MORE angry than anything else and the hand that shot out to close on his arm was strong. "What the hell is Zamara telling you?"

His arm hurt from where she dug her fingers into his flesh, but it was a good pain. He gestured that she remain silent. Zamara had much more to impart.

You—you said something. . . . Is there any chance?

It is my presence and the volume of the memories that is harming you, Zamara said, the words paining her. *In order for your brain to handle this knowledge, cells must be altered. And these alterations have caused a brain tumor. The longer I am present, the more cells are altered. The reason I was so adamant about getting into the chambers is that the crystals there might aid in removing me from your body.*

You—can do that? Just—download yourself into a crystal?

The dark templar have no preservers. But I am given to understand that they still keep the memories of what has gone before. Not in the same way, of course—but if they can store memories in khaydarin crystals, perhaps they can house me and the memories and knowledge I bear. The crystals in that chamber are the purest I have heard tell of. If we can retrieve one, or a fragment of one, and take it with us to Shakuras, perhaps one of the dark templar can accomplish the goal in time. Presently I believe the tumor could be treated effectively. But if it continues much longer, the damage will be irreversible.

Comprehension dawned. *That's why you wanted to go to Aiur rather than straight to Shakuras,* Jake said. *We had to detour here so you could—could try to save me.*

Yes.

"Jake . . ." Rosemary was looking up at him, her raven's wing brows knitted together, her full lips downturned in a frown.

I will be fully honest with you, Jacob. It . . . may already be too late. But we will try. I truly regret this turn of events. But the information I bear necessitated dire measures.

Stunned disbelief suddenly gave way to fury. *Damn it, Zamara! You keep telling me this information is worth dying for. I know you died for it. You were willing to let dozens of innocent people die for it. Hell, maybe* I'd *be willing to die for it too—but you won't let me know what it* is! *You have no right to do this to me. I thought—*

He thought they were friends.

Now she let him sense her pain, washing over him. It was her grief that stung his eyes with tears, not his own fear.

Yes, Jacob. Yes. We are. That is why I am doing every-

thing I can to both preserve this knowledge and get you to safety. You must understand us before you can understand this secret. And if you do not know it yourself yet—as Jacob Ramsey—then the secret is safe still. If you know this, if I reveal it to you—someone would be able to extract it from your memory.

You know it, Jake shot back. *Wouldn't someone be able to extract the information already?*

And then the slightly sickening thought came, wordless and starkly true: Zamara would kill them both before that happened.

I see.

He took a deep breath, disentangling himself from both Zamara's very real regret and her implacable, almost brutal resolve, and turned to Rosemary. The conversation between Zamara and him had been private; none of the other protoss had sensed it. He would share the information with them in a moment, but he wanted Rosemary to know first.

Quietly, calmly, he explained what had happened, using good old English, not thoughts. He was not as frightened as he thought he'd be. He was angry and frustrated and saddened, and all that and more crept into his voice as he spoke. Rosemary kept her hand on his arm, and her face didn't change expression as she listened. Finally, she released his arm and got to her feet. Purposefully she strode to their weapons cache and began to examine them.

"We get you in there today, and then we haul ass to get off this planet," she said bluntly. She didn't look up at him for a moment, and when she finally did, her blue eyes were burning with intensity.

"You don't get to die." She slammed the chamber into place on the rifle. "Not on my watch."

Jake was not prepared for the outpouring of concern and affection that washed over him when he told Those Who Endure. Part of it, of course, was worry for the continued existence of their preserver. He shared that worry. But there was also genuine sympathy and grief for him, Jacob Jefferson Ramsey, emanating from the minds of the protoss who surrounded him. It was almost too much to bear.

"I . . . I thank you. But I'm hopeful that Zamara's plan will work. She's not let me down yet."

"We all share that hope, Jacob," said Ladranix. "But now it is imperative that we move quickly. With Alzadar gone, the Forged will be on high alert."

Alzadar nodded. "There will be guards stationed, certainly. And since they do not know what has happened to me—it is doubtful they will settle for attempting to drive you off or capture you."

Jake noted the usage of "you," not "us."

Ladranix looked stoic. "Then we die, proudly, for what we believe in."

"No, wait," Jake interrupted. "We don't have to go in the main entrance, ringing the doorbell."

While he was pretty sure protoss didn't ring doorbells, they immediately understood the metaphor's meaning. "What do you suggest?" Ladranix asked.

Jake smiled despite the pain in his head. "I know a back entrance."

Rosemary met his eyes and grinned. She knew exactly what he was planning.

"So, we're following in the tracks of Temlaa, then," she said.

"And Khas," Jake said.

"Him too. I always liked Temlaa better."

The protoss within range of Jake's thoughts stared at him.

"Khas?" said Ladranix. "Of course . . . preservers have the memory of all protoss. You would have Khas's memories."

Jake nodded. "Yeah," he said. "But for some reason Zamara had me live those moments through Temlaa's eyes, not those of Khas."

Why'd you do it that way anyway?

Because the lessons learned by Savassan—by Khas—are not the ones that are important for you to understand. You do not need to learn as a mystic learns, Jacob. You need to learn as an ordinary protoss does. You needed to learn as the student, not the teacher.

He supposed that made sense.

"Khas and his friend and apprentice Temlaa were the ones who discovered the chambers in the first place, back during the Aeon of Strife," Jake continued. "They figured out some sort of puzzle in order to enter. With any luck that . . . security system, I guess, is still in place and the Forged got in through the main entrance."

"It is so," Alzadar confirmed. "I know nothing of any other way to enter the chambers."

"I cannot imagine that they would have been able to figure out a puzzle they did not even know existed," Ladranix said. "And this world, like all worlds must, has changed greatly over time. But there is one way to find out."

It took some time to hammer out all the details. Then the protoss began to break camp. If the gamble succeeded, they would be leaving Aiur forever. If it failed . . . then Those Who Endure would not be alive to worry about such things as camp. Jake and Rosemary helped, until finally, with only three functional vessels—and small ones at that—they were ready to depart.

The remaining templar and all the khalai who had shown promise in combat would accompany Jake, Zamara, and Rosemary to the chambers. Other khalai would go ahead to the warp gate and clear it of any zerg in the area. The rest—children and those who for various reasons could not fight as well as the others—would stay here, waiting to be ferried to the warp gate in waves. Eventually, all the Shel'na Kryhas would rendezvous at the warp gate. Zamara—hopefully—would be able to reactivate it, and they could all depart.

They were all, not surprisingly, stoic and in good spirits. No one held the cloud of failure in his or her heart. Jake found it very uplifting. All thoughts were quiet and focused as he and Rosemary entered the by-now-familiar little craft and settled in.

Jacob . . . Zamara's mental voice was hesitant.

He chuckled to himself. *I know I'm far from done with Adun and Vetraas and Raszagal.*

Every memory I give you in this fashion will further damage your brain. I am reluctant to do so, but I must.

I understand, Jake replied. *Go for it.*

"Who knew we had such a gift for stealth and secrecy," Jake said wryly to Adun.

Adun was wise about many things, but he had not yet seen enough to develop the sense of humor Jake had through the long years. He bridled a bit at the comment. "We do what is necessary," he said. "I do not relish it. This is not a game, Vetraas."

No, it was no game, or if it was it was a game as life always was, with the highest stakes imaginable. At first, the Conclave had been complacent. But recently it was as if something had changed. They were demanding more proof of the executions than simple recordings. Adun had done his best to keep them from actually attending an execution thus far, but sooner or later, they would insist on being present, and then the "game" would be over.

Or would it? The work Adun, Jake, and all the other high templar were doing with the fugitives was focused on teaching them how to mask themselves with startling efficacy. Just yesterday, Jake himself had watched, shocked, as Raszagal proudly showed off her ability to become almost invisible.

"You taught us about the concealing shadows," she said

to Adun. "We have studied hard, as I told you we would. Now we can bend light to hide ourselves."

While Raszagal was the most visibly talented student, the others were not far behind her. Knowing that their lives depended upon learning these psionic abilities, and heart-breakingly grateful to the templar, especially the executor, for saving them, they progressed with astonishing speed.

It worried Jake, how swiftly they moved. "It took us decades simply to learn how to fully share our hearts with one another," Jake told Adun. "You yourself are learning as much as teaching, for these abilities are hitherto foreign to us. Perhaps we should not push them so rapidly."

"There is no other choice," Adun replied. "The net closes in even now. And because they are utterly convinced that this is the right path, they will not relent."

Jake shared his worry.

"Soon, we will not be able to hide what we are doing," Adun continued. "Until I can persuade the Conclave that in this instance they have made the wrong choice, the only protection the dark templar will have is how well they can conceal themselves. It would be so much more efficient if I could link with them in the Khala—but of course, if I could do that, none of this would be necessary."

Later, Jake would sorrowfully muse that the events that unfolded were inevitable. He and Adun were both right. The so-called dark templar indeed had no defense other than these psionic abilities. And, they were trying to learn too much too quickly.

Jake would never know exactly what the ill-fated dark templar who accidentally brought about catastrophe was attempting. For of course he was not linked with the Khala, and every one of his kinsmen, the beasts of the rain forests, and the jungle itself for miles around were destroyed in the dreadful psionic storm that was unleashed. What was certain was that he or she had tried to do too much, too soon, and had triggered a psionic backlash in which the summoned power raged out of control. This unfortunate soul was not the only one; other dark templar presumably panicked and more and more storms were created as the students, unable to handle such power without the comfort, control, and discipline of the Khala, became the first victims of their own inexperience.

"A psionic storm?"

"Dozens of them," Zamara said gravely. "All across Aiur. All caused by inexperienced dark templar trying to wield too much power, too soon. Storms that were devastating in their scope; storms that were easily traceable back to their source by the Conclave. When they identified the bodies as those of dark templar they had been assured had been executed, they realized they had been duped by one they had trusted to do what they firmly believed was the right thing."

"So it was all for nothing," Jake breathed. "All the difficult decisions, the lies, the painful choices."

"No," Zamara stated. "The dark templar were indeed found by the Conclave, but even here, Adun's influence prevailed."

The righteous anger and confused hurt emanating from Kortanul was almost as overwhelming as the psionic storms.

"How dare you disobey a direct order? What gives you, a templar, the right to make such decisions? We are the Conclave! We know what is best!"

Adun stood his ground unflinchingly. "I am at peace with my decision. What is it you decree now, Judicator? For you know as well as I that if you publicly condemn us, you expose the very secret you were so determined to hide—the existence of the dark templar."

Jake sealed off his sudden burst of humor, lest it be detected by Kortanul. Adun had the judicator there. "We will do what you failed to do," Kortanul replied. "We will execute the dark ones ourselves."

"You shall not!" Adun's mental voice was almost painful. Jake touched his temple. "For if one of them comes to harm, I will speak openly of them. And again, your secret will be exposed."

Jake waited, still as stone. He wanted to help Adun, but he knew that any interference now would do more harm than good. This was Adun's choice; all would succeed or fail on how he handled it.

For a moment, Kortanul's mind was a careful blank. "Curse you, Adun. You know you are right. But the dark ones cannot be permitted to dwell with those of us who follow the true teachings of Khas. You have seen how dangerous they can be."

"It was unintentional," Jake blurted, unable to hold his peace any longer.

Kortanul turned to him. "That is even worse! You see how wild, how uncontrolled they are. Would you have them and this power rampage across our world unchecked?

Can you in good conscience, as one who has sworn to protect the protoss, say that is a good thing?"

Adun was stricken to the core, and lowered his head. "What . . . are you suggesting?"

"Banishment. We have already rounded them up. We will put them aboard one of the remaining vessels of the xel'naga and—

"You have such a thing?" Adun and Jake were both astonished and thought this at the same time.

"There are many things we know which you do not. It is why we are the leaders of the protoss and you merely wield the sword when we tell you to."

Except this time, Judicator, *Jake thought fiercely.* Except this time.

"Yo, Sleeping Beauty," said Rosemary, elbowing Jake. "We're almost there." Blinking sleepily, his mind mulling over the tragedy suffered by the protoss and wondering if he'd get to see the dark templar depart, Jake sat up. This was it then.

At first, he didn't see it. And then . . . ah, there it was, the crystals still towering toward the sky, glittering in the star- and moonlight, completely new to his eyes and yet completely familiar. Something inside him relaxed at the image, at the continuity it represented. Despite everything, despite the years and the wars and the zerg, these stones were still here, their luster undimmed, though perhaps they were more deeply buried in the soil than before.

"No sign of zerg activity," Varloris said. This was a

risky moment. While Zamara had blocked his and Rosemary's thoughts from being detected by the Forged, and of course the Shel'na Kryhas were able to block their own thoughts as well, a protoss craft landing on an open space was not safe. If they were noticed now, by either Tal'darim or zerg, their mission might end before it had even truly begun.

This was definitely the place. Jake knew it in his bones, in his cells, the moment he placed a foot on the soil. Here it was that Temlaa and Savassan had stood so long ago, with no inkling of what lay just beneath their feet. Here they had touched the crystals, trying to figure out the puzzle. Savassan had smashed a necklace made of shells, to point out the universal ratio, one to one point six. Jake knew better than to think he'd see fragments of those long-ago shells here, but part of him yearned to look. Just in case. He stifled the urge.

A thought struck him. *Zamara—I'm not a protoss. The crystals won't respond to me.*

You are not protoss, it is true. But your mind has been changed. Reshaped. I believe the crystals will respond to you as they would to me. If not, it is no matter, you can direct Ladranix in how to properly activate them. But . . . I know you wish to try.

I . . . I do, I really do.

Then, Zamara said, deliberately echoing words that had once been passed, then as now, mind to mind, *you do it, my student. The honor is yours.*

Jake closed his eyes briefly and called up the memory. He stood in this same place now as "he" had then, as Temlaa had. Jake opened his eyes and reached out his hand to touch the crystal, and for a brief heartbeat of an instant, it was as if a long protoss arm was superimposed on his own. Gently, he placed his palm on the cool crystal.

He felt a tingling, not a physical, but a mental one, and hope surged in him. The crystals were responding!

Moving counterclockwise, Jake touched the next crystal and held his breath. Both crystals seemed to light up faintly inside, and . . . yes, yes, there it was, that deep, barely audible hum that would grow in volume and harmony as soon as the voices of these two crystals were joined by others.

Rosemary whistled softly. "You were right, Jake. That's the same sound we heard in the temple where Zamara was trapped."

Jake barely heard her. He was enraptured with what he was doing. One to one point six. This was the secret, the code, the understanding of the ancients, of Zamara, and of Jacob Jefferson Ramsey. A perfect ratio, found in art and in nature. The xel'naga had known it. Zamara had known it. He moved, almost hypnotized, to the next crystal, and a third pure stone-voice was added to the harmony. The crystals were glowing brighter as well, the light coming from deep inside them now pulsating.

The protoss watched, their eyes wide, as an alien who housed one of their most revered minds re-enacted a scene from their long-distant past.

"This going to attract any attention?" Jake

frowned, the deep peace he found in this moment disturbed by Rosemary's practical consideration. He banished his resentment; it was a good question.

Ladranix started slightly, and the protoss keeping watch spoke in all their minds. "Beautiful and powerful though this is, my duty is to keep you safe. There is no threat."

Jake subsided back into that place as if he were diving into a deep, clear pool. He moved in a widening spiral, touching each stone and feeling it stir to life, warm and wakening beneath his hands. The song was rapturous and resonant now, and Jake didn't want it to end. But it had to—everything had an end; even things that were beautiful and timeless like the khaydarin crystals had ends—and so he reluctantly touched the last crystal and stepped back.

The humming swelled. The crystals grew brighter. A line of white energy began to form around the spiral created by the glowing crystals, encasing it in a rectangle whose ratio was the Golden Mean, one to one point six. The rectangle of earth so brightly outlined slowly began to rise, excess soil falling in a small rain, its edges smooth beneath the dirt as if cut by a laser. Behind Jake, Rosemary gasped just a little, and he felt the protoss's astonishment and awe wash over him in a warm, tingling wave.

The hole the hovering rectangle had left in the earth was no gouge, no wound in the planet's surface. It was a stairway, leading down into the heart of wonder. It looked as new, as fresh, as it had when Temlaa had beheld it so long ago; it probably had looked this way when it was first created. The walls were organic, made of earth and stone, but throughout was a striation of metal that was obviously not naturally occurring but woven in seamlessly. Glowing crystals had been embedded into the walls as well, providing illumination for any who might descend along the steps.

Jake sensed Alzadar's disquietude. Then the protoss said, querulously, "I . . . Is there no other way? This is forbidden. . . ."

Rosemary turned to him. "The only reason this area has been forbidden to you is that Ulrezaj said so," Rosemary said. "And you know for sure that Ulrezaj got you addicted to a really nasty drug, you half believe already that he lied to you, and if he is what we're sure he is, he's an abomination of pretty much everything you say you believe in. You're a templar—at least you once were. So let's go."

Jake winced, but Rosemary had done nothing but speak the truth, and it rendered Alzadar silent for a moment. The power that Ulrezaj had exerted over the Forged was strong, Jake knew, or else they would never have followed him in the first place. But it was more than the drug. Ulrezaj preyed on the deep-seated fears of the protoss—their ancient dread of abandonment, of not being good enough. Jake knew how powerful that fear was because he had been one of them. He had watched the xel'naga depart, had watched what that abandonment had done to the protoss.

He shared his thoughts. "It is an ancient wound," he

said quietly. "Because of Zamara, I saw it when it was made. Khas showed you the way—the way of unity, and trust. Honor that now, Alzadar. Trust us, as you know you can, and don't let this—this monster sway you. Aiur protoss and dark templar alike abhor what he is and what he's done. He needs you, your cooperation. Deny him that, and you begin to weaken him."

Alzadar turned to him. Jake felt himself being analyzed by a very shrewd and very strong mind. He made no attempt to shield himself or his thoughts.

"This is Jacob, not Zamara, speaking so," Alzadar said. "How is it you know exactly what to say, terran?"

Jake smiled wanly. "Because . . . I just might know you better than you know yourselves. And that knowing might be what I die for."

There was the sensation of a slight wince, and then Alzadar nodded. "I . . . will come," he said.

Jake hadn't ever given much thought to his eventual death, or the manner of it. When he did think about it, when such esoteric conversations sprang up on late nights over deep camaraderie perhaps lubricated by a smidge too much alcohol, he'd always thought that he wouldn't want to know. If he saw it coming, he had thought, he'd be so focused on that above all else that it would consume him.

It was certainly foremost in his brain now, but rather than shutting him off from life as it unfolded around him, it sharpened his desire to experience it. When Zamara had first broken the news to him a few hours ago, he'd been devastated. But at this moment he was almost hyperaware of everything. Each bite of food tasted better. The sun and moonlight on his skin were causes for wonder. The automatic functioning of his lungs, his heart, his whole body—amazing. And as he finally descended into the place where so long ago Temlaa and Savassan had trod, he was filled with a sense of awe and delight.

Zamara?

Yes, Jacob?

Whatever happens—I mean, I want to live, of course I do, everyone does, but . . . I'm glad. I'm glad you chose me. I'm glad I got to have this experience. Better to live fully than long.

The emotion that poured over him was like warm rain. It was followed by cool resolution. *I will do everything in my power, without compromising my duty, to keep you alive, Jacob Jefferson Ramsey. This, I swear.*

Rosemary glanced up at him, saw the gentle, almost childlike smile on his face, and shook her head, smiling softly herself.

CHAPTER EIGHTEEN

THE TWO PILOTS REMAINED WITH THE SHUTTLE in case they needed to escape in order to avoid being detected. They would stay in contact with the others while the party ventured down into the ancient chambers that housed xel'naga secrets. Their regret at being unable to accompany their brethren at this historically significant moment was tempered by their devotion to their duty. It was an honor to enter the chambers; but it was also an honor to serve the greater good.

Despite everything, Jake felt a surge of pleasure and excitement as he, Rosemary, Alzadar, and several of Those Who Endure descended the steps, treading in the footsteps of Temlaa and Savassan. He was not alone in his sense of awe and wonder, as he looked at the striated walls inlaid with softly glowing, jewel-toned gems. As Temlaa had done, he reached and touched them with his fingers, gasping quietly as he, as the long-dead protoss had, sensed a sort of . . . life in the very rock.

Only Rosemary, the one among them who had nothing protoss about her at all, was seemingly unmoved. The former assassin ran point for them all, along with two other protoss, hastening lightly down the steps with her rifle at the ready. Jake was grateful beyond words for her presence.

They needed to move and move swiftly, and Jake silently lamented the lost exploration opportunity. Still, when he had first "seen" this place through Temlaa's eyes, he'd never dreamed he'd be here at all. So he observed as much as he could, taking it in with his own human senses, as they quickly and quietly headed into the heart of the place. His ears strained for the sound he knew he would soon hear, the rhythmic thumping, so like a heartbeat. He smiled as finally he began to detect it.

"After so long," mused Ladranix. "Truly, the Wanderers from Afar are marvelous."

Jake didn't say anything, but he wasn't so sure. He'd seen what some of the technology could do and the desiccated bodies it had left behind. He wondered if he'd see it with his own eyes today.

"Heh," said Rosemary, speaking softly, "this is a lot faster than the way I came in."

The stairs ended, and Jake felt the cool air swirling about him. "This is the first big cavern Temlaa and Savassan encountered," he said. Rosemary waited for his nod, then moved forward. Light came up and all of them stared at what it revealed.

The beauty, the integration of the natural with the

technological, was stunning. Jake was deeply moved, and he looked around hungrily, at the softly glowing ceiling, the carved and inlaid stone formations that rose majestically from the polished floor—and over there, the control panel inlaid with small, circular, glowing gems.

"When Temlaa touched those gems in the Golden Mean order—the *ara'dor*—that wall over there opened up." He pointed. "A slab came out with six desiccated protoss bodies on it. They were covered with wiring."

He sent the memory at the speed of thought, and the protoss recoiled at the image. "Did Temlaa and Savassan ever learn why the bodies were there?" Alzadar asked.

Jake shook his head. "No. They assumed that since it was the xel'naga, they were trying to help the protoss. But . . . I gotta tell you, I'm not so sure about that."

Rosemary fidgeted slightly. "Let's keep moving," she said. "The longer we stick around here, the greater the chance someone'll find us."

Jake nodded. She was right. But he was seized with a desire to tap in the ratio, one to one point six, and see what emerged if he did so. Reluctantly, he turned to follow Rosemary. She headed off into the next chamber, but paused for a moment. Catching Jake's eye, she pointed to a smudge on the wall.

"Temlaa's markings," Jake said. Rosemary did not reply, merely regarded him with a grin that had only affection in it. Jake touched the charcoal; his finger came away blackened. He had, quite literally, touched the past.

On they went, with protoss going ahead of them and following behind, alert for any sign that might mean discovery. So far, they had been very lucky. Alzadar had told them this was a forbidden area for the Forged, and Jake dared to hope their luck would hold. The heartbeat sound increased as they went inward, following a trail of charcoal smudges and the memories of a preserver.

Jake wasn't prepared for it when he turned a corner and suddenly—there it was. He stopped dead in his tracks at the entrance to the cavernous room.

"Wow," said Rosemary softly, staring as raptly as the rest of them at the giant khaydarin crystal that hovered above them. All faces were turned up toward it, protoss and human features alike bathed in the soft glow. The crystal was a wondrous sight, and for a second it looked blurry to Jake. He blinked hard to clear his vision.

It is magnificent, Zamara agreed, *and if we are fortunate, it will mean your life.*

He smiled a little. *Then it's even more beautiful, if such a thing is possible.*

Rosemary broke the reverent stillness. "Here's your giant crystal, Prof. Now what?"

Now what indeed? Zamara wanted to get a piece of it, perhaps one of the smaller shards that he could see clustered around the base. But the crystal was a good twenty feet in the air.

"Uh . . . good question," he murmured. "Any suggestions on how we get up there?"

"It is possible that there is a mechanism to raise and lower the crystal," Ladranix said, shaking himself slightly. Like the rest of them, he was in awe of what they were seeing here.

Jake thought about what had happened to Savassan the first time the two protoss had experimented with the controls. The great mystic had almost had the very life essence sucked out of him, it had seemed to Temlaa. He grimaced. "Yeah, but I don't want to be switching things off and on randomly. Not a good idea down here."

"What is it you require?" Ladranix said. "Be specific, Jacob."

Zamara's impatience and sense of frustration washed through Jake. "She's not sure. I'm afraid this part wasn't in the script." He pointed to the small shards clustered around the base. "I think we should start with one of those."

Ladranix craned his neck, studying the crystal. "The distance is not too great for me to leap from the floor," he offered. "The crystal does not appear to have any protective field around it."

"Yeah, but your technology might not register something that advanced. No offense," Rosemary said.

"None taken," Ladranix replied.

Jake rubbed his temple, trying to ignore the throbbing pain in his head. "I . . . think that may be the only way to get to it."

Jacob, wait.

"Hang on a minute," Jake said, extending a hand to physically stop Ladranix from stepping into the room. He saw what had given Zamara pause. "Those containers—they weren't here when Temlaa and Khas were here. Those are new."

Their gaze had first gone to the crystal, drawn by its beauty and magnificence, but now that Jake had pointed out the half dozen rectangular tanks, at least three meters square each, everyone stared at them. Jake thought they looked like giant fish tanks filled with ink. He couldn't put his finger on it, but they looked sorely out of place here, their edges and unforgiving liquid darkness in disharmony with the blending of natural and artificial that surrounded them.

"This is no protoss construct. Nor do I think it is of the xel'naga," Ladranix said.

"The Xava'kai," Alzadar said quietly. "This must be their doing."

"Then we'd better find out what they've been up to," said Rosemary with her customary practicality.

Rosemary is correct. I . . . have dreadful misgivings. But we must obtain a shard of that crystal, or all is for naught.

Jake stepped forward, both fiercely curious and deeply worried. *I'm not going to like what I'm going to see, am I?*

I . . . do not believe you will.

Rosemary was already stepping forward cautiously. Jake and the protoss followed. Jake's gaze was fixed on the nearest container. Curiosity burned in him, of course. How could it not? But he was also well aware that anything that so unsettled Zamara was something he needed to have a healthy caution about so he—

Jake cried out, as did the protoss around them. Rosemary whirled, her weapon at the ready. "What is it?"

Jake had fallen to his knees and for an instant thought he would pass out at the sickening psionic buffeting he was receiving. Zamara quickly erected a barrier and he started breathing again. He looked up at the other protoss—they'd felt it too.

"The containers," Ladranix said. "It emanates from them."

All the protoss were shaken by what they had felt, but they were in control again. Jake took a deep breath. He did not want to go anywhere near those tanks.

"What do you think's in them?" asked Rosemary.

"I don't know and I sure don't want to find out," Jake said in voice that shook.

"Agreed," said Ladranix. Jake glanced at Alzadar. The former templar was highly distressed. Jake sent him a private, focused thought.

Those tanks weren't in here before, and whatever's in them is certainly not wholesome. You sense it too.

A single word, laced with pain and confusion and stubborn refusal to believe: *Xava'tor . . . ?*

"Let's get what we came for and get out of here," Rosemary said. "Those tanks even give me the creeps."

"That . . . might not be as easy as we'd like," Jake said. He pointed wordlessly. The giant crystal they had come in search of was hovering directly over one of the vats.

Rosemary swore. Jake silently echoed her sentiment. "Does the crystal have anything to do with the, uh . . . whatever's in the tanks?" she asked.

"Zamara doesn't know," Jake replied.

"So if we touch the crystal, or the vats, we could be tripping some kind of alarm. Hell, we could even be waking up whatever's in there."

Jake paled at the thought. He looked from the vat to the crystal and then to Rosemary, and shrugged helplessly. "Entirely possible. But what are we supposed to do? Zamara needs a piece of the crystal. We've come this far, we can't leave without it."

Rosemary nodded, resigned. "Well, we'll just have to be ready for anything then. Ladranix, you still think you can reach it?"

Jake realized that none of them had budged. It took almost a conscious effort to put one foot in front of the other until they were standing below the crystal—right beside one of the tanks. Jake edged closer to the open container and looked down. The blackness of the sludgy liquid was impenetrable. Faint wisps of chemically created smoke floated lazily off the surface, and he coughed.

The water rippled. Jake jumped back about a foot, staring, his heart racing. Something brushed against the side of the tank, something soft and sinuous and unspeakably *wrong*. The barrier Zamara had erected protected him from any psionic disturbance, but he didn't need that to be sickened and scared to death by the partially glimpsed *thing.*

He was not alone; everyone had taken a step back. For a moment there was silence. Then Ladranix spoke, a trained warrior, no trace of fear or worry in his thoughts.

"I can reach the crystal, although it is more challenging with the open container below me. There is no margin for error. I must leap cleanly and not fall."

"And hope you don't wake up everything in the place," Rosemary added. She, too, spoke calmly, though Jake knew she was as rattled as the rest of them. "Good luck."

Ladranix nodded. With a final squeeze to Alzadar's shoulder, he stepped forward and analyzed the task in front of him. He crouched for a moment, settling himself, and again Jake was reminded of the lethality of Ladranix's ancestors as they ran through the jungles of ancient Aiur. Ladranix sprung higher than Jake anticipated, easily reaching the hovering crystal and clinging as expertly as Little Hands the primate might.

The surface of the tank did not move.

The moment Ladranix's fingers touched the smooth surface, Jake felt his reaction. They all did. Ladranix's joy poured over them like warm honey, filled with a sense of connection, of unity, and Jake gasped with it. A heartbeat later, Zamara had erected a barrier.

You are not protoss, although in spirit you are our kin, Jacob, she said sadly. *This place—you cannot come here. Your mind cannot handle it. It would kill you.*

Jake realized that he had been close—perilously, gloriously close—to entering the Khala. The crystal had facilitated the mental journey to a degree that even Ladranix had never experienced, and Jake was fiercely envious of the protoss. He would never know such union; the closest he would ever come was that moment, seemingly so long ago now, when he had brought the human minds together for that one brief moment.

"Looks like our luck is holding," Rosemary said, providing a much-needed distraction. All she had seen, had felt, was Ladranix's successful leap to the crystal. "I guess the xel'naga never expected anyone would get here who wasn't supposed to be here. So there was no need to protect the crystal. And it looks like it has nothing to do with the creature. We caught a break."

Jake got control of himself with an effort. "Yeah," he said.

Ladranix had recovered from his surprise and now moved quickly down the length of the radiant stone toward the small cluster of smaller crystals at its base.

"This may be difficult," he said. "Jacob—I can sever a small crystal easily enough, but I will need the usage of at least one hand to hold on to the main crystal. You will have to catch it and make sure it does not fall into the vat."

Jake's stomach clenched. *I will catch the crystal, Jacob. Do not fear.*

"Okay," Jake said. "I'll try to be better at catching than I was as a kid." He stepped closer to the vat, although every instinct urged him to put as much distance between it and himself as possible.

"Careful," Rosemary warned. "Don't touch the sides at all."

He froze and realized he was only a few centimeters away from the side of the container. The sickly mist floated upward. The surface of the liquid was flat now, and he tried not to think about the thing that lurked beneath it. He swallowed hard.

"Right," he managed. He stepped back and let Zamara, with her millennia of knowledge on how to move with grace and assuredness, have control of his body.

"You may proceed, Ladranix," Zamara said. "We are ready."

Ladranix nodded, shifting his position for the best possible grip, taking his time. Jake felt him readying himself. The protoss held on with one hand and both legs, extended an arm, and closed his eyes. The golden armor around his wrist glowed softly, and suddenly the bright psi-blade flashed into existence. Ladranix bent and brought his arm down in a sure stroke. The glowing blade of focused mental energy sliced through a small shard at the base of the crystal like a knife through cheese. The severed crystal dropped, turning slowly end over end through the air, falling toward the vat.

Without his realizing it, Zamara extended Jake's arm, moving as smoothly and as easily as the protoss had, and caught the crystal in his outstretched palm.

Most immediate was the sensation of the crystal in his hand. The feelings that washed through him were startling. Shivers chased each other down his spine. Warmth flowed over him, soft as water, strong as stone. At first it was pleasant, but then the sensation grew more and more intense and Jake pulled out his shirttail to hold the crystal. He glanced at Ladranix, who had dropped down in near-silence beside him.

This is . . . extremely powerful, Zamara said, and Jake realized that she still had her shield up. The crystal had managed to penetrate it to a degree. *I hope it will be sufficient. Come, Jacob. Now we must retreat.*

"Is that gonna work?" Rosemary asked.

"She hopes so," Jake replied, tearing off a piece of his shirt and wrapping the crystal in it. He started to place the shard in one of the many pockets of his jacket, but something was already there. He took it out and stared at one of the fossilized shells from Nemaka. He'd put it in there that fateful night when he'd figured out the code, the universal ratio, that had led him to Zamara and this moment.

Jacob . . .

Jake shook his head and replaced the fossil. Hell, he might want it someday, if he made it through this alive. It would be a great souvenir. Sticking the shard in another pocket, he said, "Okay, time to get out of here."

He almost couldn't believe how lucky they had been. Those things in the vats—he shuddered, not wanting to think about them anymore. But he couldn't help it. He hadn't seen much, but even as it horrified him he found he was curious. What were they? And were they, as he suspected, Ulrezaj's doing?

He turned with the others and hurried back the way they had come. But as they passed through the first chamber they had entered, he slowed and stopped.

"Jake, what is it?" Rosemary asked, alert.

What was it indeed? There was something about this room . . . he looked around, comparing what he saw before him to what Temlaa had seen when he entered.

"There's something wrong," Jake said slowly. And then he knew. "The platforms. When Temlaa and Savassan were here, the platform was extended. It's not now. Someone's retracted it since then."

Jake looked at Alzadar, who still looked very uncomfortable. "I know how to open the alcoves."

Rosemary frowned slightly. "We just got very lucky back there, Jake. I don't like the idea of wasting time and taking chances opening cupboards around here."

Jake ignored her; ignored Zamara, who was echoing the human woman's words. His thoughts were for Alzadar.

You know what Temlaa saw, he said to Alzadar, his words for the templar alone. *Those ancient bodies could still be there. Or there could be nothing there.*

Alzadar's worry, fear, and guilt washed over Jake. *I know what you suspect . . . and I do as well. Do it. I must know. What was in the tanks could have a reasonable explanation, but . . .*

I think—I know what we're going to see there.

Gods help me, so do I.

"Jake? You listening? I said I don't think opening those things is a good idea."

"Me neither. But I think I have to."

Jake moved to the console. He looked at the rectangle of small, glowing gems, and as Temlaa had done before him, tapped out the ara'dor. The soft, sweet humming issued forth, and the crystals pulsed as each was touched in turn. When he touched the last one in the pattern, the gems all lit up, then their radiance faded.

Jake turned to the wall. Everyone mimicked him, watching intently. A glowing line appeared on the wall and moved slowly to form a rectangle of the same perfect proportions as the giant one that hid the chambers from careless eyes. Jake's heart was racing. The platform's probably empty, he told himself.

It was not.

But what he saw, despite its gruesomeness, filled him with relief. Six ancient bodies lay there. They looked exactly like the ones Temlaa had found. Jake exhaled and opened his mouth to say something when Alzadar's mental cry pierced him to the bone."

"Rukashal! Tervoris . . . Azramith . . . !"

The bodies weren't ancient after all. They were protoss that Alzadar and the others had known.

"The Xava'kai . . ." breathed Rosemary. "Guess this is what Ulrezaj was doing with his loyal followers when he took them away."

Alzadar rushed forward to the desiccated corpse of what had once been a friend, as if it wasn't already too late and somehow he could be rescued. Quick as a thought, Ladranix raced after him. He seized his fellow templar and shoved him away from the platform.

"Let me help him!" Alzadar cried. He struggled in Ladranix's grasp and to Jake's shock twisted free. Maddened with grief and outrage, his hand closed on one of the bodies.

An eerie, otherworldly wailing shattered Jake's ears. Alzadar had rung the dinner bell.

"Damn it!" Rosemary yelped, shooting the protoss an angry glance. "Let's get out of here!"

Ladranix bodily lifted Alzadar. Alzadar shook his head, recovering himself, and with one heartbroken glance back at the corpses of his murdered friends, rushed to flee with the others. As they raced toward safety, not too far now, Alzadar cried, "They are coming! The Xava'kai—they are coming. Do not shoot them, I beg you!"

No chance, then. Jake could hear them now, running swiftly and almost, but not quite, silently down the corridors. He expected Rosemary to ignore Alzadar's plea. To his surprise, she scowled, and while she did not drop her weapon, neither did she fire. Ladranix and the other Shel'na Kryhas closed in around the two humans, forming a protective ring with their bodies.

The whispering sound of running protoss increased, and suddenly there they were, moving with shocking speed, their lambent eyes fixed fiercely on Jake. Seconds later they were surrounded. There were many of them, true, but not nearly as many as Jake had expected. The thought chilled him as he realized that although the Forged had once had far greater numbers than Those Who Endure, the very being they called the Benefactor had been slowly, stealthily decreasing their numbers, faster even than the zerg would have.

Jake reached out to try to touch their minds, but they were shuttered to him. Through the circle of protoss that protected him, he stared at the others, their faces composed, their minds unavailable to him, and wondered if they would even give him a chance to explain things.

One of them stepped forward. "Alzadar, it is good to see you alive and well. And you have brought us the preserver. The Xava'tor will be pleased."

Before Jake could even form a coherent thought, Alzadar had stepped away from the other protoss and stood before his leader. He was tall and straight, his head high, and Jake realized that even if he hadn't known Alzadar had been a templar, he would have pegged him as one.

"I am alive, but not well, Felanis. For I have beheld the atrocities committed by the one we call a benefactor."

Jake's mind was suddenly filled with the images they had recently seen—the mysterious tanks in the crystal chamber, the desiccated corpses of former

Tal'darim. He realized what Alzadar had done—shared that image with the rest of the Forged. Some of them still guarded their reactions, foremost among them the seemingly implacable Felanis. Others seemed stunned, and he realized that even the Xava'kai hadn't known the end results of their labor on the Xava'tor's behalf.

Alzadar suddenly stumbled back, reeling as if from a physical blow. "You—knew," he said. "Felanis—you knew all along what Ulrezaj was!"

Some of the Forged shifted uneasily, while others ducked back, literally recoiling in horror. So unsettled were they that they broadcast their thoughts rather than directing them privately.

"These images that Alzadar shows us . . . it is true then?" one of them cried.

"An archon comprised of the souls of dark templar? Those we shunned and cast out?"

Jake wondered if the betrayed Forged would turn on their leader. Felanis appeared completely unconcerned. He drew himself up to his full height. Jake felt dwarfed by him, and even the other protoss standing beside him, all except Alzadar, looked diminished. When he spoke, he addressed not those who had asked the questions, but Alzadar himself.

"Ulrezaj is not a monster, but a demigod. He offered me the power to save myself and those who followed me. Who followed him, who understood his vision and believed in it. Ulrezaj and the being he serves are stronger than you can possibly imagine."

"Whoa, whoa—Ulrezaj has a boss?" exclaimed Rosemary, looking alarmed.

"The Sundrop has made us slaves to the very worst the dark templar represent!" Alzadar cried. "And I will not turn over a preserver to him—or to you!"

In his mind, Jake heard the silent command: *Go. Many of them are as stunned and sickened as I am. I will do all I can to convince them to turn on Felanis. I will hold them off—for as long as I may. Get Zamara to safety.*

Jacob, there is another way out—let me lead! And to everyone else, she sent, *Behind us—we will retreat. Half of you stay here and assist Alzadar. He has earned our aid.*

Zamara surged into Jake's mind. As if the movements were choreographed, half of the Shel'na Kryhas whirled around and, using only their powerful bodies, attacked the startled Forged, who initially seemed too stunned to block their passage. Jake and Rosemary followed as they fled back the way they had come, racing through rooms that no longer appeared enticingly mysterious or beautiful but now seemed like an elaborately laid trap. Explorer though he was, he'd seen enough of this place. He'd seen too much of it. All he wanted to do was jump into the small protoss ship, take off, land at the warp gate, and head to Shakuras. The horrible, otherworldly wailing sound continued, and Jake's head throbbed to its beat. Oh, God, it hurt.

They were pursued. More protoss dropped back to fight the Forged, buying Jake and Rosemary precious time. Jake was in good shape, but the protoss were faster, and it both moved and irritated him that they slowed their pace so some could bring up the rear. Rosemary was running flat out, her rifle clutched in her hands. He took the stairs two at a time, following Ladranix as they raced toward the surface, to the little ship that was—

—melted.

Jake almost slammed into Ladranix as he stumbled to a halt, peering past the suddenly still protoss to stare, disbelieving, at the pile of steaming metal and ichor that had once been a protoss ship.

Jacob!

Jake tore his eyes from the vessel to see what the protoss saw. Dozens—no, hundreds—of zerg covered the area. They were frighteningly silent; silent, so that no one could have heard them from down below and been warned to their presence.

Numbly, Jake's eyes roved over the carpet of insectoid, monstrously quiet forms. They stared back at him with soulless black eyes, some with more than two in what passed for heads. Antennae and multiple limbs waved as the zerg waited.

They were beasts brought to heel, dogs obeying a master. Yet that wasn't right; they hadn't been much more than wandering creatures, now and then turning on the protoss, more for sport than anything else. But not anymore.

Which meant that they were being controlled and directed. But who—

"Oh, damn it to hell," snapped Rosemary, breaking the awful stillness. "You again. Thought I'd killed you, you bastard."

"And hello to you too, Trouble," came a smooth, rich, cultured voice. A voice Jake had thought forever silenced. He turned from the zerg to stare at their master.

Ethan Stewart.

CHAPTER NINETEEN

IT WAS—AND YET IT WASN'T—ETHAN. THE FORM that stood before Jake bore Ethan's features, but in every other respect he looked more kin to the creatures he commanded. Jake felt the blood drain from his face as he realized that Ethan must have somehow been infested, and yet not been completely subverted. His skin was gray-green, his head bald and smooth, and he had two too many arms. The extra appendages culminated in scythelike blades that twitched as if itching for something to slice in half.

Ethan threw back his head and laughed. "You've led us on a merry chase, both of you," he said. Jake could hardly believe that ice-cream-smooth voice was issuing from that being. It seemed more wrong than Ethan's extra limbs or green skin or—yeah, those were scales down his back, Jake was pretty sure.

"'Us'?" Rosemary challenged. Her rifle was up and trained on him. "And don't worry, this time I won't stop firing until I'm sure you're dead."

"Us," Ethan confirmed. "My queen and myself. She's very anxious to make your acquaintance. Both of you. She sent me to come fetch you and bring her before you."

The guy's in love, Jake realized with a sick jolt. There was something in Ethan's voice, a slight catch—Jake knew a smitten man when he heard him. Stewart had never spoken in that tone of voice about or to Rosemary.

"But don't worry, Trouble. Despite the fact that you tried to murder me, and although my heart now belongs to her, I made her promise to leave you out of this. That is, if the professor cooperates."

The mutated but still oddly handsome—still oddly human—face turned to Jake. "How about it, Professor? I'll spare Rosemary and all your little protoss friends if you come along without a fight."

To his surprise, Jake found himself laughing. "I don't know who this queen of yours is, but anything that controls the zerg, or frankly, you, I don't trust as far as I can throw."

It was what the protoss had been waiting for—Jake's answer. He saw them ready themselves for combat, dropping into battle position, bringing weapons up, and then waiting, motionless, for the moment to explode into deadly, beautiful motion.

Jacob . . . you will not win this one. There are hundreds of zerg.

I know. He was surprised at how calm he felt. *And I know what you have to do. I only wish I knew what this secret was.*

I am sorry it must end so. I know this queen he speaks of, and she will use my knowledge to her own ends.

Jake lifted his weapon, a single pistol. It seemed so pitifully, pathetically tiny. But it was all he had. *Do what you have to do, Zamara. I'm ready.*

At that moment, several dozen zerg exploded. A horrible stench of ichor and feces filled the air, and liquids and soft pulpy bits rained down on them. Jake instinctively ducked and covered his head.

"What the—" His first thought was that somehow Those Who Endure had rounded up more ships, but when he risked a quick glance skyward he recognized the vessels as Dominion. Even as he put two and two together, he heard a voice inside his head. After speaking telepathically with protoss for so long, this contact seemed graceless and labored.

My name is Devon Starke. I work for Valerian. We've come to help you.

Help me? Valerian was going to kill me!

That was a dreadful misunderstanding. His Excellency knew nothing about your captivity until the Gray Tiger *was discovered adrift in space, its crew dead.*

In the Khala, Jake knew, no one could lie. But even among the protoss, one could lie with thoughts. And humans certainly could. Jake thought an angry, ancient Anglo-Saxon word and lifted his pistol. Rosemary and the other protoss were already attacking the zerg. Ethan had been completely distracted by the abrupt appearance of the Dominion vessels, and all was chaos.

I understand your doubt, but would you rather die at the

hands of the zerg? You know that is the only other possible outcome. Let us send you a ship.

Jacob. Zamara's thoughts overrode Starke's. *Tell him you agree.*

What?

Do it! Tell him to send a vessel large enough for all of us. Don't waste time negotiating anything else. Trust me!

Jake did trust Zamara, even though she had hijacked his brain and body, even though what she was doing to him was likely going to kill him. The protoss were the most honorable people he had ever known, and Zamara's integrity shone like a beacon. He sensed that she knew exactly what she was doing. And so he obeyed.

All right. Send down a ship that's big enough for me and the protoss. We're all getting out of here alive.

Done. We will clear an area for the ship to land.

Starke kept his word on that, at least. The strafing attacks narrowed to a small area, and within seconds a landing strip was created.

If it were not for the distraction caused by the terran ships, Jake mused, his friends would all be dead by this point and he would be in the tender-loving care of Ethan Stewart and his zerg pets. Even as it was, they were having a tough time holding off the waves that came at them. After his halfhearted attempt to get Jake to submit without a fight, Ethan was nowhere to be seen, and even as she fired, Rosemary muttered curses against her former lover.

There were several bright glints in the sky, denoting

ships taking the battle off-planet. Two of the glints grew brighter and larger and, sure enough, a battlecruiser and a dropship came into view, surrounded by fighters, which took most of the damage. The battlecruiser landed first, disgorging its contents of siege tanks and marines in full combat gear. The dropship followed. Slowly, it settled down on the uneven, rocky soil. The door slid open and more marines spilled out, firing as they came. The air was filled with the outraged shrieks and squeals of dying zerg and the rat-a-tat sounds of automatic weapons fire.

"Let's go!" Jake yelled. "Everyone in!"

Firing as they went, Jake, Rosemary, and the protoss raced for the vessel. Jake had no idea what Zamara's plan was, but she clearly had one. Did she truly think Valerian could be trusted? Was the whole thing really just, as the telepath who had to be a ghost had whispered in his thoughts, a misunderstanding?

Jake darted inside and swore silently. The ship was indeed large enough to accommodate all the protoss, but only just. They crowded in, pressing in close, packed so tightly they could barely breathe. Flattened against a wall, Jake waited for the plan to reveal itself. A second later, it did. The instant after the last protoss had wedged himself into the dropship, Rosemary hit a control and the doors slammed shut. The pilot glanced back, frowning, and was about to make some kind of protest when his face impacted with the butt end of Rosemary's rifle. Jake winced as the man's nose crunched under the metal and he toppled out of his seat. He could not get used to this violence. But even so, he was proud of Rosemary for not simply shooting the pilot. Perhaps she was mellowing.

She grabbed the unconscious man by the shirt, hauled him off, and slid into the seat. "Hang on, everyone," she yelled. The ship took off. Jake grabbed onto the back of a seat; Rosemary's liftoff wasn't the smoothest he'd seen from her.

"It'll take 'em a couple of minutes to figure out we've hijacked the ship, and until then I'm playing along. But once they catch on . . . well, you better hang on."

It was one of the most incongruous things Jake had ever seen—eighteen protoss completely out of their element, crammed into the terran space vessel. They looked sorely out of place, like a crystal on a junk heap.

"We got company," Rosemary said. "That was fast. Valerian doesn't want to lose you again, Professor." Jake peered at the console. Sure enough, already six Wraiths had floated in to virtually enclose them—on each side, in front of and behind them, and one below and above them.

"Hang on," Rosemary said, and two seconds later Jake and the protoss were tossed about as she forcefully slammed into the Wraith on their left.

"Rosemary, what—" Anything else Jake might have said was silenced as she again rammed one of the small, one-man fighters.

Professor Ramsey, what are you doing? Devon Starke

again, in his brain. *Cease this attack at once! Rosemary Dahl will listen to you!*

Jake effortlessly erected a barrier around his thoughts so that the mental conversation went one way and yelled to Rosemary, "They know it's you."

"Good" was her response, followed by another ramming of a Wraith.

This must cease or we will be forced to open fire.

When he relayed this to Rosemary, she shot back, "They might fire on us, but they won't try to kill us. Both Valerian and Ethan want you alive. You're too precious to risk serious injury to. Dropships can take whatever they throw at us, and their Wraiths are getting the worse end of the deal right now."

Wham. Jake's teeth rattled in his skull as Rosemary sought to prove her point. Then the dropship rocked violently and he realized that Devon was as good as his word. They were indeed being fired upon.

Professor, please—we truly have no wish to harm you in any way. But you cannot be permitted to elude us again. As a scientist, surely you understand what is at stake!

It was Devon and Valerian who didn't understand. Jake's own life was what was at stake. That and some profound, universe-rattling secret that Zamara had yet to let him in on. Both were more important to him than satisfying the idle curiosity of an emperor's son.

The attacks increased. Smoke started to seep into the cabin, and Jake and Rosemary coughed. "We're almost there," Rosemary said, her voice raw from coughing, her eyes watering from the acrid smoke.

"Which is good, 'cause this thing won't hold out much longer."

Another shot and the dropship listed badly. Jake wasn't sure he could hold out much longer either.

His queen was not pleased. Her anger seared Ethan as, through the eyes of her consort, she watched her quarry escape. Neither he nor she cared about the dozens of zerg who were reduced to stains on the Aiur landscape, blown to bits, impaled by steel spikes, or burnt to crisp, smoking corpses. Her supply of zerg was infinite.

Her patience was not.

"How did Valerian find them?"

"My queen, I know not," Ethan said. "But Ramsey shall not escape me a third time." They were desperate words, but they were the only ones he could muster. If Jake Ramsey and Rosemary Dahl had allied with the Dominion after all, despite everything they had seen from Valerian, then there would in truth be little Ethan could do to recover the archeologist. He had traveled here as the other zerg did, safely inside an overlord, having no need of the technological assistance of a ship despite the ability to operate one. Now he cast about desperately for a way to follow and stop Jake's escape. A swift mental command brought a mutalisk hastening toward him, and with the grace granted him by an extra set of limbs and his vastly increased strength, Ethan climbed swiftly atop it. It and its companions rose into the air, hell-bent on destroying the ships that were escorting the dropship that contained his queen's desire.

And then he laughed aloud as the dropship slammed into the Wraith next to it.

"Ah, Trouble," he said, his voice nostalgic. He should have known better. Jake and Rosemary were not going with Valerian. They'd tricked the young Heir Apparent, and were heading toward the only place on the planet where they could possibly make an escape: the warp gate.

He directed his creatures there, and secured his grip on the mutalisk as he flew to join them.

"Okay, here we—wow." Rosemary's voice was subdued. "Looks like the zerg beat us here. Some of them, anyway."

Jake strained to see. From his position, he couldn't see much, so he brushed Rosemary's mind and saw what she had seen. A battle had been fought here four years ago, almost the same one that would be fought now—escaping protoss against determined, directed zerg. The debris of that battle was everywhere, but at some point, either then or in the last few hours, the protoss had used their own fallen vessels and even zerg corpses as bulwarks. The area around the warp gate was now at least somewhat defensible, but Jake saw with a wrench in his gut that many of Those Who Endure had fallen while awaiting his and Zamara's arrival. Few were left, and more and more zerg were coming.

My heart aches too for my fallen brethren, Zamara said, *but far, far worse than this awaits if my mission fails, Jacob.*

While the dropship had plenty of armor, which had kept them safe thus far, it had no weapons. Other than whatever handheld weapons were in the lockers, they were bringing the embattled Shel'na Kryhas no new ways to hold back the increasing tide of zerg.

That's not quite right, Jacob. Valerian wishes you alive, which means that the Dominion will inadvertently aid our escape.

Even as she spoke the words in his mind, Jake knew that they were true. Valerian wasn't about to let him become zerg chow. The ship landed hard. Jake braced himself for the hell that awaited them outside.

"Damn!" Valerian pounded his fist on the desk, and Whittier jumped. "Starke, can't you bring them down?"

"Negative, sir, not without significant risk to Ramsey. Dropships are built precisely to withstand attack. Dahl knows this and is ramming the Wraiths quite severely. We're not sure where she thinks she can run." Valerian ran a hand through his golden hair, thinking furiously. Was Dahl running away from capture or toward something else? She had sent Ramsey's medical information to him early on, and Valerian had spent many an hour analyzing it. He'd seen the initial spate of abnormal and seemingly uncontrolled cell division in Ramsey's brain—bad news no matter how one looked at it—and suspected that the protoss in Jake's head had taken the professor to Aiur to aid him. Were they heading there now? Or just trying to flee from Valerian's pursuit?

It didn't matter. Healthy or not, Jake had to be captured as soon as possible.

"Ramsey must not be harmed; that's the top priority here. Direct all forces toward eliminating the zerg, and stay in touch with Ramsey. You have to convince him that we're not going to harm him. Because—damn it, it's the truth."

Starke nodded. "Yes, sir. I know it. But one can lie in a telepathic link, and Ramsey knows it. The evidence is against you."

Valerian sighed. "Do what you can, Starke. Neutralize the protoss and capture Ramsey alive. Do whatever you have to do to achieve those goals."

Rosemary leaped out first, firing with seeming abandon but with absolute precision. The others closed in around Jake, shielding him and Zamara with their bodies and their weapons as they fought. Jake felt close to losing it. All around him he heard the screams of dying zerg, smelled the stench of burning bodies and blood. He was pressed tight against the protoss. Two of them even linked arms with him and when he stumbled, dragged him forward until he could get his feet underneath himself again.

He couldn't even see where they were heading, as the protoss all towered above him. But he trusted them, and he trusted Zamara, and he let them propel him forward. He craned his neck, and through the haze of smoke he saw the outline of the warp gate high above him. Twin tides of hope surged through him—his own, and that of Zamara.

How do these things function? he asked Zamara.

The gates are xel'naga technology. Each gate is able to connect to any other active gate, unless it has been programmed not to do so. When the protoss fled four years ago, Fenix and the others who chose to stay behind disabled the gate, so that it could not open on Shakuras. Some zerg had already gotten through; more, and they would have destroyed Shakuras as surely as they did Aiur, and that could not be permitted to happen.

The cocoon of enclosing protoss bodies parted and Jake stared, horrified, at the controls. Or rather, what was left of them.

Looks like they did more than disable it.

Zamara's despair flooded him for just a second, before she exerted her usual rigid control. He didn't need to be a protoss to know it looked bad. It looked as if someone had wanted to make sure that the gate would never be reactivated, for the controls had been physically damaged.

I stood here on that day, Ladranix said, *with my old friend Fenix, and our new friend James Raynor.*

Jake opened to the memory Ladranix was sharing with him.

"We must disable the gate," Fenix said. "We cannot permit more zerg to go through."

Raynor threw him a glance. "Buddy, that's the only way off this place for us."

Fenix nodded. "Yes, it is." Nothing more needed to be said or even thought. Neither of them would put his own life before those of the innocent protoss fighting for survival even now, both on Auir and on Shakuras, both traditional protoss and so-called "dark" protoss. Ladranix watched them both, and understood why Fenix thought of Raynor as a protoss in spirit, if not in flesh.

He did not see what Fenix did. He turned to fight against the fresh wave of snapping, chittering creatures who crawled as thoughtlessly over the bodies of their own fallen as they did over the blasted soil of a once-fertile world. But he did turn to see what happened when Raynor said, "My turn to contribute," and lifted his rifle.

Jake saw in his mind's eye, as clearly as if he had witnessed it himself, what part of the console exactly Raynor melted to bits, what kind of weapon he used, and for how long he fired.

I came here planning on and capable of reopening the gate—of reprogramming it to open onto Shakuras. But I cannot accomplish both that and repair the physical damage to this in time, Zamara admitted bitterly. *As it stands now, the zerg will be upon us by then.*

Jake couldn't believe it. Had they come so far, endured so much, to be stopped by one human's well-meaning and indeed necessary blast to the controls? Zamara's knowledge rippled through the protoss. They simply nodded, then turned to the seemingly ceaseless wave of zerg that, despite the onslaught from Valerian's troops, were now beginning to gain ground.

If protoss knew nothing else, Jake thought with mingled grief, helplessness, and respect, they knew how to look death in the face.

CHAPTER TWENTY

IT WAS HARD TO SEE. THE CRUSHING DESPAIR was wrenching his gut and causing his eyes to fill. Jake blinked quickly, his fists balling, good old human stubbornness surging to the fore amidst the stoic protoss acceptance all around him. No. There had to be another way, there had to be a—

His gaze fell on a tiny figure, dwarfed by the towering protoss, firing and reloading with a grim determination.

"Rosemary," he breathed. Maybe—could she . . . He turned without thinking and charged toward where she stood, feet braced on the body of a slain zergling, firing with deadly effect into the surging tide. He sent the thought quickly, naturally, and showed her what had been done four years ago.

If you got any parts, I bet Zamara and I could fix it, she shot back in his mind.

Just as she lowered her rifle, Ladranix sent them all a chilling message. "More are coming."

Sure enough, Jake could just make out in the distance a rolling dust ball that seemed to reach up to the sky. Of course. It wouldn't have taken a genius to figure out the only place Jake would have gone, and Ethan was far from a fool. He had of course immediately redirected his zerg, and now here they were closing in, and a figure, tiny in the distance now, was perched atop one of them.

"I swear, next time I'm putting the muzzle right against his temple," Rosemary said. Nonetheless, despite her deeply personal grudge, she tossed her rifle to one of the unarmed protoss, jumped down from the embankment of zerg bodies, and hurried over to Jake. Another protoss came with her, and Jake realized that they were communicating quickly and privately. Rosemary, it seemed, had lost most of her reluctance to have her mind read. Perhaps it was only the direness of the situation, but Jake was glad of it.

"Okay," the young woman said. "What do you need me to do, Zamara?"

Zamara moved into the forefront, linking swiftly with Rosemary. Jake was not technically inclined at the best of times, and now he paid scant attention to them, more worried about the fighting raging about him.

Any warp gate can open onto any other, Zamara was telling Rosemary, explaining it to her as she had to Jake. *What Fenix did was program it so that it would not be able to open onto Shakuras, so the zerg could not follow and devastate that world as they had Aiur. What James Raynor did . . .*

. . . was physically damage the controls so that they'd be extra-hard for anyone else to tinker with. Rosemary's thoughts as she examined the panel, sharp and pure and bright, stood in contrast with Zamara's almost muted, rich mental voice. *Not a traditional panel, is it? I wonder if I can do something to jump-start it . . . maybe bypass or reroute the pathways to make a direct connection. It seems almost to be growing in there. Wait . . . I think I understand now. . . .*

Jake's body was standing beside Rosemary as she and Zamara worked together. He watched as he placed his hands on the surface of the portal. It was dark now, and it reminded him somewhat of the xel'naga temple whose mystery had set his feet on the path that had led him here. He was not a religious man, but he felt a deep prayer welling up within him that soon this surface would thrum to new life, that his friends would make it through, that this mission would succeed—that he would live.

Rosemary needed no more handholding. She was using tools fashioned from crystals as if she had been born with them in her small hands, and her face was knotted in concentration. It was a delicate task, and while Rosemary could be a blunt instrument, she could also be surprisingly deft. Now that Zamara had given her an understanding of the physical aspect of the xel'naga and protoss technology, that knowledge, together with an intuitive grasp of how a human would choose to target something he didn't quite understand, made her an effective partner. Zamara's powerful intelligence was now freed up to the more esoteric task of . . . awakening the gate.

Jake watched as Zamara directed her psionic energies into the crystals that seemed to lie at the very heart of xel'naga technology, almost calling to them softly. Again he was reminded of how alive the walls of the temple had felt beneath his fingers the closer to the green center he went. He did not think he would ever understand xel'naga technology.

Jake turned his consciousness away from the project and toward the immediate situation. He knew that neither Zamara nor Rosemary could rush, but at the same time, he was painfully aware that time would soon be running out.

It ran out faster than he expected.

It was the sudden stillness that first alerted him that something was wrong. His physical eyes were on the task before him—Zamara's task—but even she paused and lifted Jake's head for a long, searching moment. The zerg, who hitherto had seemed as ceaseless and undefeatable as the incoming tide, suddenly stilled as one. Jake/Zamara sensed that the protoss were puzzled, but seized the opportunity to make fresh new inroads, and the Dominion ceased its battling not one whit. The zerg simply stood there, frozen in place, letting themselves be shot to pieces or vaporized.

What the . . . ?

And then the first scout saw it. The image sped throughout the protoss via the Khala at the speed of a single thought. Jake's mind all but seized up at it, and even Zamara reeled.

It was enormous. It was darkness visible, like Satan's hell from Milton's *Paradise Lost,* a swirling blackness that yet was somehow radiant. It glowed and crackled, and even in a simple mental picture Jake instinctively knew that the power the thing exuded and controlled would obliterate every living being gathered at the warp gate.

Ulrezaj. *Here.*

Somehow Jake had thought the abomination safely far away, mentally controlling and enslaving the Forged—he understood that term now—and having them be his Xava'kai, making them do his dirty, obscene work for him. Ulrezaj had been a threat, yes, if he had sent assassins to kill Zamara for what she knew. But for some reason Jake had never thought the monster within striking range, had never thought of him as a real and present danger like Valerian or Ethan or the zerg.

Now Rosemary, too, had stopped. Her blue eyes were wide, and for the first time since Jake had known her she looked scared. He didn't blame her. He was terrified.

He could see the monster with his own eyes now, a huge swirl of glowing darkness on the horizon like a cancer.

Something brushed Jake's thoughts, a tiny, almost pathetic breeze of hope amidst this flood of despair and inevitability.

"We are coming, Jacob. Not all of us are his Hands."

"Alzadar!" he cried. The news rippled throughout the protoss and indeed, a few seconds later, six small protoss ships appeared in the skies. Their appearance seemed to rouse the zerg from their paralysis. Perhaps Ethan sensed that this new threat was the greatest, or perhaps he knew that Ulrezaj, unlike himself or Valerian, had come to kill rather than capture. Regardless, the zerg turned as one and began to move to attack Ulrezaj. So did the Dominion vessels.

The giant dark archon, comprised of not merely two powerful dark templar but seven, rebuffed their efforts as if the attacking zerg and Dominion ships were mere flies. The air shivered as if a heat wave pulsed through it and fully a dozen mutalisks went down, surrounded by the dark energy consuming them. Another blast of dark psionic energy rippled forth on the earth, and zerg fell over like dominos tipped by a careless hand. The Forged themselves were not engaging their former master in battle; they were simply trying to make it to the warp gate. Ulrezaj, however, was not inclined to let them escape so easily. Jake was rocked by pain as he helplessly watched two of Alzadar's tiny ships be destroyed before they could safely land behind the front line of the battle—two ships filled to capacity and beyond with the Forged, who had resisted the power of a dreadful drug and their own deep-seated pain and fears to follow Alzadar and come to help save what remained of their people.

Inside him, he felt Zamara stir unhappily. *Every time a protoss dies, his or her memories become my own. Each thread is a glorious part of a complex tapestry. It is sometimes difficult to manage . . . so many at one time from one place.*

Jake was humbled—by the preserver, by the protoss, by everything around him. Damn it, they weren't going to die here! He felt Zamara return to her task at hand, although he knew that she and indeed all of them now thought it a futile gesture. As futile a gesture as what Adun had attempted, trying to shelter the dark templar, to teach them skills they could never possibly—

Adun.

Jake felt a shiver run down his spine. *Zamara . . . you said you showed me these things for a reason. Adun's story—it was to show that the protoss are really one people, and that their split was due to fear and ignorance.*

Yes. I am taking you to Shakuras, the world that the dark templar settled after they were expelled from Aiur so callously. You needed to understand the division, and the attempt to heal it.

No, more than that. Don't you see? We can fight this dark archon after all! We can do what the dark templar did!

He thought of the psionic storms unleashed by the dark templar, the raging, out-of-control energies that had whirled across Aiur's surface so long ago, attracted by mental energy and destroying everything in their wake.

Jacob—the powers the dark templar wielded are not known to traditional protoss. Those Who Endure are not dark templar.

What about the Forged? The Sundrop—sure it was used to keep the Tal'darim docile, but it also cut them off from the Khala, remember? It changed their personalities. Altered them. What if—what if that was what Ulrezaj was going for? What if he was actively manipulating them to make them of better use to him in those experiments? Preparing them somehow?

. . . Such a thing had not occurred to me. I will converse with Alzadar. If he will let me probe his mind . . .

Jake waited, fidgeting. A few seconds later Zamara was again in his thoughts.

Your theory is correct. Alzadar's brain chemistry has been altered—permanently or not, we do not know. I also spoke with some of the others who are still actively addicted to the Sundrop. Their chemistry is even more greatly altered.

He fanned their hatred and fear of the dark templar . . . and all the time he was trying to turn the Forged into them, Jake said.

So it would seem. But they are untrained and undisciplined, and the psionic storms that so devastated Aiur in Adun's time were uncontrolled.

Maybe—the storms would go right to that thing out there? Jake asked. *Directed or not?*

Yes. Yes, it could work—but there is one more thing you need to know if you are to teach the Forged and Those Who Endure to do such a thing.

We don't have time!

We do. We must.

And before he fully understood what was happening, Zamara was unfolding yet another memory in his mind while she and Rosemary worked desperately to repair the warp gate.

It was wrong. Jake knew it, Adun knew it, the templar knew it. And yet wrong as it was, it was still better than watching dark templar corpses stiffening in the green light filtered through the canopy. At least the dark templar were still alive to be exiled.

Anger and a great sense of hurt rolled off the assembled Conclave in waves. Mixed with it was a partial sense of satisfaction and relief—at least the heretics would no longer endanger the protoss people with their refusal to link with the Khala. Jake watched grimly as dozens—hundreds—of the banished protoss moved slowly up the ramp of the curving, luminous vessel that was the last ship left behind when the Wanderers from Afar departed this world. It had taken the protoss centuries to even get inside the xel'naga ship, and it still held mysteries. The ship had been the template for much protoss technology, and it was a testament to how strongly the Conclave believed they were right that they would surrender such a prize in order to be rid of the dark templar.

Raszagal was boarding now. She lifted her robes so as not to stumble, her head held high, as always. He saw her pride, even now, although as she was not and would never be in the Khala, he could not feel it.

Raszagal, I am so sorry, *Jake sent, for her and her alone.*

She turned to regard him. Do not be. You did what you could. This, we know.

And then—

"Adun! We expressly forbade you to attend!"

Jake felt his friend's thoughts, as calm as those of Kortanul were agitated. Adun mounted the platform on which the Conclave members stood and sketched a brief bow. "I know, Judicator. And yet again, I respectfully disobey. These people trusted me. It is my duty to see them off safely."

"Duty! What does a templar who deliberately deceives the Conclave know of duty? You pollute the word!"

The little line of refugees had come to a halt. Every one of the dark templar was looking at Kortanul and Adun. Tension was in their bodies and their eyes. The templar guards began to move forward, and Jake sent a thought to halt them.

"Please move aside, Kortanul," Adun said gently. "I ask to escort them onto the ship, and to see them safely launched. Nothing more."

"You ask too much!" Jake could hardly believe it, but the judicator, a full head shorter and much less powerful than Adun, actually shoved the high templar off the platform. Adun executed a graceful turn as he fell, landing smoothly. An uproar went up from the other Conclave at Kortanul's actions and their thoughts washed over Jake. Whatever Adun had done, painful and wrong as it was, the Conclave knew he believed it to be right, just as the Conclave believed their decree of banishment to be right. Lost in his outrage, Kortanul had gone too far for even the Conclave.

"Touch him not!" Raszagal's youthful broadcast slammed into Jake. She was stronger than even he had thought, and he had not thought he underestimated her.

"He has shown nothing but the best of what we can achieve! He—"

Kortanul, twisted with zealotry so violent that the rest of the Conclave recoiled from it, whirled on Raszagal. Jake saw the girl stumble and fall to her knees. At the same moment, pain from several of the Conclave washed through him as the more adept dark templar responded. Jake sent the order to fall back and protect Adun and the Conclave. As his templar guards fell back, the Conclave members, now convinced that their own lives as well as the protoss as a race were in danger, began to attack. Jake saw several dark templar fall and he saw the panic begin to spread through them. Their untrained mental powers were no match for the combined might of the Conclave. But they were still a very real danger. If in their defense, one or more lost control again, it would surely create a psionic storm.

Adun said nothing, merely rushed forward, arms spread out, head thrown back, eyes closed. A radiant blue glow emanated from his wrists, and then moved to encase his entire body. Such Jake had seen before; such, he had even done. But what happened next—

The glow expanded like smoke, moving forward to encompass the now-panicky line of dark templar who, until the outbreak of violence, had been walking toward the ship. Now they were running full out, and the cloud of blue settled down upon them and embraced them.

What was he doing? How was he doing it? Jake tentatively inclined his thoughts to Adun's and was sent reeling backward. Not from an overt attack, but from the very power—and the very unfamiliarity—of what his friend was somehow managing to do.

Jake sensed the energies that were familiar to him through centuries of focusing his powerful mind. And there was something else, something strange—familiar yet completely alien to him.

"Both . . . he's using both types of energies—the familiar energy of the templar and the . . . shadow-stuff of the dark templar!"

"Precisely."

"But—if a protoss had already used the dark templar energy—why is it so feared and shunned and—"

"Watch."

Recovering, Jake could only stare at his friend in awe. What was Adun managing to do? What kind of breakthrough in psionic power had he just achieved?

The dark templar were seemingly as confused as anyone, but they understood protection, and they moved forward into the vessel. When the last ones had nearly made it through—a party of elderly protoss and small children—the curving, graceful doors of the ancient xel'naga vessel began to close.

Adun stood, back arched, hands up to the sky, eyes now open. He was swathed entirely in the radiant blue cloud, and as Jake watched, Adun's armor, too, began to glow.

And his hands . . . and his face—

Blue light everywhere, glorious, intense, too much to behold. Jake had to look away but he could not bear to, could only stare in stunned disbelief and wonder as Adun himself glowed like a star in the night sky, bright, magnificently bright; but stars that burned so brightly always—

"—burn themselves out," Jake breathed.

Bright, too bright; Jake squinted, but he saw what happened. Saw, and for the rest of his life wondered at it. Tried to understand it, and failed.

Adun's form glowed as brightly, as truly, as a star falling to the ground, transient in its glory, but breathtaking. For a moment, the light came from him, but as Jake watched, it began to consume the executor. Before Jake's horrified gaze his friend began to disintegrate. And a moment later, he was gone.

A mental cry of shock and anguish went up among the assembled templar and Conclave. And although Jake did not feel it, he knew that the dark templar were stunned and confused and in pain as well. The blue glow that had taken Adun with it when it departed was gone, and after a few moments, some of the appalled Conclave channeled their grief toward the beings that, Jake realized, they believed had caused his death.

"Go!" he shouted to the dark templar. "Hurry!"

They snapped out of their paralysis and the last few ducked quickly through the door before further harm could befall them. The door closed right before the first rush of angry Conclave had made it up the ramp, at once sealing the exiles safely away from the anger of their former brethren and entombing them. Their destiny lay in the hands of the gods now.

Nothing was left of Adun's body. Jake reached into the Khala, frantically searching for his old friend, trying to fathom what had happened. For the first time, there was no trace of Adun's bright and shining spirit in the Khala. He was—gone. Utterly, inexplicably gone, and already the stories were beginning to grow around him, mere moments after his—death? Ascension? What in the world could they even call it?

Jake bowed his head, even as the ship lifted off, bearing the dark templar away from the only home they had ever had and into the face of the unknown. Taking with them, Jake suspected, the truth and the true greatness of what Adun had done.

"Adun, my friend . . . will this world ever see your like again?"

The grief Jake felt was not entirely that of Vetraas or the long-ago Conclave. Much of it was his own. Adun had not made the choices he had easily or lightly; he had struggled with his conscience and done the best he could to save innocent lives, going against a code of forthrightness in order to attempt to teach others how to integrate into society without compromising their beliefs.

Jake understood now why Zamara had shown him this. He was limited in his thinking. He'd thought that merely by having the protoss conjure up the storms that had once devastated their world—because every one of them had more experience than the dark templar—all would be well. But bearing witness to

Adun's final act of heroism had put that idea in context. Not only had Adun tried to bring together traditional and dark protoss by teaching the dark protoss how to use their psionic abilities, at the very last, he had understood that both types of power were necessary. Both types of *protoss.*

The storms alone weren't enough.

There was no time for planning, or first attempts. They would have to succeed the first time or fail spectacularly, both Forged and Those Who Endure, human and protoss and preserver together. The only thing they had going for them right now was the fact that neither Valerian nor Ethan wanted them dead. They would have to defeat Ulrezaj, or at the very least drive him back enough so that everyone could safely escape.

I cannot guide this. My attention is needed here—I am close to awakening the gate to Shakuras. And your mind—cannot handle another experience with the Khala without my guidance.

They will have to do it themselves, Jake sent back. *They are protoss.*

He sent the thought to the protoss, complete with the memories of Adun and Vetraas. The entire exchange took a heartbeat. He felt their stunned awe, their anger at the deception, but now was not the time to react. Now was the time to do what Adun had done—embrace the two types of protoss psionic powers, the wild and the regimented, the dark and the light.

The Forged, with the exception of Alzadar, were still suffering from the dampening effects of the Sundrop. They could not enter the Khala. They could share thoughts, as the dark templar could, but until they had cleansed themselves of the drug they could not share emotions.

But they had also been changed by the Sundrop. They, like the dark templar had done so long ago, potentially could summon storms of devastating power.

Those Who Endure would be their guides, their lifelines, their protectors. They could draw strength and calm and support from one another as they linked to the Forged to shield them from the storms once they were created. They could not individually use both types of power, as Adun had, but as a group, as a united species—

The earth trembled and nearly everyone, zerg and protoss and terran alike, lost their footing. Ulrezaj was nearly upon them and Jake felt wind and electricity stir his hair as the atmospheric effects from Ulrezaj's outer nimbus reached them. Dark tendrils of shadow began to snake across the ground, and protoss and zerg jumped away to avoid them. Those that did not . . .

A little time to prepare, begged both Alzadar and Ladranix, but Jake was implacable.

"There's no time!" he screamed, reverting to habit in this moment and shouting the words aloud as well as thinking them. "Start figuring it out *now*!"

CHAPTER TWENTY-ONE

VALERIAN STARED AT THE JUMPY IMAGES THAT were coming in on the view screen. He had patched in feed from six different ships, including the one that carried his ghost. On the screens now was something that looked like—like radiant darkness.

"What the hell *is* that?" he demanded of Starke.

"Sir, I—can't rightly tell you." Starke's voice was shaking and uncertain. "It is extremely psionically powerful, and the energy readings from it are off the scale."

Valerian could see that. Spurts of dark energy seemed to erupt from the being like magma, and anything that was in their path—even in their general vicinity—was destroyed. Including one of his ships, he surmised, as one of the screens suddenly went dark.

"It's—*aaah*!"

In all the time Valerian had known the man, Devon Starke had never raised his voice above a calm, reasoned pitch. To hear him cry out in pain startled the youth. "Devon—what's happening?"

"He—it—them—he doesn't see me as a specific threat, or else I'd be"—a growl of pain—"dead."

Valerian watched the swathe of destruction this monstrous thing was causing and did not doubt that statement for a second. "Stay out of its way. You're too valuable to lose."

"Aye, sir."

"What is it targeting? Is it after Jake?" Valerian stared raptly at the figure, a glorious swirl of death and darkness and destruction. Valerian thought it was a very good thing that his father wasn't present. Mengsk Senior would probably happily sacrifice Ramsey and the protoss entity inside him in exchange for somehow being able to trap and harness this dark storm of energy. It would make a powerful weapon.

"Everything, sir. He's fighting the protoss and the zerg alike. He's moving directly for the warp gate, though. My guess is that he wants Ramsey, just like the rest of us."

That day when he had sat with Jake Ramsey in his study, discussing the temple and toasting the discovery of wonder, Valerian had never anticipated it coming to this—a bitter, bloody fight between three races and a monster on an all-but-dead world. He had not yet developed his father's callousness when it came to sending men to die, but gave the orders even as he felt a wave of regret.

He would make it up to Jacob Ramsey. Somehow.

"See to it that the thing doesn't get him" was all he told Starke.

* * *

"A dark archon!"

Kerrigan's voice in Ethan's mind cracked like a whip. She was surprised, and angry at being surprised, and he quailed slightly at her wrath. "Yet nothing so simple as that, I think. Where did it come from?"

"I know not, my queen, but we are engaged in battle with it now."

"Is it attacking you or the protoss?"

"It seems to be bearing down upon Ramsey and the gate," Ethan confessed haltingly. "It seems we all have an interest in the professor."

"But there is only one faction that can prevail, and that must be ours. Use our forces fully, my consort. We are fortunate in that it does not matter, nor do we care, how many of our soldiers fall, so long as we obtain our goal. The preserver inside him is valuable beyond measure to me. She must not be allowed to die here."

"She shall not," Ethan vowed. His queen's consciousness left him, flitting away to other things, other minions, and he sagged slightly.

She was his world. She had made him, improved him, re-created him to serve and love her, and so he did. Part of him knew that he was not choosing this of his own volition, but he did not care. She was his queen, he adored her, he would die for her, and killing for her was a joyful task.

* * *

"Got it!" yelped Rosemary. The look she flashed Jake, obviously intended for both him and Zamara, was filled with triumph and pleasure.

"I have nearly completed my task as well," Zamara said. "Once I am finished, we will have six minutes to get everyone through before a self-disabling sequence is employed."

"Whoa, wait, we've only got six minutes once it's set?" Jake turned and looked out to where the battle was still taking place. The realization suddenly hit him: There was no way that everyone was going to make it through. Many of his friends would die here.

Ladranix, of course, read his thoughts. "Four years ago I stood in this very spot, with Raynor, and Fenix, and dozens of my people, who stood to hold back the tide that threatened to wash away everything I loved. We have a saying, Jacob Ramsey: 'My life for Aiur.' I thought to give it then, but such was not my fate. I lived to help protect and defend those who could not protect themselves. But today I stand ready to fulfill that destiny, for I believe it to be mine."

"Ladranix . . ." Jake was not in the Khala, not as the protoss were, but he did not have to be for the templar to feel his emotions.

"I can think of no greater honor than protecting a preserver, or of aiding my people. Truly, I am glad that I did not die that day so that I might stand here at this moment."

"I will fight alongside you, as we have before," said Alzadar. "I will atone for what I have done. What I have unwittingly enabled. The obscenity that marches upon us now was fed in part by my hand. My servitude—my willing, foolish, blind servitude—aided him. I will find redemption when my blood is spilled to stop him. I wish to greet the gods a templar again."

"Brother," said Ladranix, with deep sincerity, "you are already redeemed. But I understand. It will be an honor to die with you." He extended his hand.

"My life for Aiur," said Alzadar.

"*Our* lives for Aiur," replied Ladranix simply.

With no more words, the two protoss hurried to join the others. Jake looked after them for a long moment, then turned to see Rosemary watching them as well. There was respect, admiration, and a hint of sorrow on her beautiful features.

Rotten time to fall in love, he thought, then turned his attention to the gathering protoss.

There was in truth little time. The accidental allies of protoss, zerg, and Dominion were slowing Ulrezaj, but only for the moment. Debris from both Dominion and protoss vessels, crushed or smoking or actively burning, littered the ground, bits and pieces of metal entwined with chunks of flesh from zerg mowed down in numbers almost too vast to comprehend. The remnants of Those Who Endure and the Forged clustered together as far back behind the fighting lines as possible, reaching out toward one another, physically joining hands as they mentally began to link minds.

Jake didn't know if it would work. Nor did Zamara, nor Ladranix, nor any of the others who, on his word—his, not even Zamara's, honestly—were willing to open themselves to the wildness they feared and mistrusted on such a deep level.

But Jacob, truly—there is little else we can do. There are insufficient numbers for disciplined tactics to achieve much more than senseless death. The only hope is the most desperate gambit. Your instincts were sound.

Could the templar control and direct the storms their Forged brethren were going to summon? Or would the energies spiral out of control, wreaking dreadful havoc upon the very people they were supposed to protect? There was no way of knowing, no way of telling—only the doing of it.

"Zamara doesn't need me anymore, so I'm going to the front," Rosemary said, almost casually, reaching for her rifle and running with a lithe, even gait toward the makeshift bunker walls. Jake watched her go, wanting to call her back, yet knowing that she was too valuable not to utilize. He wished he could do something. It wasn't his world, but it had become his battle.

Ulrezaj came on. Implacable and inevitable he was, and Jake despaired to see it. Even if the templar could coordinate in time, how could anything short of a nuclear blast stop this thing? It was huge, and awesomely, devastatingly powerful. Adun had called upon the powers of both Aiur and dark templar to weave a protective shield about those he had sworn to keep safe as they fled into the xel'naga ship. Jake knew a very little bit about the dark templar, but not what had happened to them after that pivotal moment in history. Where had they gone? What had they learned? How had they come to Shakuras? Zamara hadn't told him that story yet. He was sad to think that he would never live to know it. Never live to know so many stories of these people he had come to respect and love. Never know what it was like to kiss Rosemary Dahl. He—

It was like a song.

For a few seconds, he couldn't fathom what was happening. And then he understood.

They were doing it.

Those Who Endure and the Forged were now joining minds, one group grounded in the Khala, which had served them so well when they were in desperate need of order, the other disconnected from that ancient place in the mind and heart, but linked secondarily to it. Dumbly, Jake stood, mouth slightly open, and let it wash over and around and through him. The screams of dying zerg and wild creatures of this world, the boom of exploding vessels, the sound of weapons fire—it all receded before this *song* of unification. He didn't hear it with his ears, but he felt it, felt it down to his cells, felt it pulse through him with every contraction of his heart.

And then the song took a wild turn.

Energy rose up like a blue mist from the huddled figures, and Jake's breath caught. Their bodies arched, from ecstasy or pain or both commingled. The mist swirled like a little galaxy before his eyes, coalescing and crackling and growing stronger.

Then Ulrezaj paused.

Hope shot through Jake with an almost painful intensity. And then he felt the powerful focus of the monster's intense regard. The blue swirling galaxy, the nascent psionic storm, shivered and all but dissipated in the face of the dark archon's directed will. Jake cried out—what, he did not know; but it was a plea, a prayer.

And then the cloud split, and split again, and again, until each psychically joined pair of protoss had their own small, comparatively weak energy field. As Jake continued to watch, every heartbeat a wild plea, some of the clouds were extinguished as if a careless hand were pinching out a candle flame.

Those protoss fell, crumpling silently.

But others did not fall. They redoubled their efforts, and their energy fields increased. Swirling, spiraling, growing, pulsing. Again Jake felt the monster's angry attack, and more protoss died in silence.

Suddenly Jake realized what had happened. The protoss who had passed had not done so in vain. They hadn't been snuffed out, erased, as he had thought. They had freely given their life energies to the others in this moment, in this union that the protoss had never before attempted.

My life for Aiur.

Ulrezaj realized it as well, and Jake staggered from the force of the creature's anger. But this time, the remaining joined pairs did not waver. The small galaxies that enveloped them suddenly surged, and grew stronger. A wind came out of nowhere. Jake shivered and his hair stood on end, crackling with static electricity and something other, something more than simple physics could explain. He thought of Adun, standing to protect the dark templar, of the energy that flowed in and around and through him.

And suddenly the song reached a crescendo.

A huge crash deafened Jake for a moment as he was blown off his feet. He hit the earth hard. His body felt almost burned and he couldn't breathe for a moment. Power surged and snapped above him, and for a moment he thought the protoss had lost control. These storms were beasts they sought to tame and the creatures had turned against their masters, struggling and straining to break free, and for a second—the briefest, longest second in Jake's life—they succeeded. Then the protoss regained control, corralling the power of the mental storms and sending them to attack.

Ulrezaj halted as the blue nimbus of the storm began to feed on his dark energy. As it grew, he shifted back, and began to fight it in deadly earnest.

Now! cried Zamara, as the gate behind them came to life. Those protoss who were not actively engaged in the fight were galvanized into action. They turned and raced through the gate, running with that lithe, graceful speed that Jake remembered from his time as Temlaa. Half of the protoss ships that were attacking Ulrezaj curved smoothly in mid-flight, disappearing through the gate as well. The other half remained, the attack not slacking, engaging the enemy from all sides as to split his attention from the wildest, deadliest weapon the protoss could manage—the one created from joined minds and spirits. Jake realized they weren't planning to retreat at all. He was looking at flying, golden coffins.

The storm grew in force almost faster than the protoss could flee to safety, and Jake wondered if they had cut it too close; had inadvertently created their own deaths. Some of the protoss worried about that too.

We are protoss. We cannot be divided any longer. Stand strong and focus!

Jake felt Ladranix and Alzadar respond then, their unique mental voices blazing in his mind. The storm swelled, roiled, heavy with lethal energy, and then—

They finally released it.

Dozens of zerg screamed in agony as they seemed to explode from the inside. The storm cut the very air with its power, the sonic boom rattling Jake's bones. The breath seemed to be sucked out of his lungs for a moment as he watched, unable to tear his gaze away.

The storm surrounded the dark archon—Ulrezaj, the "Benefactor"—in a cocoon of destruction. Jake felt a visceral stab of deep satisfaction as he saw the thing lurch to a sudden halt and falter, taken aback by the intensity of the assault.

"Sir, they're escaping through the gate." Starke's voice revealed his strain.

"Stop them!"

"It's all we can do to stop this dark archon from killing them. The protoss are doing something—I'm not sure what, but it's giving the thing pause."

Valerian stared at the various screens that were flashing jumpy, static-flawed information. It was obviously madness down there. He couldn't tell what was going on even as he saw it unfold.

Suddenly all the screens went dark. Whittier gasped and let out a sound perilously close to a squeal of horror.

"Starke, what just happened?"

Silence.

"Starke? Devon! *What's going on?"*

Ethan went flying. The whirlwind had slammed into him and the beast he was riding like a blow from a giant's fist. Pain shuddered through him and he fell, tumbling down, bound by gravity despite the fact that he was the consort of the Queen of Blades, had been made glorious and nearly perfect. He felt his flesh shivering, puckering, and it was only the several-deep piles of zerg corpses that broke his fall. As it was, he was bruised and battered, despite his vastly increased strength and resilience.

Feet and hands and scythe-blades sinking into carnage, Ethan struggled to rise. He cried out in rage.

The gate had been opened, and the protoss were fleeing in a mass exodus. Ramsey was still there, for now.

Enough of relying upon beasts. He would leave such machinations and manipulations for his queen, whose skills were best suited to it. He rose, scythe-arms flashing, hungering as if they had a will of their own, and moved purposefully forward. He would slay Rosemary Dahl and bring Kerrigan Jacob Ramsey himself.

We must go, Jacob.

Zamara reached out to Rosemary as well. Jake saw the assassin's head whip up before she fired one last time, clearly reluctant to leave without seeing the enemy destroyed. Jake shared her feelings. He hesitated, watching the battle continue to rage, watching the legacy of Adun unfolding before his very eyes. Ulrezaj had been brought to a full halt now, his attention entirely focused on defending himself from the onslaught of unified, fiercely directed protoss mental energy.

The image of the drained protoss husks and the briefly-glimpsed creatures in the tanks flashed in his mind. The knowledge of what the Sundrop had done to Rosemary, to Alzadar and all the others—

Fall over, you glowing dark bastard. I want to see you topple.

Jacob!

Zamara's thoughts cracked like a whip in his mind, and Jake started violently. She was two heartbeats away from physically commandeering his body and forcing him to flee. Rosemary raced toward the gate at a flat-out run, pausing only to turn and yell over her shoulder, "Jake, come on!"

Then she, like the protoss, was gone.

Still, Jake could not bring himself to move. His friends were dying out there.

Dying to save me and the knowledge I bear. Dying to save you. Do not let their sacrifice be in vain!

"Ladranix—"

No words met Jake's mind when it brushed Ladranix's. Nothing so confined or limiting as that—just a feeling, of respect, and affection, and pride.

Then Ladranix was gone.

"No!"

Alzadar's grief and fury sang in Jake's mind as the remaining protoss fueled the storm with everything they had. Zamara's thoughts grew harsh and Jake gasped as pain shot through him and his body was usurped by the preserver. His legs began to move, bearing him closer to the blue mist that whirled within the oval confines of the warp gate.

He fought her as he had not done for a long time now, not since the beginning, and if for only an instant, he was stronger, Jake turned his head just in time to see Ulrezaj's whirling motion turn erratic, the fierce blackness fluctuate. Had they gotten him?

He guessed he'd never know. All he knew was that the bitter gamble had paid off, and that the cost was dear indeed.

But Zamara was right—he couldn't let their sacrifice be in vain.

His head aching, his eyes filling with tears, and his heart swelling with pride at the courage of the people who had made him so welcomed, Jacob Jefferson Ramsey raced toward the warp gate and jumped through.

The Dark Templar Saga will continue in
Book Three

ABOUT THE AUTHOR

AWARD-WINNING AUTHOR CHRISTIE GOLDEN HAS written more than fifty novels and several short stories in the fields of science fiction, fantasy, and horror.

Golden launched the TSR *Ravenloft* line in 1991 with her first novel, the highly successful *Vampire of the Mists,* which introduced elven vampire Jander Sunstar. *Vampire of the Mists* was reprinted in trade paperback as *The Ravenloft Covenant: Vampire of the Mists* in September 2006, fifteen years to the month after its initial publication.

She is the author of several original fantasy novels, including *On Fire's Wings* and *In Stone's Clasp,* the first two in her multi-book fantasy series from LUNA Books. *In Stone's Clasp* won the Colorado Author's League Award for Best Genre Novel of 2005, the second of Golden's novels to win the award.

Among other projects are over a dozen *Star Trek* novels, including *The Murdered Sun, Marooned,* and *Seven of Nine.* She's authored the *Dark Matters* trilogy, and continued the adventures of the crew of *Voyager* in *Homecoming, The Farther Shore, Spirit Walk: Old Wounds,* and *Enemy of My Enemy.*

An avid player of Blizzard Entertainment's *World of Warcraft* MMORPG, Golden has written several novels for the game, including *Lord of the Clans* and *Rise of the Horde.* And no, she won't tell you her characters' names.

Golden has had the remarkable opportunity of writing much of this trilogy in a place that to her feels alien indeed—Flinders Island, Tasmania. She currently lives in Orange County, California, and has joined the writing team at Blizzard.

ORIGINAL NOVELS BASED ON THE HIT VIDEO GAME!

Liberty's Crusade
by Jeff Grubb

I, Mengsk
by Graham McNeill

Heaven's Devils
by William C. Dietz

The Dark Templar Saga: Book One: Firstborn
by Christie Golden